Only fate

ONLY YOU SERIES BOOK TWO

USA TODAY & WALL STREET JOURNAL BESTSELLING AUTHOR
CHARITY FERRELL

Editor: Jovana Shirley, Unforeseen Editing, www.unforeseenediting.com
Proofreader: Jenny Sims, Editing 4 Indies
Sensitivity Reader: Jill McManamon
Cover Designer: Lori Jackson
Cover Photographer: Wander Aguiar

eBook ISBN: 978-1-952496-85-1
Paperback ISBN: 978-1-952496-86-8

PROLOGUE

Essie

"You know, one day, my charm will win you over," Ethan says from the driver's side of his Jeep.

I laugh, giving him my best *you're crazy* expression. "No way. I'm immune to it."

"You'll be Mrs. Leonard. Mark my words."

I throw my head back. "I think you'll have *plenty* of Mrs. Leonards."

He taps his thumb against the worn steering wheel to the beat of the music. "Oh, come on. The football star falls for his tutor. That's romantic as fuck."

I shake my head at him, fighting back a smile. "Stick with the *football star falls for the cheerleader* trope. That seems to be going well for you."

The sudden glare of headlights in the starless night interrupts us, nearly blinding me. I shield my eyes from the oncoming truck's bright beams.

"Jesus," Ethan says, flashing his lights at them.

I squint, struggling to see the truck, and then scream.

The truck isn't in its lane.

It's in *ours*.

Ethan blasts his horn. "What the fuck?"

"What's it doing?" I yell.

The truck's tires squeal as it speeds toward us.

"Dial 911!" Ethan orders, swerving into the opposite lane.

The truck does the same.

I fumble for my bag on the floorboard. My hip smacks against the door when Ethan switches lanes. It's like we're in a game of chicken against our will.

I empty my bag in my lap, grab my phone, and my hands shake as I dial the numbers.

"Nine-one-one. What's your emergency?" a woman asks on the other line.

"A truck keeps trying to hit us!" I scream into the speaker as Ethan curses in the background. "It won't stop swerving into our lane!"

"Ma'am, can you state your location?"

Before I can reply, Ethan swerves to the side of the road. The truck follows, crashing into us head-on.

The impact throws me forward. I hit my head on the glove compartment and cry out in pain.

As the truck speeds away, it sideswipes my side, sending the Jeep crashing into a light pole. My ears ring as I see the truck's taillights fade away in the rearview mirror.

When I peer over at Ethan, he's not moving.

I scream his name, fighting to release my seat belt and climb over to him.

His body is still, and he's not breathing.

I check his pulse.

He's gone.

"No!" I say, smacking his chest, like I can somehow bring him back to life.

I stop when a sharp burning smell fills my nostrils. Glancing in the mirror, I see fire blazing up the Jeep's tires. As sparks hit my door, I back away on the seat.

It takes only seconds for the sparks to turn into flames.

Ethan's door is caved in, and it'll take too long to crawl over him.

"Oh my God!" I yell, my adrenaline kicking into overdrive.

The door is lodged shut, so I kick it.

It doesn't budge.

I kick *over and over and over* until it finally opens.

Taking a deep breath, I throw myself out of the burning Jeep.

An intense heat sears my skin, and I scream out in pain.

Then, everything fades to black.

1

Essie

Ten Years Later

"We're sorry, Essie," Laurence says with no apology in his tone. "Adrian was the better candidate."

"Better candidate?" I throw out my arms. "He's been here for *two months*. I've busted my ass for this firm for *three years*. One of those without pay."

For six months, my bosses at Adaway and Williams at Law led me to believe I'd score the junior partner position at their law firm. Today, they told me they'd chosen someone else.

Who did they choose?

A man who completely obliterated my heart.

First my heart.

Now my promotion.

What else does he want?

A freaking kidney?

Charles, his partner, fakes a smile. "Another position will open next year."

I force back tears and follow my bosses out of the boardroom. They don't say another word as they move to their shiny offices, and I head back to my sorry excuse for a cubicle.

Angel, my cubicle neighbor, pokes his head over my partition. "Did you get it?"

I shake my head.

"Sorry, girl. I bet Adrian did. You didn't stand a chance after he gave them World Series tickets."

I stop myself from sitting. "I'm sorry? World Series tickets?"

He nods. "They were box seats too."

Oh, hell no.

I stand from my chair and head straight to the corner office that should be mine. Angel and my other coworkers follow me.

It's one thing to earn a promotion, but to *buy one*?

That's the ultimate smack in the face.

When I reach the doorway, I find him sitting behind the desk.

Adrian Castillo.

The certified thorn in my side.

A man who's made me experience every emotion in the world.

Happiness, then love, and then heartbreak.

Our lives once secretly revolved around each other's.

But now, we act like two people who hate each other. No one knows our history, nor will they ever.

Starting today, he'll also be my boss.

A pang forms in my chest.

Don't do it, Essie.

Don't freaking do it.

Unfortunately, I do it.

Adrian stares at me from across the room when I burst inside his office without knocking. A smirk spreads along his gorgeous tan face in slow motion.

He looks so much the same yet different than he did years ago in college.

Manlier.

Instead of baggy, wrinkled sweatshirts, he's wearing a black suit with a black tie. His cuff links are new and expensive. The green hue in his eyes is more pronounced now that he's swapped his black-rimmed glasses for contacts. His dark hair is shorter and not as wild as it once was. I hate how tamed it is now. He used to run his fingers through the thick strands while concentrating on a problem he couldn't figure out.

I like that he's not the same man I fell in love with.

But I hate that there are still traces of him there.

Since he joined the firm, I've done everything to avoid him: take the stairs—my glutes will thank him for that—come into work early, and leave later.

"You bribed them?" I cross my arms and stand in front of his desk.

His smirk stays as he scratches his cheek. "What are you talking about?"

"You gave the partners baseball tickets in exchange for *my promotion*."

He shrugs. "Gifting tickets to your bosses isn't illegal. You're an attorney. You should know that."

"Yes, but some might consider it unethical."

"Who's some?" He points at me. "*You?*"

"*Me* and ..." I peer at the doorway, where my coworkers stand, and wait for backup.

They give me nothing.

I throw my arms out toward them.

Sorry, Angel mouths as he straightens his tie.

Everyone else stares at the floor while slowly backing away.

There's seriously no coworker loyalty in this place.

Their stepping away makes more sense when Laurence and Charles charge into the office.

Laurence's gaze drifts from me to Adrian. "What's going on here?"

For what seems like the first time since I was hired here, I finally find my voice with them.

Finally decide to stick up for myself.

"You're sellouts." I signal to them. "I'll be sure to let

everyone know all it takes for a promotion around here are sports tickets." I stand on my tiptoes to see the people behind them. "You hear that? Start saving up the little salary they give us to buy Super Bowl tickets!"

Laurence's pudgy face reddens as he shuffles farther into the room. "That's slander, young lady."

"Slander?" I huff, grabbing a globe from Adrian's desk and playing with it in my hands. "Let's talk about slander then, shall we?"

Adrian reclines in his chair, enjoying every minute of my breakdown.

I point at Laurence with the globe. "Is it slander to tell everyone your mistress is your son's ex-fiancée?" I talk over Laurence as he attempts to cut me off. "Or that she had your baby two months ago, and your family has no idea? In fact, she attended you and your wife's vow renewal last summer."

Laurence balls up his fist as sweat builds along his forehead. "Essie, this is out of line."

I turn my attention to the next man on my shit list. "And, Charles—"

"Essie"—Charles's voice rattles—"this isn't—"

I interrupt him. "Charles is on probation for six months because he used a client's money for personal expenses. Boy, does the man love to fly on private jets and eat expensive sushi."

I glance at Adrian. "And *you*."

Adrian straightens in his chair, making a *you have the floor* gesture. "Take your best shot, Esmeralda."

I wince at him using my full name. "Adrian ..." There's a pause, and my stomach tightens when his eyes level on mine. "You know what you did."

While I'd love to put him on blast, doing so would also put *me* on blast. I'm already doing enough damage to my reputation as it is. From the way Laurence is glaring at me, I'm certain it's almost *escort Essie out of the building* time.

"What did he do?" Angel asks, poking his head through the doorway.

Oh, now, he wants to have a voice?

"Yes, Essie," Adrian says, folding his hands together and resting them along the back of his head, "what did I do?"

"That's enough," Laurence yells, spit flying from his lips. "Essie, clear out your desk. You're fired."

"And good luck ever finding a job in law again," Charles adds, shoving his glasses up his narrow nose. "We will let *everyone* know of your behavior."

I refuse to look at Adrian, but if I had my guess, he's smiling pretty from his new office chair. It's one of those pricey ergonomic ones.

"Yeah, well … I quit," I tell them.

A little delayed and not as climactic as I hoped, but at least I said the words.

Without waiting for a reply, I storm out of Adrian's office.

"You should've quit *before* the firing," Angel says, following me on my return to my cubicle.

I blow out an upward breath. "I just had to make sure I said it."

He chuckles. "You said that *and* more."

Unfortunately, I didn't think about the walk of shame post-firing. I want to shrivel up and melt into the floor as everyone stares at me while I pack my cubicle. Charles stands in the corner, arms crossed, waiting to interfere in case I get in the mood to spill more company secrets.

I say goodbye to my old coworkers and leave, carrying a single cardboard box with random belongings. All I have to show for my hard work here.

A box, a scene, and unemployment.

Adrian doesn't bother telling me goodbye—thank God.

The muggy spring weather smacks me in the face as I walk outside. When I drop the box into my car's passenger seat, it slips off the edge. The urge to scream bites at my throat as I watch the items tumble onto the floorboard. As soon as I'm inside my car, I burst into tears.

2

Essie

They say there are many ways to deal with life changes. Pinterest told me to take time to reflect.

My mother told me to embrace change.

But the best advice was given by my best friend, Amelia.

"Time for tequila and nachos," she told me over the phone.

That's why we're gathered around a table at Down Home, the neighborhood pub.

Down Home is where we toast our accomplishments and wash down our failures. Both are welcome, and neither is looked down on.

"Screw Adrian Castillo," I announce, raising my shot glass. "And screw Adaway and Williams."

Amelia follows my lead and lifts her glass. "Yeah, screw them."

My cousin Callie and our friends Mia and Ava do the same. The five of us have been best friends since our births.

"Screw them," we say together. "Cheers!"

Tequila spills as we clink our glasses. When I knock back my shot, I cringe as the alcohol slips down my throat. I'm used to having my tequila accompanied with a little margarita mix.

Though being unemployed sucks, I'm proud of myself. The

partners worked us ragged and pitted us against each other for promotions. Every day I was there, I was miserable.

Setting down my glass, I sigh. "You know what will get those jerks back?"

"What?" Amelia asks before shoving a cheesy nacho in her mouth.

"Starting my own law firm here in Blue Beech." I lean in closer, as if I'd just pitched them the best idea in the world.

Not that they wouldn't support me. I could tell them I was moving to the forest and planned to live off strawberries for the rest of my life, and they'd ask when they could visit.

Starting a law firm from scratch is hard, but it's always been a dream. It's expensive, and it can take years to build a decent client list. Some attorneys don't make a penny during their first few years. But I've always been a go-getter.

"You won't have much competition since Adaway and Williams is an hour away," Mia inputs. "Terrance Nelson is the only attorney in this town, and given his age, he's bound to retire soon."

"Terrance handles all the legal stuff for the brewery," Amelia adds, picking cheese from her black hair. "Last week, he said he was looking for someone to take over his firm. It's like destiny." She raises her hands and makes a spirit fingers gesture.

Amelia and her boyfriend, Jax, own the local brewery in town. She didn't always have ownership in the pub. Jax co-owned it with Chris, his best friend and Amelia's fiancé. After Chris's death, he left his share of the brewery to Amelia, and at the time, considering she and Jax hated each other, they both spent months trying to convince the other to sell their share.

During their time arguing and healing from their loss, they fell in love. Honestly, I think they'd had feelings for each other long before Amelia and Chris even started dating. It took time for her to admit her feelings for him.

Falling for your deceased fiancé's best friend isn't exactly ideal. But now, they're happily in love and run the brewery together.

Callie arranges our empty shot glasses at the end of the table. "You could ask him to refer new clients to you or buy him out."

"If you can't join them, beat them," Mia says, pulling a tube of lip gloss from her Prada bag. "Revenge is best served as competition."

"I'm proud of you," Mia tells me when she pulls into the driveway of my parents' house. "You stood up for yourself."

I solemnly smile and nod.

The reality of leaving the firm is now fully hitting me, thanks to the tequila.

Instead of making me forget my problems, it only caused me to remember them more, like a nonending movie replay.

Drunk Essie is an emotional Essie, which is annoying.

Which is also why Mia drove me home.

"Do you need help getting inside?" she asks.

I shake my head and step out of her red Mercedes. "Thank you for driving me home."

"Take two Advil and drink lots of water," she calls to my back before I shut the door and walk toward my parents' backyard.

When my parents built their house, they added two pool houses on the back of the property. Though I refer to them as cottages. One for me and one for my twin brother, River. They said we could design them and live here as long as we wanted.

I went with a cute cottage aesthetic with pastel colors. The furniture consists of antique pieces I've gathered while estate shopping with my mother. Everything here has character—from the baby-blue chest with hand-painted doves in the entryway to the asymmetrical, handcrafted forest-green velvet couch to the English oak coffee table.

I kick off my boots and start stripping out of my clothes on my way to my bedroom. I flip on the light, and nausea swirls in my stomach when I look in the mirror.

My scarred skin.

After all these years, I still struggle with the sight of it.

I feel defective.

On the outside, everyone sees me as this confident attorney.

But inside, I'm far from that.

What's worse is that every time I see myself naked, it's a reminder of that night.

I hurriedly button my pajama shirt and toss my dirty clothes into the hamper.

Just as I settle in bed, my phone beeps with a message.

I glare at it while reading the text.

Adrian: We need to talk.

He hasn't texted me in years. I only have his number because the firm required us to share ours with everyone.

I reply.

Me: I never want to talk to you again.

Adrian: Don't expect for that to ever be a reality.

I fight with myself on whether to answer but decide ignoring him is the best option. There's nothing that kills assholes more than silence.

"Please let it be a reality," I say, patting my pillow and making myself comfortable. "Don't let him find another way to barge into my life."

But I should know that he always finds a way to blindside me.

3

Adrian

"Let me get this straight," my mother says, staring at me wide-eyed from across the table. "They promoted you … and then you quit?"

We're at Isla Dulce, my *abuela*'s favorite restaurant. It's the only place around that serves true, authentic Puerto Rican dishes.

"That's exactly what happened." I snort back a laugh and down my bourbon.

I should've turned down Laurence and Charles's offer as soon as they congratulated me. I had no idea Essie was in the running, but when she barged into my office, I knew exactly what it was for.

"I'd have gotten sick of those assholes sooner or later." I raise my glass for a refill as the server passes, and he nods.

My abuela grins. "I think you leaving that firm is fate."

"Fate that he's now unemployed?" my mother argues.

My abuela keeps her brown eyes on me. "You don't need those idiots to be a successful attorney. As a matter of fact, I have the perfect opportunity for you."

"Your ideas are always trouble," my mother says with a sigh. "Trouble that I always have to bail you out of."

"Oh, hush, Paula." My abuela flicks her hand through the air. "You can't blame a woman for wanting to have some fun."

"Fun?" My mother scowls at her. "Arguing with your HOA over pink plastic flamingos in your lawn or starting a farm in your backyard might be fun *for you*, but it's a headache for me since I'm the one who always has to bail you out. They have your picture with the words *Valeria Guzman is trouble* hung up on the community bulletin board."

My abuela laughs. "Who are they to tell me I can't have pet goats? Unless they're paying my bills, they need to keep their nose outta my business. Also, I scribbled out my name on that bulletin and replaced it with the HOA president's."

My mother massages her temples. She has a folder full of situations she's had to bail my abuela out of. Like me, she's an attorney, which works in my abuela's favor.

The server drops off my drink, and I'm grateful the conversation is no longer about my lack of employment.

An older man, wearing black suspenders and a white shirt, stops at our table. "Apologies for my tardiness. I hate this city traffic." He smiles down at my abuela. "I texted but figured you'd forgotten your phone at home again."

My abuela's face lights up as she peers at him. "Of course I did."

They grin at each other, and the man's wrinkled face brightens.

What the hell am I missing?

"This is Terrance, my boyfriend," my abuela introduces before I have the chance to ask.

I choke on my drink and tap at my chest to force the liquid down.

"Boyfriend?" my mother asks as Terrance holds out his hand toward her. "Since when do you have a boyfriend?"

"Since I wanted one," my abuela replies, rolling her eyes dramatically.

My mother shakes Terrance's hand. "Paula. It's nice to meet you."

I stand and do the same when he offers me his hand. "Adrian. The grandson."

Terrance smiles and clasps his free hand over our joined ones. "I've heard great things about you, Adrian."

"So, how did you two meet?" my mother asks Terrance as we sit.

"Remember the neighbor I sprayed with the hose after he ran over my petunias?" my abuela asks us.

"Sure do," I reply, remembering her calling and asking me to come over and give the guy a knuckle sandwich.

My abuela reaches out, taking Terrance's hand in hers. "He sent his grandfather over to talk to me—an attorney scare, if you will—but let's just say, he didn't get me in trouble the way his grandson had thought he would. Terrance asked me out on a date that very day. And now, five months later, here we are."

My mother swats her black bangs from her face. "And you're telling us now?"

"I needed to be sure Terrance was a keeper before introducing you." She leans toward Terrance, shutting her eyes and resting her head on his shoulder. "I never thought I'd find love again after Ricky."

My *abuelo* passed before I could meet him. From what my abuela has said, he was a great man, and they were madly in love. After his death, my abuela left Puerto Rico with my mother and moved to the States.

"Now, Terrance," my abuela starts, hugging his arm, "Adrian is no longer working at that snotty firm."

"Adaway and Williams, right?" Terrance asks me.

I nod.

"I wouldn't want to work for them either."

"Terrance also practices law," my abuela says. "But he's retiring."

"I started my own firm ages ago," Terrance adds. "In my hometown."

My abuela focuses her attention on me. "He's looking for someone to take over his practice. I think it'd be perfect for you."

Ah, this is why she was so excited about me quitting the firm.

Small-town law?

I don't know how interesting that'd be.

But if Terrance has an established firm, it'd save me work.

Terrance nods toward me. "I'm open to having you work for me and then possibly taking over the firm. You can stay with your grandmother and me while we work out the logistics."

My mother holds up her hand. "Can we backtrack to you two *living together?*"

"We're getting married," my abuela says, casually dropping the bomb before whipping her attention back to me. "Now, Adrian, what do you think?"

I scratch my cheek. "Can I have a day or two to consider?"

"Of course," Terrance replies. "Let's meet this week. I can show you around the firm and town."

"Where is this town?" I ask.

"Blue Beech. Have you heard of it?"

I lean inward, a smile spreading over my face. "I sure have."

Blue Beech, Iowa.

I'll never forget the town Essie always talked about.

Those two words are all Terrance needed to say to convince me to accept his offer.

"When can I start?" I ask.

4

Essie

"I need waffles smothered in maple syrup and coffee with too much sugar," I say, plopping down across from Amelia in the red leather booth at Shirley's Diner.

She laughs. "Already ordered for you, babe."

I blow her a kiss. "That's why you're my bestie."

Amelia's wearing a black polo with the Down Home Brewery logo stitched on the left side of the chest. Her hair is down in long dark brown curls—her daily hairstyle—and her lips are a vibrant red.

Shirley's has been a Blue Beech staple for decades. Her parents started the diner, naming it after her, and the diner has been passed down through generations. Now, Shirley's daughter, Ruth, and granddaughter, Margo, run it.

I grew up eating pies, drinking milkshakes, and hanging out with my friends here. Some places just feel like home. Shirley's is one of them.

Margo delivers our drinks. "Two iced coffees with extra caramel and whipped cream. Waffles will be up shortly, ladies."

We thank her, and she rushes over to the booth behind us.

Amelia pushes her hair away from her face and takes a sip of her coffee. "*Soo*, Tipsy Essie talked about opening her own firm last night. How does Hungover Essie feel about that this morning?"

I dip my finger in the whipped cream and lick it off. "That's too big of a question to ask this early in the morning."

"You used to wake up at four o'clock when you worked at your old firm."

"And I hated it."

"Don't be mad at me for interfering—"

"What did you do?" I interrupt.

"I emailed Terrance last night, asking him to give me a call about a contract he was looking over for the brewery. When he called me back this morning, I asked if he still planned to retire." Her voice turns into a squeal. "He said yes!"

I can't stop myself from smiling.

"When I asked what he planned to do with the firm, he said he'd either sell it or pass it down to someone." She takes a slurp of coffee. "Did you know that he's getting married? I didn't even know he had a girlfriend, and that's hard to keep secret in a town this small. He did say she isn't from here though."

"Calling him today was on my to-do list. I just wanted to make sure I was organized first."

"You've got this, Essie." She gives me a thumbs-up. "You're the most determined person I know. You'll take Blue Beech legal by storm."

"Yes, because the crime here is booming."

"You do family law. Crime isn't even something you deal with."

"Technically, I do *all* law. Family is just what my old firm specialized in."

My original dream was to become a prosecutor, but that's not an easily earned job. For years, I've looked up to prosecutors. They're the reason I don't live every day in fear.

"Family law. Criminal law. Animal law. *Business law*— because you can guarantee we'll hand you everything brewery-related," Amelia says with absolute certainty. "Not to mention, everyone loves you and your family here."

Eh, debatable.

"*Some* people love my family," I correct.

The Lane family has had its ups and downs in Blue Beech.

People once referred to the Lane family as Blue Beech's Kennedy family. It was meant to be a compliment, but as our family scandals spilled, we started to fall on the gloomier side of that comparison.

My grandfather caused our name downfall. It was before I was born, but gossip never dies in a small town. He went from the highly respected mayor to a disgraced one after people found out he had a secret baby, paid the mother hush money for years, and was involved in countless other scandals.

"Oh my God," Amelia gasps, nearly spilling her coffee. "Speaking of Terrance, he just walked in. If that's not a sign it's meant to be, I don't know what is."

I turn to find Terrance speaking to the hostess as she grabs menus and leads him to a booth on the other side of the diner.

"Go talk to him," she adds, swatting my arm.

"I'm usually not one to believe in fate, but you might be right." I shoot her a smile before sliding out of the booth and walking his way.

"Mr. Nelson," I say when I reach his table. "I'm sorry to interrupt, but I planned to reach out to you today."

"No interruption at all, Essie," he says, unrolling his silverware from the napkin.

I take a deep breath. "I heard you planned to retire and are possibly selling your firm. Would you consider selling to me?"

Terrance's bushy brows furrow. "I'm sorry, but I already have someone interested." He smiles. "If things don't work out, I'll reach out to you."

A lump forms in my throat, a twinge of hopelessness hitting me. "Is it someone local … if you can disclose that?"

"My fiancée's grandson. He's not local, but the plan is for him to move here."

There goes my hope of no competition.

"Oh, and there he is now," he adds.

I follow his gaze, and a heaviness expands in my chest.

No. No. No.

My head starts spinning.

My heart pounding.

Adrian—*yes, Adrian freaking Castillo*—strolls in our direction, dressed in dark jeans and a white V-neck tee. The look reminds me more of our past rather than the expensive suits he sported at the firm. I got so familiar with the suits that I forgot how attractive he was like this.

Don't get me wrong.

He's hot as hell in suits, but this? It makes him more relatable.

More desirable.

It doesn't give him that asshole-attorney vibe.

I peer down, taking in my floral maxi dress and boots. Thank God I took the time to curl my hair, pushing it back with a rhinestone clip, and brushed a few coats of mascara on my lashes before coming here.

Heads turn as Adrian passes, coming our way.

Jaws drop.

Women giggle.

Jesus.

He's a newbie.

They're like circus animals here, especially *hot* newbies.

He acts like he doesn't notice any of it.

Instead, his eyes are glued on me, as if he's incapable of looking anywhere else.

"You've got to be kidding me," I mutter, my face burning hot.

Adrian smiles, not appearing nearly as surprised to see me as I am him.

This damn man.

He's my new recurring nightmare.

Was he put on Earth to make my life a living hell?

If only I could go back to the past. I'd never spoken to him before the night I showed up at River's dorm. If I'd fled and gone with my original plan of calling an Uber, I'd never have known what it felt like to have him rip apart my heart.

"Good morning, Terrance," he says, offering him a head nod before returning his attention to me. "Essie, what a surprise."

Surprise, my freaking ass.

Adrian traces his finger along his thick bottom lip. "I didn't expect to see you here."

"Really?" I cock my head to the side. "Pretty sure you knew I lived here."

If he's trying to hold back the arrogant smirk on his face, he's failing.

I narrow my eyes at him. "Can I talk to you in private?"

"Of course." He glances over me to Terrance again. "If you'll excuse me for a moment."

Terrance, looking majorly confused and wrinkling his forehead, slowly nods.

He and his late wife worked at the firm for years. I'd job-shadowed his wife in high school. He's always been a kind man … but now, I'm holding a little grudge against him.

He's bringing Adrian into my space.

Adrian is stealing yet another opportunity from me.

Call him the damn job swiper.

Swiper, no freaking swiping.

Now, curious stares are on both of us as Adrian follows me toward the door. Not only is he bombarding me in my town, but he's also making me the gossip topic for the next month. That's another reason I need him to stay far, far away from me.

The sun beats down on us as soon as we're outside, and Adrian pauses to hold the door open for a couple.

As soon as he steps to the side, I whip around to face him and cross my arms.

"Why are you here?" I snap.

"Meeting with Terrance," he replies, as if it's obvious.

Okay, it is, but it was a valid question.

I can't stop myself from shoving his shoulder.

It does nothing. He doesn't even fall back an inch. Instead, he steps closer into my space. The smell of his cologne seeps into the air. I pick up a faint scent of masculinity with notes of mint and cedar. It's a smell that makes you stop in your tracks, wanting to smell more.

The smell of a professional, sophisticated man.

Not the cheap body spray of a college kid who spends too much time studying and hardly ventures out into public. That reminds me of our good times—when we locked ourselves in the library, enjoyed late-night dinners in diners like Shirley's, and sat in his car talking for hours.

"Shouldn't you be living your best life in your new office at Adaway and Williams?" I seethe. Saying their names puts a sour taste in my mouth.

"I quit." He shrugs, like it's no big deal.

I wince. "Why?"

"That's none of your business."

"Considering it was a promotion I wanted, I think it is."

"No, it isn't." He drags a hand through his hair, and my fingers tingle at the memory of when I used to do it when my anxiety got the best of me.

"And now, you're coming to steal another opportunity from me."

He raises a brow.

"I wanted to buy Terrance's firm."

For a moment, he's quiet, and from the look on his face, I know he didn't expect that. It's not like I released a freaking public announcement.

"Why don't we partner up and run the firm together, then?"

"Uh, I think the fuck not."

He bites into the corner of his lip. "Damn, your mouth got dirtier and your attitude crazier. It's sexy as hell, Essie."

Desire bleeds along his words, and chills run up my spine.

It takes me a moment to slap my attitude back in place. "Too bad I can't say there're any pros to this new Adrian. Your assholery definitely isn't *sexy as hell.*" I waggle my finger at him. "And don't call me sexy again."

"Seriously"—he spreads out his massive palms—"we can be partners. I'm sure Terrance wouldn't mind, and I'm okay with sharing the business. Consider it an apology for what happened at Adaway and Williams."

"You know what a better apology would be?" I don't give him time to answer. "You staying away."

"That sounds like it'd be a half-assed apology. I like to go for more grand gestures."

I hold up my middle finger. "How's this for a gesture?"

He shakes his head. "Consider it a peace offering. An olive branch."

"How about I snap that branch, then?"

He runs his hand through his hair. "Come on, Essie—"

"No," I say, cutting him off and holding my finger in his face. "You disappeared for years. No returned calls, texts, emails, *nothing.*" I drop my hand. "What makes you think I'd ever trust partnering up with you?" I shuffle to the right a few steps, away from the listening ears of customers walking into the diner.

He inches closer, and I shudder when his body brushes mine. "Don't act like you were perfect. You completely changed after that night. Both of us are to blame."

I turn my face, refusing to look at him as sadness hits me. "I won't be your partner, Adrian. I'll be your competition. I'm starting a firm here."

"*From scratch?*"

"From scratch."

"That's not easy."

"I grew up here. The residents like me and my family—"

"That's egotistical to assume they won't like me."

"They will choose me over a stranger who walks into town with the only intention of making money off them for legal issues."

"That's not my only intention here."

"What's the other then? To make my life hell?"

He opens his mouth to answer, but I put my finger in his face again.

"You know what? Don't answer." I blow out a harsh breath. "Please, just stay away from me, and if you have a heart and ever cared about me, you'll tell Terrance you don't want his firm and never come back here."

"I won't do that, Essie," he says to my back when I turn around. "I'm here to stay."

"Then, stay away from me," I mutter.

I don't wait for his reply before rushing back inside the diner. People stare, and I try to return to my booth as casually as I can. Thankfully, my food has arrived.

"Um, who was that?" Amelia asks, glancing over my shoulder. "He looked familiar, and obviously, you know him. You stomped out of here like he'd told you Netflix shut down."

At this point, I'd rather have Netflix shut down than Adrian in Blue Beech.

And this is coming from a stream queen who watches Netflix every night before bed.

I snatch the syrup bottle. "That was Adrian."

"*The* Adrian?"

I nod.

Amelia met Adrian once, years ago, but he's changed so much. He has more muscle now that he doesn't spend all his time cramming for exams and speaking with me at all hours of the day and night.

I peer over my shoulder when I hear someone in the booth

behind me whisper, "Who is that?" in the same tone as Amelia did.

Everyone's eyes are on Adrian as he joins Terrance at their booth. They shake hands, and he sits across from him.

Adrian looks good.

And me? I'm scarred.

"I take it him meeting with Terrance isn't a good thing?" Amelia asks.

"He's taking over Terrance's firm," I say.

He and Terrance haven't finalized the deal, but Adrian made it clear he's taking it.

Amelia freezes mid-bite, and syrup drips onto the table. "What? *How*?"

"Terrance's future wifey? That's Adrian's grandmother."

"Oh, how the plot thickens. What are you going to do?" She finally shoves the bite into her mouth.

"What did we say before? If you can't join them, beat them." I smother my waffles with syrup. "I've made my decision. I'll start my own firm."

"I like it." She wipes up her syrup spill with her napkin.

We brainstorm firm ideas while eating. It takes every ounce of my restraint not to turn and look at the back of Adrian's head. But I still hear people around us talking about him.

Amelia asks Margo for the check when we're finished.

"Not necessary," Margo replies, shaking her head before smiling toward the diner's other end. "The gentleman with Terrance paid for your meals."

I slap my napkin on the table and start to stand. "I'm going to kill—"

Amelia grabs my elbow, pulls me back into the booth, and shoots me a *not here* look.

I force a smile. "Thank you, Margo."

She appears as confused as Terrance did.

As everyone else in this damn place.

Margo pats the back of the booth. "Let me know if you need

anything else. If not, have a great day. It was nice seeing you two."

"You probs don't want to announce you want to kill your future competition," Amelia says, leaning in closer.

"So, just kill him, but don't announce it. Got it."

"This will be interesting," Amelia says, leaning back in the booth. "Possibly more entertaining than when Jax and I wanted to kill each other."

I push my plate away from me. "Yes, but there will be no happily ever after for Adrian and me."

A twinkle shines in her eyes. "You never know."

No one knows about my past with Adrian.

And they never will.

It's a secret we keep to ourselves.

5

Essie

I did it.
I freaking did it.
Lane at Law.

Is the name kind of generic? Yes.

It's not like you can tap entirely into your creativity. No one will take *Boho Love Law* or *Sparkly Butterflies at Law* seriously.

My office is a brick building fifteen minutes from downtown and less than a minute's walk to Down Home Pub. It's also not close to Terrance's—soon-to-be Adrian's—firm downtown.

No thank you on being near him.

I tapped into my savings, and my parents covered the remodeling costs. Since the space was an insurance office before, not much work was needed.

River and Jax put a fresh coat of paint on.

A local carpenter replaced the old tiled floor with wood and installed new cabinetry. And because I have the most supportive parents in the world, they surprised me with brand-new computers and anything techie needed for a business.

I throw my arms out and spin around.

My own firm.

Somewhere I don't have to run myself ragged for self-centered men who see me as beneath them. It might take a while to acquire clients, but I'll work my butt off. I posted an ad for a paralegal but haven't hired anyone yet.

I straighten items on the antique desk I found at an estate sale last week. Just as I'm about to start my computer and go through paralegal résumés, the door chimes. I leave my office to find Archie Jetson, the local florist, holding a bouquet.

Archie offers me the flowers. "A delivery for Ms. Lane."

"Thanks, Archie," I say, taking them from him with a smile. "Who sent these?"

"There's a note on the card." He grins and plucks a flower petal from his thick beard. "You have a good day now."

I thank him again, set the flowers on the front reception desk, and admire them.

The sweet honey bouquet.

My favorite.

The bouquet has blooming sunflowers, blue thistles, and pink snapdragons. I shut my eyes and press my nose against the sunflowers, inhaling their scent. I gently take the pink card sticking out from between the stems. There's a note written in black ink.

GOOD LUCK WITH YOUR FIRM.
WISHING YOU THE BEST,
ADRIAN

I play with the card in my hand.

Is that sarcasm?

I hold the vase in both hands, lift it off the counter, and walk toward the empty trash can. But I can't bring myself to throw them away.

"They'll give the office life," I tell myself to justify keeping them.

6

Adrian

"Congratulations," Terrance says, shaking my hand. For the past three months, I've worked with him at the firm, familiarizing myself with the office and the two employees, Monica and Ralph. Monica is the paralegal, and Ralph is the secretary.

Terrance won't retire for another three months, but he's giving me his business. The man must really love my abuela to trust me with a firm he spent decades building.

I could've rejected the offer. Essie thinks this is another opportunity stolen from her, but she doesn't know that if I hadn't agreed to take over the firm, Terrance had someone next in line who wasn't her. The grandson of one of his former law school buddies.

I haven't seen her since the diner, but I heard she opened her firm today. I couldn't resist sending her a bouquet of her favorite flowers. One night, while we had been spread out on a blanket in the park, she'd told me that her favorite flower shop here made the prettiest sweet honey bouquet.

"Let's celebrate with drinks and dinner at Down Home Pub," Terrance says, snapping me out of my thoughts. He grabs his tweed blazer off the back of his chair. "Valeria and Paula will meet us after they finish with the real estate agent."

My abuela put her house on the market. It was a surprise to all of us since she used to tell us stories of when she'd bought it, pride deep in her voice. My mother is still worried about her rushing into such a major decision with a man she's known for less than a year.

But from the time I've spent with Terrance, I think he seems to be a stand-up guy. Like my abuela, he knows the pain of losing a spouse since his wife passed away from a stroke five years ago.

We leave the office and slip into Terrance's old Volvo. He turns down the classical music as we buckle our seat belts. The pub is a short drive from the office and even closer to Essie's new firm. During my lunch break, I couldn't stop myself from plugging the address into my GPS and sneaking in a quick drive-by.

I love the convenience in Blue Beech. There's little traffic, and nothing is more than fifteen minutes away. Although I was born in Iowa, when I was five, my mother moved us to California when she got a position teaching law at a university. We didn't return to Iowa until I was seventeen to be closer to my abuela.

It's six o'clock on a Thursday, but the pub's parking lot is already crowded. When we walk inside, the dim lighting provides a comfortable vibe. In the corner, a band plays a Tom Petty cover. The place is a little divey but has character with Blue Beech memorabilia and old beer ads on the walls.

People wave at Terrance and stop me to introduce themselves.

I meet a Wayne, who says he might need to sue his neighbor.

A Jessica, who offers to give me a tour of Blue Beech.

A Capria, who offers to have me over for dinner so I can try her famous pie.

Since I've started venturing around town, this has happened

often. My abuela made sure to note that multiple women had pointed out I didn't have a ring on my finger.

After I decline Jessica's and Capria's proposals, Terrance and I sit at a four-top table near the back.

"The fried tenderloin is my favorite here," Terrance says, swiping a menu from the basket in the middle of the table. "They have the best french fries too."

When the server, whose name tag says Alicia, comes, Terrance orders the tenderloin while I go with a BLT.

I flip the menu to check out their drink specials. "What are your beer options?"

"We only serve Down Home Brewery beer here," Alicia replies with a smile.

"It's good stuff," Terrance says before ordering a glass of Alicia's recommendation.

I return my menu to the basket. "I'll have the same."

I'm usually more of a bourbon or whiskey drinker, but I don't want anything strong. The local ale seems to be the preferred drink in Blue Beech.

Alicia tucks her pen behind her ear. "I'll be back with your drinks, and the food should be up shortly."

"I was never a beer man until I tried Blue Beech's ale," Terrance says. "This pub has been in the owner, Maliki's, family for decades. His son opened Down Home Brewery, and this place hasn't served any other beer since."

Alicia returns with mugs spilling over with beer. It's tastier than the cheap, watered-down shit I tried in college.

Terrance and I share law school stories. He tells me about life in Blue Beech and how he raised his two sons here. While neither no longer lives in Blue Beech, his grandson is a vet who splits his time between here and Anchor Ridge, a town nearby.

While my abuela is loud and sarcastic, Terrance is chill with a monotone voice. She wears bright, patterned clothing, and his wardrobe consists of beige and blazers that belong in the '80s.

Our food arrives at the same time my mother and abuela join us.

"No, you cannot fire your real estate agent for suggesting you take better care of your houseplants," my mother says as they sit.

"Fine," my grandmother argues with a huff as Terrance kisses her cheek. "If he's so worried it'll *detract* buyers, he can go water them his damn self."

I take a bite of my sandwich and listen to them bicker about agents and whether she'll drop the price if necessary. I nod, pretending to agree with what they're both saying, but freeze when I hear, "Cheers to Essie for starting her new firm!"

I turn in my chair so fast that you'd swear someone punched me in the back of the head, and I search the pub for Essie.

When I find her, my body relaxes, and I smile. Essie's beauty has always captivated me, and it's no different now. Her brown hair is loose in curls, and she's wearing a pink top with a tight black skirt. I wish I could see her killer legs, but the crowd cuts off most of my view of her.

There's more to her than beauty too. Essie is wicked smart and kind—albeit not to me now—and our humor has always matched.

She used to be mine.

Sorrow hits me as I remember what I lost.

She raises her shot glass and toasts to her success with her friends. I can't stop myself from lifting my mug and doing the same.

My abuela smacks my arm, breaking me from my trance. "Who's that pretty girl you're staring at?"

"Essie Lane," Terrance answers for me.

"Do you know her, Adrian?" my mother asks, texting while keeping her eye on me.

I nod. "She's my old dormmate, River's, sister."

"Hmm," my mother hums. "Small world."

"Essie just started her own firm," Terrance adds. There's no animosity in his voice about it. "She used to work at the same firm as Adrian, Adaway and Williams."

My mother blinks at me and sets down her phone. From the look she gives me, I'm positive she thinks I came here for Essie.

Technically, I did.

But I won't share that with her.

Terrance straightens the napkin on his lap. "Essie is a nice young lady. Very smart."

"Hmm," my mother hums again.

The moment Essie leaves her table, I slide off my stool.

"Be right back," I hurriedly say before strolling in her direction. I keep my eyes glued on her while weaving through the crowd.

And that's how I *conveniently* run into Essie.

"Whoa," I say with a little too much dramatics when my shoulder *accidentally* brushes hers.

I pretend to be headed in the opposite direction, and she cut me off.

She steps back, and, damn, do I wish there was better lighting so I could see more of her face. I inhale her sweet perfume, a mix of mandarins and flowers. It's what she wore in college.

"Adrian," she says with more hatefulness than I'd like. "Why are you here?" Her voice grows more agitated. "This is *my* town."

I hoped she'd be in less of an *I hate Adrian* mood since she's celebrating a new milestone in her career. Apparently, she's still on the *ownership of Blue Beech* mentality.

"I wasn't aware this was Essie Beech." I shove my hands into my pockets and lean back on my heels. "The sign at the town limits states otherwise."

Sometimes—and it's probably not a good idea—I enjoy pushing her buttons. Especially when she attempts to force herself to forget all the feelings she had for me years ago.

She crosses her arms. "You knew I lived here. So, yes, it's my town."

"How would I know you *still* lived here?" I slide closer as the band plays louder. "Is this how you treat all the new Blue Beech residents?"

"Only the unwelcome ones who come here to mess with me."

"I'm not here to mess with you."

"Then, why are you here?"

"I told you, for my abuela and to try something new."

"I have an idea if you want to try something new. I hear they need a salesperson for World Series tickets. Rumor is, you're good with getting rid of those."

I smirk. "Nah, I'm not a baseball fan, which is why I gave the tickets away. I'd rather try somewhere new, like a small town."

"Are you moving here for good?"

"When I find a place, yes."

We shuffle a few feet away from the bar as it grows busier.

Essie blows out a long breath. "Why are you doing this, Adrian? You can start a firm anywhere. Why where I call home?"

Because wherever you are feels like home to me, is what I want to say, but I hold myself back.

Instead, I say, "What if I want to call it home as well?"

"Too bad. I called dibs here when I was in the womb."

I decide to go with a different angle. "It's not like I woke up one morning and said, *Gee, I think I'll move to Blue Beech.* My abuela lives here, and now, I work here. No matter what, I'd be here, even if you weren't."

I hate that I'm lying to her.

No way in hell would I have taken Terrance's offer if she wasn't here.

"And what's up with the flowers?" she says, her words coming out faster. It's what she does when she grows agitated. It's also something we worked on in college because she wanted to slow her talking—*pack a better punch with them in courtrooms.* "Did you send them to create bad juju in my office?"

I shake my head. "The flowers were a genuine gesture. I want your firm to succeed, Essie."

"Sure," she drawls out. "*I want my competition to do well,* said no one ever."

"There's plenty of business to go around, *and* as I suggested before, we can always merge."

She scoffs. "I'd appreciate you finding another pub to hang out at. This is my safe space, which means Adrian-free."

I glance around. "*This* is your safe space? If I recall correctly, your safe space used to be quiet libraries and places where people wouldn't talk to you."

"I could go for the *don't talk to me* right now."

"Sorry, Esmeralda, but you can't lay claim to a public place."

She holds up a finger as if counting. "A, this isn't a public place. It's a private business owned by my uncle." Another finger rises. "B, don't call me that." She makes a shoo gesture. "Now, find your own safe space."

"Oh shit. Adrian, is that you?" River asks, interrupting us. He stops at Essie's side—his height nearly three inches taller than her—and points toward me with his beer. When Essie gives him a dirty look, he shuffles back a step. "Shit, sorry." His attention returns to me. "I forgot I'm supposed to hate you for reasons my sister won't tell me."

River and I got along in college, but I wouldn't consider us close friends. While I kept to myself and studied, River made the best of college life until he dropped out. I'm almost positive he went to college for the experience and left when he was tired of it.

Essie elbows River. "Uh, promotion stealer, remember?"

River dramatically glares at me. "Yeah, you rat bastard, you." He claps my shoulder. "Sorry, man, it's twin rules. If she hates you, I hate you by proxy." His tone says he's far more entertained than worried about hating me.

"Swear to God, I'm never having your back again," Essie grumbles to River.

"Sis, you know I one hundred percent always have your back." River laughs. "The problem with this time is that I know you two don't really hate each other. You're just too much alike."

"Negative," Essie says, her gaze traveling to me. "I'm not morally corrupt."

"You two kids have fun," River says, chuckling while he leaves us and wanders toward the bar.

As soon as he's out of earshot, I hold my hand out. "Truce?"

She flicks her hand against my extended one as if it were an annoying gnat. "Uh, no."

"Come on." I throw my head back.

"I never give in that easily, Adrian. You should know that by now."

Without another word, she turns and walks away from me.

I watch her, shamelessly staring at her plump ass, before focusing on the others who do the same as she passes. I want to shove them away, tell them eyes off what's mine, but that'd probably get me banned from this place.

"I see you and Pretty Girl had a nice little chat," my abuela says when I return to our table.

For a man who was just practically told to fuck off by a girl, I'm not feeling as discouraged as I had when I tried speaking with her at Adaway and Williams. Something about this town has a feeling of hope, of forgiveness, of happiness. I want to find that here with her.

"You know what would be adorable?" My abuela doesn't offer me a chance to answer her question. "If you two got a case against each other."

Adorable? No.

Fun? Probably not.

A way to be around Essie more? Absolutely.

Essie and I don't speak the rest of the night, but we keep catching each other staring.

I want her to forgive me.

This time, I want to have the strength to make her mine.

I want Essie's hate toward me to turn back into love.

7

Essie

Crime in Blue Beech is the equivalent of it in Mr. Rogers's neighborhood.

Marriages last lifetimes.

People respect their neighbors.

I definitely have my work cut out for me here.

But this morning, Brielle Huxley called me for divorce representation. I had gone to school with her and her husband, Rhett. They were high school sweethearts who married and had two children. Rumor is, Rhett was caught cheating with the nanny.

Brielle walks into my office, dark circles under her eyes and her blonde hair pulled back into a messy bun. She drops her Chanel bag on the floor and collapses on my patterned pink chair. "I want to take him for everything he has, Essie."

Cheating rumor definitely true.

"I have faith in you," she adds.

I stare at her from across my desk. "Does Rhett have representation yet?"

She nods. "As soon as I told him I was leaving his ass, he called an attorney. Terrance's new guy. I forget his name." She flicks her manicured fingers through the air. "Rhett said he was some hotshot attorney in the city before moving here."

I gulp when she mentions Adrian but then hold back the urge to roll my eyes at her referring to him as a *hotshot attorney*. Don't get me wrong. Adrian is a great attorney, but like me, he fell victim to Laurence and Charles. Neither of us was ever given a decent opportunity to show our strengths there.

"When can you start?" she asks between chomps of chewing her gum. "How long until I can divorce this bastard?"

"I can start right away." I grab a notebook and pen. "Tell me everything I need to know and what you're asking from Rhett."

"I want half his money and a court order that forbids my children to be around his mistress."

"Is she a danger to them?"

"No. But we hired her to babysit our children, not screw my husband."

Understandable from her point of view, but I doubt the court would agree she's a danger to the children if Brielle trusted her with them before.

We talk for the next hour, and I take notes while Brielle fills me in on their marital problems, Rhett's infidelity, their finances, and how she thought their future would be different.

After she leaves, I debate on whether to call or email Adrian.

I decide on email.

The less personal, the better.

But there's a slight problem with my plan.

The only email addresses I have for him are his old college and Adaway and Williams ones. Which means I have to call Terrance's office and ask for it.

"Hey, Essie! How are you?" Ralph asks after I greet him. "I heard you opened a firm here. That's awesome! But everyone knows there will never be a law firm secretary as fabulous as me."

Ralph works with Terrance and at Down Home Brewery. Years ago, when I was in high school, I used to babysit him for extra cash.

"There will never be anyone in this town as fabulous as you," I say with a laugh.

"What can I do for you?"

"Can you give me Adrian's email—"

"One sec," he chirps. "I'll transfer you to him."

"Wait!" I shriek. "No—"

It's too late.

I lose him. The line rings twice and then stops.

"This is Adrian."

Goose bumps spread over my entire body at the sound of his voice.

It's the perfect mixture of masculine and sincerity.

"Hey." I exhale a steady breath. "It's Essie."

"Essie." He slowly repeats my name, his voice deepening as it ends.

Heat crawls up my spine.

No. No.

The mere simplicity of this man's voice shouldn't turn me on.

I clear my throat to empty my thoughts.

Doesn't work as much as I hoped for.

"I'm representing Brielle Huxley in the divorce from her husband, Rhett," I tell him, my voice growing more professional, "one of your clients."

"Rhett said she didn't have representation."

"She does now, and we expect Rhett to pay her attorney fees."

Brielle worked in the office of Rhett's plumbing company, but he only paid her minimum wage. She spent her paychecks on bills, so she has no savings. Even with the discounted rate I gave her, she can't afford legal bills.

"Rhett won't go for that," Adrian says like he's suddenly Rhett's bestie.

"His attorney had better talk him into it then."

"I don't work for you."

I can't help but mock his words and roll my eyes. "She wants primary custody. Alimony. Half of everything."

"How about we discuss her demands over drinks tonight?"

I frown. "How about you pay attention to what I'm saying, and that won't be necessary?"

"I'll come to your office then."

"You are banned from my office. No jerks allowed." I drum my fingers along my forehead. "All I need is your email so we can discuss the case professionally."

"Don't want to do drinks? Understandable. You probably need to eat after a long day's work. We can meet for dinner, and I'll write my email on a piece of paper for you. Shirley's. Seven o'clock."

"You're not bribing me with dinner so I can get your email."

"It's not bribery. I forgot my email, and only food will help me remember."

I open my mouth to scream at him but shut it. This is my time to show Blue Beech what I'm capable of, and having dinner with the attorney I'm up against isn't professional. I need to win so that people want me as their attorney, not him.

"The children are to have no communication with the mistress," I tell him as if the dinner invite never existed.

He chuckles. "She is their former nanny and has been around the children for years."

"Potato, potahto," I drawl out. "I'd advise your client to work with Brielle because we don't plan to go easy on him."

"He has a prenup, Essie."

"He also had an affair. I'll need a copy of that prenup so I can pick it apart."

"I'll bring it to dinner tonight."

"There will be no dinner tonight. You can email me at—"

"Tonight," he interrupts. "The diner. Seven. I'm not emailing you anything."

He hangs up.

Are you kidding me?

There's an urge to call him back to get the last word.

But I don't even have his direct line. No way am I having Ralph, one of the biggest gossipers in town, know I'm calling Adrian again.

Adrian thinks he's winning here, but he's so wrong.

I'll convince him to leave my town, just like he left me all those years ago.

8

Adrian

This is something I never foresaw in my future.

I'm sitting alone in a small diner, "Greased Lightnin' " playing in the background, while being stood up by a woman.

Other diners stare at me in interest.

Some try to hide their nosiness. Others do it shamelessly.

I've never felt like more of an outsider.

It doesn't help that the people in the booth over have been discussing me like I don't have ears and am the latest episode of their favorite show.

"Why would he randomly move here?"

"His grandmother is why! She's marrying Terrance."

"Is he single? I wouldn't mind marrying him!"

"Daphne, you're married."

"Shit, I forgot about that."

A few times, I've wanted to turn around and tell them I moved here for my abuela *and* to get my girl back.

I bet that would make them shut up.

Margo stops by my table for the third time and taps her pen against a notepad. "Ready to order yet or still thinking?" There's a hint of pity in her tone, like she knows I'm being stood up.

"I'll, uh …" I open the menu. "Take another coffee." My gaze scans the options. "And a club sandwich with fries."

Margo offers me a sympathetic nod and shuffles toward the counter. She yells my order to the cooks through the small window.

I don't want another coffee, and my appetite is nonexistent, but I also don't want Margo to kick my ass out for taking booth space. Chances are, Essie isn't coming, but I'm too nervous to leave. There's still that chance she *will* come, and I don't want to be gone if that happens.

I pick up my phone, play with it in my hand, and consider texting Essie to ask if she's coming.

That'd sure make a man look desperate.

More desperate than moving to a new town to win her back?

"Adrian?"

I peer away from my phone to see Ava standing at my booth. We've only been introduced once, years ago, but I still recognize her.

I rest my phone on the table. "That's me."

"I'm Ava." A smile cracks at her lips. She's trying not to show she's about to give me shit. "Essie asked me to pick up whatever you had for her. Something about an email written on paper?"

Ah, she sent a courier.

I run a hand through my hair. "The paper is for Essie's eyes only. Sorry." There's no hiding the disappointment in my voice.

"She couldn't make it. Something came up."

"Something like?"

"A hot date."

My back straightens against the booth. "With who?"

Even if she told me a name, if it was someone local, I still wouldn't know who it was.

I grab a sugar packet, tear it open, and dump it into my coffee that I know I won't be drinking.

"You wouldn't know him." She holds out her hand, but her

face softens when she notices my reaction to Essie's rejection. "Sorry, I'm only the messenger."

I gesture for her to sit, but she doesn't. "Did Essie tell you to do anything else?"

"She said not to conversate with you or like you. Oh, and if possible, throw a pie at your face."

"Well, good thing I haven't ordered pie yet." Relaxing in the booth, I drape my arm along the back of it. "What does Essie normally order here?"

Her brows scrunch together. "Why?"

"Since she bailed on dinner, I'll order her a meal to go, and you can drop it off to her, along with the paper. I never go back on my word to buy someone dinner."

Ava pauses, contemplating my offer. "Fine, but I'll tell Margo the order and wait at the counter for it. And I'm *only* doing this because we never turn down a Shirley's meal."

I wanted Ava to sit here and wait for Essie's food so I could pick her brain apart and ask all the questions about the girl I'd lost.

Instead, I'll be here in this booth, rehashing all my regrets.

Ava walks to the counter and talks with Margo. After Margo rings Essie's order in, she delivers my food. I pick at the toasted bread while watching Ava wildly text on her phone. My guess is, it's with Essie.

Ava points toward me when Margo hands her the food. I give them a thumbs-up.

"I told Margo to charge the sandwich to you," Ava says, stopping by my booth on the way toward the exit.

"Wait," I call out.

She spins around to face me while narrowing her eyes. The poor girl is doing her best to hate me for her best friend.

"Forgot this." I snatch the folded paper I prepared for Essie from the table and hold it up.

"Thanks," she mutters, returning my way to take the paper.

I jerk it back, most likely looking like a straight asshole. "Has Essie been dating this *hot date* for long?"

Something inside me tells me the date excuse is straight bullshit.

According to my Essie social media stalking, there's no mention of a boyfriend. She was also guy-free at the pub. If she is dating someone and they didn't show up to celebrate her firm opening, she should dump his ass just for that.

"Oh, it's *realll* serious," Ava says with a smirk. "In fact, I'm already picking out my bridesmaid dress. Pretty soon, their wedding will be all this town talks about. You should probably leave so you don't have to see it."

Some people are good at lying.

Ava is not on that list.

I snatch a fry and point it at her. "Maybe I'll stay so I can crash the wedding. Give this small town some excitement."

She smirks. "I'll make sure we have extra security on her big day then."

" I'd better make sure I'm the groom."

"You sure are cocky." She steals a fry from my plate.

"Nah, not cocky. Determined."

She snatches another fry and walks away without another word.

If Essie thought I'd simply hand over my email address, she was so wrong. She should know me better than that.

I lean back in my booth, deciding that I need to take this Blue Beech thing a step further. It's time for me to look for a place to live here.

9

Essie

"Okay, I think this man is a psychopath, like the Riddler from *Gotham*," Ava says, walking into my cottage, kicking off her sneakers, and handing me a takeout bag from Shirley's.

"How do you know about *Gotham*?" I ask.

"Your brother was obsessed with that show. But I must admit, the Riddler was always my fave. There was just something about him." She dramatically sighs and fans her face. "Team Villain over here." She holds up a folded paper. "Sorry, I couldn't resist reading this. Hate me for it later."

"*Of course* you couldn't," I say, faking annoyance. "I take it there's more on there than a simple email?"

"Oh, his email is there, but I highly doubt *give me another chance Essie at groveling man dot com* is a legit email."

I snatch the paper, holding it in my mouth, and untie the takeout bag, moving into the living room. I drag the food containers out of the bag and unfold the paper while collapsing on the couch.

Ava follows my lead.

Two glasses of red wine sit on the coffee table. After she left to meet with Adrian, I poured them for us while waiting for her return. That was after she called me a chickenshit for not meeting with him myself.

Next to the wine is a bowl of popcorn.

À la Olivia Pope.

I ignore the food and mutter, "What the hell?" as my eyes skim what Adrian wrote on the paper.

At the top is the false email, written in blue Sharpie.

Underneath the email, he wrote out a bulleted list in red Sharpie.

"They're all our inside jokes," I say.

No wonder they didn't make sense to Ava.

"Not going to lie, babe, but something that sweet does fall into the groveling category." She pulls her thick hair up into a ponytail and clasps a tie around it. "I also need you to explain some of them to me, please and thank you, because they sound *very* interesting."

I grip the paper tight and read off the first bullet that's a song quote.

She holds up a finger. "That one I did know, and I love that he's quoting Tay Tay. Though he doesn't give off Swiftie vibes."

"In college, Adrian asked for my favorite playlist. I sent it to him, and 'Treacherous' was on it. He listened to it and said those lyrics reminded him of me. After that, before he drove to see me, he'd text me that quote."

"This guy needs to stop being romantic before *I* fall in love with him."

"Ava!" I lean forward to smack her shoulder.

"Kidding, kidding," she sings out. "He has his shit together too well. Not my type. I prefer workaholics with subpar communication skills."

"True. I mean, your ex did cut people and then stitch them back up."

She snorts. "He was a *surgeon*. God, you say it like he was a serial killer." She picks up a glass of wine, hands it to me, and then grabs hers before nodding toward the letter. "Now, keep cracking the cutesy little inside joke codes for me."

"A simple twist of fate," I read off.

She blinks at me, the glass rim against her lips, waiting for me to explain.

"Lyrics from 'Simple Twist of Fate' by Bob Dylan." I shut my eyes, remembering the conversation we had about it. "The song was his mother's favorite. She listened to it during every car ride when he was growing up, and just like 'Treacherous,' he said it reminded him of me."

"I'll have to add that to my Essie and Adrian Fall for Each Other Again playlist. Do you mind if I make that public?" The smirk on her face doesn't leave, even when she takes a sip of wine.

"You make it public, and I'll make your Pet the Kitty playlist public."

"Okay, that's rude. It's not my fault River found my *pleasuring myself* playlist and renamed it." She leans forward and grabs a handful of popcorn. "I do have to give him props for creativity, though."

I throw my head back, bursting out in laughter.

One thing about hanging out with Ava is that you know you're going to laugh. It's why she and my brother are so close.

Nostalgia hits me as I read off the list.

"Oh, I know that one," Ava says. "*Legally Blonde* quote. I think you made me watch that movie more than your brother did *Gotham*."

The list fills nearly the entire page, giving me reminders of our favorite foods and little comments we made to each other, and the last item is a link. Ava types it into her phone, and it's a list of all the books Adrian and I read together—from fiction to legal books.

I only spent a few months with Adrian in college, but we had so many memories. I suck in a shallow sigh to stop tears from filling my eyes.

I miss so much of this.

"Now, come on. You have to admit that was cute," Ava comments when I'm finished.

I carefully fold the note, tightening the creases, and place it on the table. "Yes, but a slow loris is cute until it bites and kills you." I snatch my wine and chug it.

"Those are cute, but hate to say it, their eyes creep me out. They're like two huge boba pearls." She scoots closer, noticing my change in emotions, and settles her head on my shoulder. "I know you never told me the entire story of what happened between you two, but sometimes, giving someone a second chance is okay, Essie. Sometimes, the second time around is when you truly show someone everything about you."

A tear slips down my cheek as I whisper, "That's what I'm afraid of."

She kisses my cheek. "I'm here for you, no matter what."

I slowly nod before reaching forward to finally open the food containers.

Ava and I spend the next three hours watching *Emily in Paris* while sharing the nachos, grilled cheese sandwich, and carrot cake.

10

Adrian

I follow Terrance's Volvo down a curvy, narrow road. We're about twenty miles outside downtown Blue Beech, and I haven't seen a house in miles.

He makes a sudden left, and I curse when one of my wheels hits a pothole before we reach a gravel lane that leads to a two-story home with a wraparound porch perched on a hill. It's an old house, but you can tell it's in the middle of a remodel. Half of it looks done, while the other half still needs some TLC.

A man and woman dressed in matching denim overalls wave to us from the porch as we grow closer. I park, and they walk down the three wide steps to meet us.

"Pete," the man says, holding out his hand. "This is my wife, Agnes."

"Adrian." I shake his and then Agnes's hand.

Pete runs a hand through his graying beard. "Terrance said you're looking for somewhere to stay. Our loft above the garage is open. If you don't mind a little dust, the place is all yours. It's private, and we won't bug ya."

"Thank you." I clasp my hands and tip my chin toward them.

"Make sure you're careful while driving here at night," Agnes says, and I notice one of her overall straps is undone and behind her shoulder. "It's easy to get lost."

"The place is furnished," Pete adds. "It's outdated furniture, but, hey, it's furniture."

"It'll do," I say, grateful.

"Rent is eight hundred a month. If you need us to go lower, we can. We cover all utilities."

Finding a rental in Blue Beech has been harder than trying to learn Terrance's filing system—and the man still hasn't learned that technology is his friend. There was hardly anything available, so Terrance asked around and found me this.

The hour-drive commutes to my condo late at night are taking a toll on me and my dog, Tucker. Tucker stays with my abuela while I work and then rides home with me later. I can only allow him to stick his head out the window at midnight for so long until enough bugs start blowing in our faces.

On the drive here, Terrance told me Pete was one of his closest friends. He and Agnes used to live closer to town, but Agnes wanted to buy a horse, so they bought this place for the extra land.

"You allow pets, right?" I ask.

"What you got?" Pete asks. "A dog? Cat?"

"Dog. Golden retriever."

"Dog is fine." He removes his hat and wipes the sweat building along his forehead. "We got an old dachshund. You might see Greta running around here at night. She don't bite but appreciates a good slice of bacon and belly rubs."

"Sounds like she and Tucker are a lot alike then." I smile.

"That mean you'll take it?" Agnes asks.

"I'll take it."

"We're glad to have you." Pete claps me on the back before handing me a key. "Agnes always makes breakfast. If you're hungry in the morning, stop in. Now, let me show you your new place."

I grab my duffel bag from the trunk, and Terrance and I follow Pete. We trudge up creaky, old stairs that lead to a door on the second story of the garage. The air is musty when we walk in, and Pete starts opening windows.

I drop my bag onto the leather couch. There are plenty of rips, but thankfully no stains. Pete wasn't lying when he said the place was dusty, but it's not too bad. There's a box TV that I'm sure was made while I was in Pampers and a metal-framed bed, but the appliances aren't too outdated.

"I'll let you make yourself comfortable," Pete says. "Let me know if you need anything." He tips his head toward Terrance before leaving. "See you next week for poker night."

Terrance shoves his hands inside his pockets. "Your grandmother is making dinner tonight. If you're not busy settling in, stop by."

I gesture to the duffel bag. "Not much to unpack here."

I'm not selling my condo until I'm one hundred percent positive I'm staying in Blue Beech. I'll give it six months. If Essie doesn't forgive me by then, I don't know if I can live in the same town. With how small Blue Beech is, we're bound to run into each other, and that'll only be a harsh reminder of what I fucked up.

Terrance grins and takes his hand from his pocket to offer a thumbs-up. "Glad to have you staying here in Blue Beech."

After settling in, I sit on the couch and drag my MacBook from my bag. But I don't turn it on. Instead, I drop it next to me and wander to the plywood bookshelves on the wall. I run my fingers along the spines of old yearbooks. Blue Beech High yearbooks, each year dating back to the early 1950s.

Essie and I graduated from high school the same year, so I immediately grab the one dated with her senior year. I flip through the pages to find her picture, via alphabetical order by class, but it isn't there.

River's is.

She's missing.

I check the class photo.

She's also missing.

As far as I knew, Essie attended school here for every grade.

11

Essie

"Of course Rhett's attorney is hot," Brielle whispers when we're at the conference room doorway at Terrance's law firm.

Yes, I will call it Terrance's firm until the day I die.

Never Adrian's.

I frown, hating that Brielle is right.

Unfortunately, this isn't the first time I've had to hear women gush over him. They did it at Adaway and Williams too. And now, he's the main topic of conversation here. According to Amelia, a few women have already asked him out.

The boardroom is all business with its bland cream walls and long, chipped table. The wall paintings and Berber carpet are outdated. It also smells like a concoction of three different colognes.

Adrian and Rhett stop talking when they notice us.

Rhett glowers, dressed in a floral button-up, like he's ready for a Hawaiian cruise.

Adrian, wearing a sleek black suit, stands from his chair and extends his hand toward me.

"Essie Lane," I say in the most professional tone I've ever used in my life.

Adrian smirks. He gently takes my hand and sweeps his thumb across it, causing me to shiver. "I'd like to say we already know each other pretty well, Essie."

I quickly jerk my hand from his hold and ignore Brielle's side-eye.

"Brielle ..." She pauses, unsure which last name to use, and I smile when she decides on her maiden. "Hermaker. That asshole's ex."

Rhett doesn't bother standing. He stays in his chair and pushes his chest forward. He thinks he has this in the bag. What a scumbag, dragging his high school sweetheart and the mother of his children through hell over money.

In high school, even when he was with Brielle, he asked me for a blow job once. When I told her, he said I lied, and she didn't believe me. Another time, during sophomore year, he tried to corner Mia against a wall at a homecoming party. She kneed him in the nuts and threatened to castrate him if he ever looked at her again. I'm sure the nanny wasn't the first time he cheated.

"Just accept my terms, Brielle," Rhett says as soon as we sit across from him. He huffs. "This is a waste of my time. I have better shit to do."

"Like what?" Brielle asks, spit leaving her lips with that one word. "Screwing the nanny?"

"Get over it and move on." Rhett clenches his jaw. "I sure have."

"That's easier said than done," Brielle fires back. "But maybe the next guy I marry won't last only three seconds and have a penis smaller than my pinky."

I cover my mouth to stop myself from laughing.

Adrian snorts, resulting in a glare from Rhett.

Not in the mood to listen to their bickering, I open my folder with Brielle's information. "Let's start with spousal support."

Rhett releases another huff. "She can get a damn job."

"The only job she's had for years was working for you, in

and out of the home," I say, beating Brielle from talking more shit. "She needs assistance to provide and care for your children while getting on her feet." I sigh. "Come on, Rhett. Let's be fair here."

"If she needs something for the children, I'll buy it," Rhett argues. "But I don't want a dime going to her. We're done, so I have no responsibility to care for her any longer. Give me custody if she's too broke to care for their needs."

"As if you'd care for them," Brielle sneers. "You never even changed a diaper, you lazy bastard."

Rhett finally looks in his wife's direction. "That's what the hired help is for."

Brielle winces. "Oh, *now*, you think that's what hired help is for? Before, you thought the nannies were only there for you to fuck."

Rhett holds up his hand. "I didn't sleep with anyone until we separated."

"Bullshit." Brielle raises her voice. "Everyone has seen you gallivanting around with the nanny. It's humiliating!"

"She's there for the children."

"The children are with me!" Brielle yells. "Now, *you* quit wasting *my* time. I want half of the business because I was there with you every step of the way."

Rhett grits his teeth. "My family has run that plumbing business for generations—"

"And it was barely surviving when you took over. I gave you my savings and the inheritance from my grandparents to keep it from bankruptcy. You had nothing when we married, and you'd probably still have nothing if it wasn't for me."

"She has a valid point," I add.

Rhett's icy glare cuts to me. "Shut up, Essie."

"Whoa," Adrian snaps, turning to Rhett. He leans in, his face close to his client's. "One thing you won't do here is disrespect anyone in this room. Don't speak to either of these women like that. Now, stay calm, Rhett."

"Whose side are you on here?" Rhett pounds his finger into his chest. "You're *my* attorney."

Adrian doesn't flinch at Rhett. "Attorney or not, you will respect all parties in this room, or you will leave."

Rhett cunningly stares at Brielle. "She doesn't have bills and lives with her parents, and I disapprove of the living conditions there. That alone should give me custody."

"There is nothing wrong with my living conditions," Brielle argues.

Rhett scoffs.

"Is it what they're used to? No. But that's where I grew up, and I had no problems."

He looks at Adrian. "It's terrible."

"You liar." Brielle's chin quivers as Rhett starts to wear her down. "Don't you dare insult my parents."

This needs to stop.

We won't come to an agreement today.

These two are toxic together.

"How about this?" I say. "We'll do a home walk-through and take pictures to prove it's suitable for the children."

A phone rings, and Rhett slides his hand into his pocket to dig it out.

"I have to take this." He narrows his eyes at Brielle while walking toward the door. "We'll be in touch."

"Fucking asshole," Brielle snarls as Rhett disappears from the room before slipping her gaze to Adrian. "Where's the restroom?"

"Out the door, to your right," Adrian replies with a hint of a smile.

I stand at the same time she does, and Brielle nearly trips on her black heels as she dashes out of the room.

"Your client might be more immature than you," I tell Adrian while shoving papers inside my folder before pressing it against my chest. "Ava gave me your *email address.*"

He smirks, rising from his chair and moving around the

table. "I've been wondering why I haven't received an email. I waited all night in the diner for you. So long that Margo felt so bad for me that she dropped off a free slice of cinnamon apple pie at my table."

"I didn't *forget* about it because I never agreed to go," I say, a sudden chill sweeping up my body. "Thank you for the food, though. If you'd given me a real email address, I'd have emailed you my thank-you last night."

He stands in front of me, cutting off my path to leave the room. "It's a shame."

I tighten my hold on the folder. "What is?"

"That your"—he pauses to lower his head so it's level with mine—"*hot date* didn't feed you."

Hot date?

Oh, I'm going to kill Ava.

She should've at least given me a heads-up about her lie.

My mouth falls open, and for a moment, I'm lost for words.

I clear my throat when they come to me. "He did feed me, but we were *sooo* exhausted by the end of the night that we needed another meal. He told me to thank you for the carrot cake. It's his favorite."

"Ah, and what's this guy's name?" he asks in amusement.

"You don't need to know that. The last thing I need is you stalking him like you are me."

He chuckles, not at all offended. "Stalking? No. This is called *winning your girl back.*"

"That's what all stalkers say."

"Did you read the rest of the paper?"

"Yep, and none of the inside jokes made sense. You must've been thinking about the wrong girl."

"How did you know they were inside jokes, then?"

Dammit.

He strokes my cheek. I know I should pull away, but I can't.

"Which inside joke was your favorite?"

I narrow my eyes at him.

"You know what I listened to on my drive here?"

"Cardi B's 'WAP'?"

"I don't even know what that is, but no. 'Simple Twist of Fate.' "

I shut my eyes, feeling my heart thump. "We have to keep this professional, Adrian. We'll never go back to how we were in the past. *Never*."

His face turns slack. "Essie, please give me a chance to explain myself."

I take a step back, his hand falling from my face. "No. And no more dinners, flowers, or forced encounters. *Please*." I hate that my tone turns almost begging, but I also hate that I'm about to lie to him even more. "I've moved on."

Adrian lowers his voice. "But what if I haven't?"

I gulp and glance away, positive if we make eye contact, I'll break. "You're eight years too late to tell me that."

12

Adrian

"Listen, you need to keep your cool," I lecture Rhett over the phone.

Never have I not wanted to work with a client before. I woke up this morning contemplating advising him to seek counsel elsewhere. We worked with some serious assholes at Adaway and Williams, but Rhett doesn't listen to any advice.

Unfortunately, he's the only tie I have to Essie right now.

The only excuse I have to see her.

So, I'll have to suffer through his bullshit.

Terrance also passed the case down to me. It'd look pretty damn bad if I ran away from the first client he'd handed over to me at his firm.

"You ever been married, Adrian?" Rhett asks.

I reach into a drawer and grab my phone charger. "No."

"Don't. Now, you need to deem Brielle an unfit mother."

I shove the charger into my computer and my phone into the other end. "You can't deem someone unfit because you don't like them."

"She takes antidepressants. Can't we use that against her?"

"Does she have an addiction problem? Has she ever been rehabilitated?"

"Well … no … but can't antidepressants make you unfit?"

"No, they can't." I hold in the urge to add *jackass* to the end of my sentence. "Meth? Yes. Abuse? Absolutely. Antidepressants? Negative."

And fuck this dude for shaming a woman for how she coped with him putting her through hell.

"I talked to a friend," he says, almost rambling now. "He said he did that with his ex-wife. Surely, there's a way for you to twist the truth."

"That won't work with Brielle."

"Don't forget who's paying the bill here. I have a lot of pull in this town. If you're good to me, I'll send you more business."

I grit my teeth, and my jaw aches. "You need to remember I have a successful career with or without you, Rhett. Choose your words wisely or look for representation elsewhere."

He goes quiet for a moment. "I want you present during the home tour and at *every* interaction I have with Brielle. You'll see what I'm talking about when I say she shouldn't have custody of my children."

"Are you fighting for custody? I wasn't aware of this."

"I know I don't want to pay her a penny of child support."

"Custody of two children is an enormous responsibility, Rhett."

"That's what nannies are for."

His smugness makes me cringe.

"I'll draw up custody papers, then." I wait for him to stop me and roll my eyes when he does.

"Why don't we see how the home tour goes first?"

Rhett doesn't want custody. He wants to be an ass.

Unsurprisingly, Brielle's parents' home is far from what Rhett described. From his depiction, you'd think it was something you'd see in a horror movie.

Sure, it's not an extravagant home, but unless it's like an episode of *Hoarders* inside, I want to kick Rhett's ass for wasting my time.

Better yet, maybe not.

I'll just bill the asshole double for every minute I'm here.

I duck out of my car and look around at the white picket fence, garden fairies, and freshly trimmed yard. Essie and Brielle are standing on the porch.

Everyone's attention moves to Rhett as he pulls up to the curb in his yellow Jaguar.

A Jaguar that costs as much as his annual salary—a number I recently discovered when reviewing their divorce documents. The man is living well beyond his means.

The home's front door swings open, and an older woman steps onto the porch. She hugs Essie, and when she turns her head to peer at Rhett, her eyes tighten.

Rhett tosses his keys in the air as he joins me. "Here we go. Her mom is a basket case, FYI."

I silently nod and follow as he struts toward the porch.

The woman—my guess is Brielle's mother—shuffles to the corner of the porch to rest her elbows on the wood railing. She flips Rhett the bird, and he shakes his head while murmuring words under his breath that I can't make out.

Rhett and I walk in first while Brielle and Essie follow. The air smells like freshly baked bread, and the interior resembles what you'd find in a small-town bed-and-breakfast.

Rhett glances at me, noticing my lack of concern, and squishes his nose. "The children, they share a room." He attempts to shove an ounce of disgust into his voice. "They have their own rooms at my home."

"Yes, but they unfortunately have an asshole father there," Brielle argues behind me.

During the tour, Rhett shakes his head and makes snarky

comments about random shit. There's not one problem I can write in a report to convince a judge to remove the children from this home.

"That concludes the tour," Brielle says, slapping her arms to her sides when we return to the front porch. "Now, go, Rhett, and never come back."

Rhett squares up his skinny shoulders. "Before I go, we need to discuss the birthday party. You have your party here, and I'll have mine at the house."

Brielle winces. "I worked my ass off for that party with the planner."

"Sure, but you no longer live there," Rhett argues. "Don't worry. I'll ask my mother to send you photos."

Essie and I retreat inches from our clients, allowing them space to hash this out but remain within earshot to hear the conversation.

Brielle moves closer to Rhett and stands on her tiptoes so they're eye level. "If you don't want me at the party *I planned*, then the children won't be there either."

"That's bullshit," Rhett screams. "I forked out a lot of money for that party."

"Either I'm in attendance or none of us are."

Rhett cradles the back of his balding head before throwing it back. "Fine, whatever." His gaze locks on me. "My attorney will also be there. Saturday afternoon. Two o'clock. My house."

Brielle parks her hands on her hips. "My attorney will also be there, then."

I peer at Essie and can't help but smile. "Looks like I'll see you at the party."

"Can't wait," she grumbles.

13

Essie

How bad would it look if your attorney called in sick?
It wouldn't look professional.

Especially if Adrian shows up and I don't.

People could look at him as the better attorney.

I have to suck it up for the sake of my career and attend the birthday party.

Rhett lives in the same neighborhood as my grandmother. It's the wealthiest subdivision in Blue Beech, but his home is smaller compared to the others. I'm sure the HOA will be all over his ass about his poorly manicured lawn.

I turn off my car, groan, and text the XOXO, Gossip Girl chat.

> Me: I'm going in. Wish me all the luck.

My phone immediately vibrates with replies.

> Callie: Good luck! You got this.

> Amelia: Sending you my love. If anyone says anything rude, I'll knee them in the balls next time I see them. If it's Rhett, I'll do it twice.

Mia: Ugh, I can't believe you didn't cancel on those assholes.

Ava: Make sure to give Adrian a hello and goodbye hug. Maybe trade some more inside jokes. IYKYK.

Mia: Ava, WTF?

Callie: UM, I DON'T KNOW!

Amelia: Inside jokes? What inside jokes?

Ava: The ones Adrian wrote in a love letter to Essie.

Me: It was not a love letter!

Callie: Aw, love letters are cute! Please tell me he sprayed it with cologne, like in Legally Blonde? That'd be the cutest.

Me: IT WAS NOT A LOVE LETTER!

Ava: You can read it out loud to the class next time we have a girls' night.

Mia: Can I cancel that night then? Hard pass on anything love-note related. Let me know when we can talk shit about him. I'm already RSVPing to that party.

Callie: I can't wait until you fall in love, and I can throw it in your face, Mia.

Mia: That will be the day I ask you to plan my funeral.

Amelia: Send a picture of the letter!

Callie: Yeah, proof, or it didn't happen.

Ava: Oh, it happened! Ugh, I should've taken a picture. I apologize for my negligence. I'll do better next time.

> **Me:** Ava, you're officially last in line for top friend.

> **Ava:** The line has 4 other people. That's, like, one whole Kit Kat. I think I'll be fine.

They're still texting each other as I slide my phone into my purse. I grab the two birthday cards from the passenger seat, shove them inside my purse, and step out of my car.

I went simple with the gifts for their twins, Wes and Jes. Gift cards to the local bookstore.

A DJ is playing music in the backyard. I'm pretty sure it's some Kidz Bop version because it just said *door* when the real lyrics say *whore*. A woman is dressed up as the Little Mermaid and another as Buzz Lightyear.

Kids are running everywhere, climbing in the bounce house and cannonballing into the pool.

The party is definitely divided.

Brielle's family is on one side, and Rhett's is on the other. Although Brielle's side is smaller than Rhett's. Rhett is drinking beers with a group of guys we went to high school with. I spot the nanny —Brielle has shown me pictures—next to Rhett's mother, talking.

I drop the cards on the present table and head in the direction of Brielle and her mom.

"Thank you for coming, Essie," Rita says with a smile when I join them at their table.

I wasn't that close with Brielle growing up. She was a cheerleader and sporty, while I was a nerdy gamer. But we did attend a lot of the same birthday parties and girl outings.

Brielle is on one knee, talking to a hysterically crying kid and pointing toward the jump house.

She glances at her mom. "Can I get your help for a minute?"

Rita pulls herself up from the chair. "Of course."

She and Brielle scurry off, and not knowing what else to do, I sit.

There's an eerie sense of someone watching me.

I glance around the yard, and my gaze collides with Adrian's. He's at a table with an older couple. He nods, listening as they speak, but his attention is half focused on me.

Goose bumps crawl up my arms, and I run my hand over my jacket sleeves.

Has he been watching me since I got here?

He says something to the couple, and they burst into laughter. The woman taps his hand in a kind gesture, and he stands. Adrian waves to them and grabs two drinks—one with a princess theme and the other *Toy Story*—and a knot forms in my stomach when he starts walking in my direction.

He sets the drinks down on the table and grips the back of the chair beside me. "Is this seat taken?"

"No," I say, keeping my voice low. "But I'm enjoying a moment of silence and not accepting chair neighbors."

"What if I want to talk about our clients?"

Eyeing him suspiciously, I motion for him to go ahead. He pulls out the chair, sits, and directs all his attention on me.

"Sooo …" I drag out the word. "What about our clients?"

Other than the fact that they're a hot-mess express.

"I forgot." He fights back a smile, and I narrow my eyes at him. "Plus, I've also heard it's unprofessional to speak legalities at parties. Serious conversations are for boardrooms. Parties are for fun."

I stare at him in annoyance. "Since you lied about your reasoning for sitting and you're not going to speak legalities with me, shouldn't you be on the other side of the party? We're the Anti-Rhett Club over here."

"I think you know I'm not a Rhett fan." He slides the princess cup closer to me.

"God, he's such an asshole," I groan.

"I can deal with assholes. It's part of the job. But the shirts? Those are what I'm struggling with."

I throw my head back, laughing.

Rhett is dressed in another one of his Hawaiian shirts, this one a neon green.

I'm never one to knock someone's sense of style. I'm all about self-expression. But he always looks like he's ready for someone to shove a margarita in his hand and a lei around his neck. It makes him look fun, and he's *far* from fun.

"I'm telling Brielle to ask for all the flower shirts in the divorce," I tell Adrian before motioning toward the table. "Jot that down somewhere."

"He'd probably give her the house before sacrificing the shirts."

"Thank you for that inside information. Please tell Rhett he has twelve days to vacate the premises."

"Nope, I told you, we don't speak legalities at parties."

I cross my arms. "What do we talk about, then?"

He drums his fingers along his chin. "How about what you're doing later tonight?"

"Eh, probably burning your *inside jokes* note," I say more teasingly than I should have. I gulp, realizing my mistake, and grab the cup. My lips pucker at the sweet strawberry lemonade when I take a sip.

He smiles in amusement. "Why would you do that?"

"Ava read it and ratted me out to my friends, and now, they want to read it."

"It's pretty much written in code. They won't understand it."

"Do you honestly think they won't decode a Taylor Swift lyric?"

"Fair point." He looks around, draping his arm along the back of my chair. "What was your favorite birthday party growing up?"

There's a brief silence before I answer. I didn't walk into this party expecting to have a conversation with Adrian. Though this is how it was in the past too.

We'd spend hours asking each other question after question.

"When we were ten, River let his friend use my video game controller. It was decked out and hard to find, and I'd spent days gluing rainbow rhinestones onto it in a specific pattern. His friend ended up being a sore loser and threw my remote into the pool, ruining it. I refused to speak to River for a week, and our party was that weekend. I insisted we have separate ones. With that short of time, my parents decided the only thing they could do was hold parties on opposite sides of the yard." I laugh and can't stop myself from grinning at the memory.

"River convinced my friends to ditch my party and go to his side. I was furious, but when I stomped over to pour punch over his head, I found it was all a setup. He'd put up a table with a *decorate your own controller* station. And that year, his gift to me was a controller, the same as I'd had, with the same rhinestone design. My mom said he had stayed up all night working on it."

Sure, as twins, River and I fought, but we never stayed angry with each other for long. One of us would end up sliding a goofy note under the other's door, or my mother would help us bake the other's favorite dessert as an *I'm sorry*.

"I'm a little disappointed you never showed me your rhinestone skills," Adrian says. "I had plenty of stuff we could've decked out in my dorm room."

I chuckle. "My brother definitely would've known something was up then."

"The rhinestone artwork would've confirmed we were dating."

I wince at the word *dating*.

We never used the term, but our actions fit the definition in every way. It was nice having our hangouts and conversations in secret sometimes. It was something that only belonged to us.

We were too busy and didn't want to put a label on anything between us.

We were Adrian and Essie.

No labels. No devotions. No expectations.

I gulp as we stare at each other.

Adrian's smile is contagious, and like a yawn, you can't stop yourself from doing the same.

This is so much like old times.

When everyone and everything else faded.

Our trance is broken when a ball flies over our heads.

"Sorry!" a kid yells, sprinting toward us to retrieve the ball and throwing it in the air before catching it. "My bad."

"What's your favorite birthday memory?" I ask Adrian.

"My eleventh birthday. My mom and abuela took me to Puerto Rico to meet my family there. My abuela gave me a tour of where she and my abuelo had lived before she moved to the States. It was eye-opening and taught me a lot about my family and what to be grateful for."

A twinge of sadness passes through me. Adrian never met his father or grandfather. One night, he told me how he wished he could've known them, even if for a day, for the memories.

I can't stop myself from reaching toward him and resting my hand on his. He uses his free hand to cover mine and squeezes it.

"I miss this," he whispers.

"Miss what?"

"Talking with you." His thumb runs over my hand. "You've always been a comfort to me, Essie. Like home, where I belong. When we shared the highs and lows of our lives, it always put me at ease. No one knows me as well as you do. I don't think anyone ever will."

This is dangerous.

Not only is it bad for my heart, but people might also be watching.

Brielle or Rhett might see there's more to Adrian and me than simply two attorneys against each other.

"Time for cake!" a kid screams.

I yank my hand out of his hold and fall back in my chair.

Disappointment crosses Adrian's features as I wipe my palm over my face.

Maybe taking this case against him wasn't such a good idea.

My goal was to win, but now, my goal is to protect my heart from him.

14

Adrian

One of the hardest things to do is grieve someone who's still alive.

If only Essie and I had been alone during our last conversation and not at the party. If we had been somewhere private, I could've explained everything to her. She needs to know why I fled.

I was too immature to face my problems. I lost who I had been, and it took me a while to find myself again. I'm not entirely the Adrian she'd created a bond with forever ago.

After leaving the birthday party, I drive to my abuela's.

Their home is a simple ranch with yellow siding and a large porch. I smile, noticing the personal touches she's already added to the home. Pink flamingos are scattered across the lawn. A decorative duck, wearing a polka-dot raincoat, sits on the bottom porch step, and a sign with the Puerto Rican flag hangs on the front door.

My abuela sits on the porch swing, knitting, and Tucker lies at her feet. He barks when he sees me, dashing in my direction, and his tail wags.

"Hey, buddy," I greet, petting him while we walk toward the porch.

"Hi, honey," my abuela says when I kiss her cheek.

"Good afternoon," I reply at the same time the front screen door opens with a slight creak.

A guy who looks to be around my age, wearing faded jeans and a tee, steps outside and joins us.

He smiles in my direction. "Adrian, right?"

I nod.

"I'm Foster, Terrance's grandson." He holds up his hand as if to stop me before I ask a question. "Not the one who ran over your grandmother's petunias. That'd be my asshole brother."

He laughs, extending his hand in my direction, and I shake it.

Tucker plods over to Foster, using his nose to nudge his knee, and Foster pets him.

My abuela gestures toward the patio furniture on the other side of the door. "You two have a seat and get to know each other. Adrian, you're staying for dinner."

Foster congratulates me on taking over Terrance's firm. I was unsure how his family would react to him giving me the practice. It's relieving to see Foster being so cool about it.

"Tomorrow night is the grand opening of Down Home Brewery's second location in Anchor Ridge," Foster says. "I'm stopping by. You should come, meet people, network."

"That sounds good," I reply.

Maybe Essie will be there.

That's what my life has become.

Going to places in hopes that Essie is there.

"So, Paula, how is everything going at the Prison Exoneration Program?" Terrance asks my mother from across the dinner table.

The Prison Exoneration Program—PEP for short—is a criminal justice nonprofit my mother cofounded with an attorney she went to law school with. The PEP works to release wrongly convicted individuals. She's always wanted me to follow in her footsteps at the nonprofit, but I want more experience. The PEP holds people's innocence in their hands, and I'd never want to let anyone down.

My mother sets down her fork and wipes her mouth before answering, "Last week, we won a case for a man who had been in prison for sixteen years for a murder he hadn't committed." She sighs, and there's that familiar sadness in her eyes when she talks about her cases. "Sixteen years of his life wasted because prosecutors wanted to point their fingers at the easiest guy they could blame."

She's shared plenty of her cases with me, and honestly, it's fucked up. I can't imagine getting locked up for a crime I hadn't committed—to suffer the consequences of someone else's actions.

A few times, she's come to me for advice and questions. I love that she trusts me enough to help her with something so important.

"If you ever want to throw a case my way, I'll definitely help," I tell her.

"I appreciate that, and I'll most likely take you up on that offer." Her gaze returns to Terrance. "Not that I'll take him away from putting everything he has into your practice, of course."

Terrance repeatedly shakes his head while running his fingers over his gray mustache. "Oh, no, no. I wouldn't mind him helping at all. I think your organization does great things."

She thanks him and takes a sip of her red wine.

We make small talk for the rest of dinner, and Foster says he'll text me the info about the brewery opening.

"Goodbye, my sweet great-granddog," my abuela sings out to Tucker.

She gives him head kisses, and he returns a slobbery one on her cheek.

15

Essie

Tonight is the grand opening of Down Home Brewery's second location in Anchor Ridge.

An old Johnny Cash song plays in the background when I walk inside. This building is larger than the one in Blue Beech, but Jax and Chris went safe the first time.

Customers are mingling and drinking.

Some are yelling their orders to the bartenders.

Smiling, I take in the space. Amelia gave me a tour a few weeks ago, but the place wasn't finished. Long picnic-style tables and stools are the only furniture, except for the stools at the bar. She wanted the brewery to feel like a family gathering.

I say hi to a few people, shuffle through the crowd, then walk outside to the beer garden.

When Amelia told me they were putting one in, I said, "What the hell is a beer garden?"

"Just wait," she replied eagerly. "You'll love it."

And she was right.

Plants and greenery provide a serene atmosphere, and the patio furniture has similar tables to the ones indoors.

I beeline straight to my friends.

"This place is incredible," I sing out before hugging Amelia. "I'm so proud of and happy for you two!" I hug Jax next.

Amelia's cheeks blush. "Thank you."

Jax stares devotedly at her.

Their happiness and how they helped each other heal is inspiring.

"Hey, Sis," River greets, lifting me off the ground in a hug.

I hug Callie, Ava, Mia, and Easton next. Easton is Mia and Ava's cousin.

Hugs for everyone!

This is our circle.

We might have disagreements, but when it comes down to it, we always fully support each other.

Amelia and Jax leave to talk with customers and local journalists who came for the opening. A news crew is filming inside.

We order pizza and nachos, and I sit beside Callie. As soon as the server delivers our food, I snatch a cheese slice and drop it onto my plate.

"How was the party?" Mia asks, sipping her beer. She's normally a martini girl, and Down Home is the only beer she'll drink.

Instead of telling them about my talk with Adrian, I dive straight into the gossip. "Everything was fine until it was time to unwrap presents. Brielle and the nanny—a.k.a. Rhett's mistress —bought the kids the same thing."

Callie covers her mouth with her hand.

"You're joking?" Ava asks.

I shake my head. "Literally the most awkward moment of my life."

"Did Brielle freak out?" Callie asks.

"Nope," I reply. "She stayed surprisingly calm until Rhett, with his big mouth, said, 'Look at that. Great moms think alike.' "

Mia twists the gold bracelet on her wrist. "Please tell me Mistress Nanny also has children?"

I shake my head again.

Callie gasps.

"What a scumbag." Mia rolls her eyes. "Give me Brielle's number so I can tell her to hook up with Rhett's hot cousin."

Ava holds up her crossed fingers. "Let us hope the nanny learns how lame Rhett is and dumps his ass."

"Oh, she will," Mia says with absolute certainty.

"On a brighter note," Callie chirps, waving at me, "did you bring the love letter?"

River looks up from his phone. "Love letter?"

Easton—who, like River, was glued to his phone—peers at me.

I squirm in my seat. "I've told you a million times, it wasn't a love letter! It was a sheet of paper with his email address written on it."

"Refresh my memory and tell me *what* his email was again?" Ava stuffs a nacho into her mouth.

"I can't recall," I mutter. "I'm a busy woman who gets lots of emails."

"*Give me another chance Essie at groveling man dot com,*" Ava tells the table.

"That's pretty smooth, I have to admit," River says. "I might need to use that line."

Ava glares at him mid-bite. "For *who*?"

"You, of course." He puts his arm around Ava's shoulders, but she pushes it away.

"I usually don't partake in your gossip, but I'm here, so I might as well." He acts out a *give me more* motion. "I had no idea you and Adrian were close enough for him to have anything to grovel for." He looks over at Easton. "Groveling means you fucked up."

"Thank you, Captain Obvious," Ava grumbles. "Being a father doesn't limit Easton's vocabulary to Dr. Seuss quotes."

"Yeah," Easton says, rubbing his brow and feigning offense. "I've advanced to Dr. Seuss *and* Junie B. Jones."

"Oh my God, I loved those books growing up," Callie says.

Mia waves toward Ava and River. "Can you two go bang somewhere so we can continue our Adrian-Essie conversation?"

"Mia!" I tear a piece of crust off my slice and toss it at her. She shrugs.

"I personally have no issue with them arguing." I try to sound as indifferent as I can. "Argue away, you two."

"Because that means you're off the hook," Mia comments.

"Mark my words: you and Adrian will be dating soon," Ava says.

Callie lifts her beer in agreement.

"Blue Beech is boring as shit," Mia comments. "That has to be his only reason to be here."

I scowl at them. "He's here because he's a stalker ... *and* let's not forget, his grandmother also lives here now."

"He isn't a stalker. He's your soulmate," Callie says dreamily.

Mia's gaze falls on Callie with disapproval. "What did I tell you about being a hopeless romantic?"

"That *hopeless* and *tragic* are synonyms," Callie says with a sigh.

"All love stories end in tragedy or death," Mia adds. "No matter who you are."

Something I love about my circle of friends is that we're always honest with each other. Mia's comment wasn't meant to sound offensive. She and Callie are the closest despite them being complete opposites.

I'd describe Callie as *cutesy*. She wears flowy dresses, lives by positivity quotes, and is the sweetest of everyone in the group. She was literally voted *Sweetest Classmate* in the school yearbook.

Mia dresses in high fashion and always matches her outfit to her mood. She was voted *Most Likely To Move Away From Blue Beech*, which she did, but then returned.

Her hair is black, while Callie's is a strawberry blonde.

Callie is a hopeless romantic, but Mia would rather have her inheritance drained than trust a man with her heart, per her words. And her inheritance is massive since her mom is one of the biggest stars in the world. She literally has a star on the Hollywood Walk of Fame.

River halts mid-text and lowers his phone to smirk at me. "Look at that. It's as if speaking of the attorney summoned the devil."

I wrinkle my nose in confusion. "Huh?"

River returns to his texting. "Your least favorite attorney is here."

I turn in my seat, and my heart skips a beat when I see Adrian. I narrow my eyes as he introduces himself to Amelia's parents while standing beside Foster.

Jesus, will this man ever give me a break?

He's going to end up running *me* out of Blue Beech.

"How does he know Foster?" Callie asks.

"Foster is Terrance's grandson," Ava replies. "I had no idea he was back in town."

"Why do you care if he's back in town?" River raises his gaze to glare at Ava. "Do you plan on hooking up with Foster again?"

Ava rolls her eyes. "Better him than you."

My brother is so dumb.

Ava never hooked up with Foster.

They went to prom together one year, and River is still butthurt about it.

"Definitely, because that means he's the one who has to deal with your attitude," River argues. "I'd much rather hook up with Daisy fucking Duck than deal with you."

Ava rolls her eyes again, more dramatically this time. "Such a well-spoken man. I'm sure you would because Daisy fucking Duck won't quack out that you're a poor lay." She glares and swats her hand toward River's phone. "How about you shush and go back to texting whatever random girl you met online?"

There's been plenty of talk about Ava and River hooking up, but I've never asked either of them if it's true. Nor do I plan to.

It's their business, and hard pass on hearing about my brother's sex life.

"Jesus," Mia groans. "This is why I only hook up with randoms out of this damn state." She exhales a long breath through her cherry-red lips. "And you need to get over yourself right now because the man Essie wants to murder just walked in. I think that takes priority over two people who randomly hook up when they're bored."

Mia's comment is so Mia.

She is both the meanest and most understanding person in our group.

Whenever we're in a tough situation and we don't want to be judged, we turn to her.

Ava and River continue their arguing. I tune them out to focus on Adrian. He's dressed in khaki pants and a white button-up. He pushes his glasses up his nose while easily talking with people.

A part of me hates that I love he wore his glasses instead of contacts.

It reminds me of our old days.

The longer I stare, the harder my heart races, like it's pleading for him to come over and heal it. I want to reach inside my chest and smack at that stupid organ of mine. My heart needs to hold a grudge against him. Years ago, I was ready to share mine with him, but he left before I even fully had the chance.

I refuse to put myself in that situation again.

This heart of mine is locked up and waiting for a deserving man.

One who doesn't vanish without so much as a goodbye.

When Foster and Adrian end their conversation with Amelia's parents, they walk over to us. My eyes lock with Adrian's.

His face is relaxed, while mine is rigid.

My breaths become shallower as he grows closer.

"Hey, guys," Foster says when they reach us.

River rudely jerks his chin up and returns his attention to his phone.

"This is Adrian," Foster introduces.

Callie waves at him.

Mia raises a brow.

Ava smiles. "Long time no see."

Adrian laughs.

"Nice to meet you, man," Easton says.

He must be out of the Adrian-and-me drama loop.

Easton is normally the last one to learn about drama and gossip. We don't take it personally. He's a single dad who spends most of his time taking care of his little girl, Jasmine, since her mom isn't in the picture.

Foster sits next to Easton, and Adrian slides down the bench until he's directly across from me.

I attempt to ignore him and act like he doesn't exist.

He orders one of Down Home's ales by name, which surprises me. I massage my temples to ward off a headache while Adrian makes conversation with River about their times in college and how River took nothing seriously.

Still pretty much sums up my brother.

A hint of my anxiety eases when my parents stop at our table. I stand to hug them. But that anxiety immediately returns when I sit and Adrian stands.

"I'm Adrian," he says, extending his hand toward my mom and then my dad's. "We met when I roomed with River in college."

Dear God.

He's acting like we're on a date and introducing himself to the parents.

I stretch my leg under the table and jam my foot against his shin.

He briefly looks at me before turning his attention back to my parents.

"Adrian," my dad says, furrowing his brows in thought. "The Adrian who took over Terrance's law firm?"

Adrian blinks in surprise at my dad's question.

I wildly grin, loving this.

"That'd be me." Adrian clears his throat and swings his hand in my direction. "Did Essie tell you I offered to merge our firms so we wouldn't be in competition with each other?"

I hold back my eye roll at his response.

It was a good one, darn it.

But hopefully, my parents will see right through his game.

"I believe Essie enjoys the independence of her own firm right now," my mom says in her best teacher tone. She shares a friendly smile with him before turning to me. "Dinner tomorrow night. Don't forget, honey."

I nod. "I'll be there."

"Your mother and I probably won't stay late, so we'll see you at home," my dad adds, smacking a quick peck on the top of my head.

"You have to see this," my aunt Sierra says, rushing over to my mom's side. She gently wraps her hand around her elbow, towing her across the room toward my uncle Maliki. My father follows them.

My aunt Sierra is my father's older sister. She and my uncle Maliki are Jax's parents.

Adrian smirks and covers his chest with both hands. "Look at me, winning your parents over."

He's too cocky for my liking.

I cross my arms. "I hardly call that winning my parents over."

He settles back onto the bench across from me, and that smirk of his grows. "How'd they know about me taking over the firm? Talking about me to your parents, are you?"

Leaning forward with my elbows on the table, I lower my voice. "I talk about you the same way I talk about menstrual cramps and shredded coconut. All nauseating."

He mirrors how I'm sitting and gets too close, our mouths almost touching. "I guess I'll have to change that, then."

"Good luck," I huff, drawing back. "My heart doesn't believe in second chances."

"Hearts don't decide on second chances. Your trust is what does that."

"Then, *my trust* doesn't believe in second chances."

"*Trust me* when I say I'll convince it otherwise." He smirks as if he'd just stated pure, factual information.

We're interrupted by the lights lowering in the garden, and the music softens.

"Oh my God," Ava says, trying to see more by craning her neck over Foster's shoulder.

Callie gasps and covers her mouth with her hand.

"I love this," Ava goes on, and I follow her gaze to see Jax kneeling in front of Amelia, proposing.

The crowd around them has similar reactions to ours.

Jax and Amelia pay no attention to the people and are in their own world. Amelia gazes down at him, and they keep their eyes locked on each other. A silly grin is on her face as he talks to her.

"Speak up!" someone shouts since Jax is keeping his words private.

Jax ignores him.

I love that even though the proposal is public, he's saving those personal words for only her.

What I don't love is that I have to look away from the happy couple and search the area for whoever asked that.

Who interrupts such a romantic moment?

"Yes!" Amelia shouts. "Oh my God, yes!"

The patio erupts with people cheering and clapping.

She leaps into Jax's arms when he stands. He holds her tight, wrapping his arm around her waist, as if she's his entire world.

Honestly, I know she is.

Their love is truly beautiful with everything they've gone through.

I sigh, dreaming of having a love like that someday.

They kiss, and when they finally pull apart, their parents shuffle toward them. Joining my uncle Maliki and aunt Sierra are Amelia's parents, Lola and Silas.

"I can't wait to help plan her wedding," Callie gushes.

"I can't wait to help plan her bachelorette party," Mia says with a smirk.

Aunt Sierra and Lola are in tears when I get a better view of them. Amelia's eyes are red and watery, but she's holding herself back from fully releasing all her emotions. Like me, she likes to keep them in check publicly. We're the cool kids who cope with our emotions privately.

"Why didn't you tell me you were proposing?" I playfully push Jax's shoulder when it's my turn to congratulate them.

Jax clears the sweat off his forehead. "I kept it from everyone but my father and Silas—since I had to ask for his permission."

I perform a *zip-it* gesture across my lips. "Uh, I'm great at keeping secrets."

"I wanted it to be a surprise, and as much as I trust you all, anyone could've easily slipped up. Hell, I almost slipped up, and so did Silas."

Amelia laughs and shakes her head. "Leave it to my father to almost leak my boyfriend's proposal."

I snatch her hand and admire the gorgeous oval solitaire diamond ring. "It's perfect. Congratulations! I'll be at the condo sometime this week with wine and snacks to celebrate, girls' night–style."

After hugging them both, I move away to make room for the next person waiting to congratulate them. Jax and Amelia's story proves that love can be rediscovered, even by broken people. The difference between Amelia and me is that the man who fixed her wasn't the one who'd caused the damage.

Can the same person who broke your heart be the one to fix it?

Or do they just inflict more harm and create additional scar tissue?

Instead of returning to the table, I stroll outside the patio to the side of the building, needing fresh air and a mental break.

The sky is black and star-filled.

My favorite kind of night.

Leaning against the building, I close my eyes and sigh.

"What kind of wedding do you think you'll have?"

I jump, and my eyes shoot open. If I didn't recognize the smooth voice that asked the question, I'd be more freaked out.

I spot Adrian under the streetlight as he comes toward me.

"What kind of wedding do you think you'll have?" he repeats, stopping in front of me.

I wince at not only his question but also his nearness.

It takes me a moment to reply. "Huh?"

I comprehended what he'd asked perfectly, but the response isn't simple.

It's personal. Too personal to share with a man who hurt me. I should've known venturing off alone would lead to him following me.

He rests his palm near my head against the building. "Do you have a dream wedding?"

Honestly, I've thought about what kind of wedding I'd want if I had one, but I've never been the girl who had a *dream wedding* in mind.

I always answer, "Marrying someone who loves me," whenever asked that question.

"I don't know." I turn my head to glance away from him, and even though I shouldn't, I ask, "Do you have one?"

"I do."

My curiosity takes over. "And?"

There's a pause before he softly slips his hand under my chin, causing me to whimper. He caresses my cheek with his thumb and turns my head to meet his gaze. "One with a woman I desperately care about and have feelings for. One *with you*." He stops my attempt to look away from him.

"Don't say things like that." I should push him away. I *need* to push him away, yet for some reason, I can't. That doesn't mean I can't hit him with the truth, though. "Especially when it's bullshit."

He doesn't pull away, like I hoped. "It's not bullshit."

I take a deep breath and shut my eyes. Staring at him is agonizing, and what I'm about to say will hurt us both.

"We were friends." I articulate each word slowly. "That's it." I casually shrug. "Then, we stopped being friends."

He jerks his shoulder back, as if my statement had smacked him. "We were never just friends, and you know that." His voice turns shaky. "Who was the first person I texted when I woke up in the morning? The first person *you* talked to?"

I tremble at his question and refuse to answer.

"I was, and you were mine. Who was the last person I talked to before going to sleep?" A laugh escapes his lips. "Hell, on the nights we actually slept and didn't stay up all night talking to each other?"

I gasp at the reality of his words, my throat closing up like an allergic reaction.

"Y-O-U," he spells out.

"Adrian," I whisper.

We ignore the commotion and people passing us. Like Jax and Amelia, we're fixated on each other.

"Who was the person I slept in my car for? The person who made me study harder because, half the time, I would daydream about a girl instead? It was you, Essie. It's only ever been you." He inches closer but maintains a safe distance, afraid to push me too far. "I've never given attention to anyone like that. Nor will I ever because whenever I try, it only reminds me of our connection and how nothing could ever come close to it. And, goddamn, I know you feel the same." He drops my chin to lower his hand and rests it over my heart. "Don't you remember? The fights over who would hang up first? The nights we sat in my car, saying nothing but everything at the same time? I care about you and want to fix what broke between us."

His words sting.

My heart batters against my chest at the memories. They were some of the best moments of my life, and as much as I've tried to push them out of my thoughts, sometimes, they still continue to linger there.

But his words also piss me off.

Why is he playing these games with me?

I shove him away. "Bullshit. If you felt that about me, what was that at the firm?"

He runs a hand through his hair. "I went to the firm because I knew you worked there. I had no idea they'd choose me for the promotion. So, when you quit, I quit." His broad shoulders slump. "I just want to have a conversation with you, Essie. *Please*. Let me explain everything to you."

"I needed your explanation years ago. Like I told you before, it's too late now."

He hangs his head and inhales a deep breath.

I push myself off the wall and move around him. "I need to go. I'm missing my friend's engagement celebration."

"Can we meet up later?" His voice drips with defeat.

"Of course." I fake enthusiasm. "Absolutely."

"You're lying."

"Maybe. Maybe not."

"You definitely are."

"Consider it more of an *I'll change my mind later* thing."

"Please." He clasps his pleading hands together. "Five minutes. That's all."

"Fine." I check the time on my watch. "Five minutes, Adrian."

"I know I saw my attorney come out here!" a woman yells, interrupting Adrian before he gets the chance to speak. "Essie!"

Brielle rounds the corner, storming toward us with Rhett

behind her. They must've been inside since I didn't notice them on the patio. She halts, glancing around.

"There you are," she shouts, her voice slurred. "Call the cops on Rhett for me."

"Call the cops?" Rhett spits through his teeth. "I haven't broken any laws."

Brielle faces Rhett, shoving her finger so hard into his chest that she almost falls into him. "Stalking is against the law, asshole."

"Stalking?" Rhett raises his voice. "I ain't no stalker!"

"I'm so ready to get rid of these two," Adrian grumbles next to me, rubbing his temples.

Our moment is gone as we watch Brielle and Rhett argue like two children.

Rhett is pissed Brielle is on a date with a guy he gave swirlies to in middle school. Brielle tells him it's better than screwing the nanny.

They go back and forth until I say, "Come on, Brielle. I'll take you home," in exhaustion.

Adrian icily stares at Rhett.

I grab Brielle's hand and refuse to look at him while we walk by.

Brielle sobs as I guide her away from Rhett and toward my car.

"He's here to give me a hard time because I'm on a date," she says as I help her into the passenger seat. She imitates Rhett's voice, and I can't help but laugh. "*You're a married woman. You shouldn't be on a date.* Even more embarrassing, my date left me in the middle of Rhett's scene."

"I'm sorry," I tell her while backing out of my parking spot. "I wish I could say it'll be over soon, but you have many years ahead of dealing with him."

The car falls silent until she asks, "Are you having some kind of affair with Rhett's lawyer?"

"No."

"It seems you're always alone together, and you two always seem stressed at the other's presence." She softens her voice. "Essie, I know what heartbreak looks like. I lived it day in and day out. Hell, I *still* live it, even after leaving Rhett."

"We have history, sure, but that's over now."

She lays her hand on my arm. "You love him."

I shake my head repeatedly. "I don't."

"And he loves you." She pats my arm once before pulling away. "I could see that as a conflict of interest."

Great. Another job lost because of Adrian.

"But I won't because I know you have my best interests at heart." Brielle slouches in her seat and wipes her face. "Words of advice from an almost-divorced woman: The heartbreak will never disappear. It will cling to you and sometimes suffocate you. You can put a Band-Aid on it, but there's no cure."

16

Adrian

The Past
College

It's three in the morning on a Saturday night, and what's this college kid doing?

Cramming for an exam.

I glance away from my laptop when someone knocks on the door. River is gone for the weekend, and I'm not expecting company.

Nearly all the company we get is his anyway.

I ignore the knocking.

It's not for me and will end soon.

We live in the dorm known for parties and drunk idiots banging on doors.

Once, we woke up to a guy who lived down the hall, passed out on our floor. He'd pissed his pants, and he was drooling on one of my pillows. After that, River and I made sure to lock the door at night.

When the knocking turns into pounding, I slam my laptop shut and climb out of bed. Since I've been staring at a screen for the last five hours, I adjust my eyes while walking toward the door.

I swing open the door and lose a breath.

The most gorgeous woman I've ever seen stands in front of me.

I blink.

Is she real?

Or did I fall asleep while studying?

Oh, she's most definitely real.

I study her, entranced.

She must be here for River.

My guess, she's around my age.

Her cinnamon-brown eyes are puffy and swollen.

Silence stands between us while we stare at each other.

She hugs herself tightly, wrapping her arms around her body.

She's wearing a pink floral dress with brown cowgirl boots.

I swallow as the sudden urge to comfort her strikes me. It's surprising since I'm not a hugger. It was a trait inherited from my mother. My mother believes we should save hugs for moments of success.

You learned a third language? *Hug!*

You graduated from high school? *Hug!*

You made the Dean's List? *Hug!*

She stands on her tiptoes and attempts to peer past me into the room. "Is River here?" she asks through restrained sobs.

I shake my head and grip the doorknob. "He's gone for the weekend."

She wipes a tear from her cheek with her arm. "He probably went on that stupid trip even though my parents told him not to."

My parents?

It clicks.

She must be River's twin sister, Essie.

He has a few photos of her, but I've never paid too much attention to them. But now looking at her, I see it.

Her hand shakes as she fishes her phone from her pocket. "I've tried calling him a hundred times, but it went straight to voicemail. It's probably dead. For someone so tech-savvy, he seriously sucks at keeping his phone charged." She focuses her gaze on the phone, as if waiting for it to ring. "And I took an Uber here, so I'll need to book another."

"Do you think booking an Uber this late is safe?" I retreat a step. "I can drive you."

I need every second I can to study and don't have time to drive her, but I also want to help her.

"You don't …" She squeezes her eyes shut. "You don't have to do that."

I step back a few more paces and signal for her to come in as two guys in jockstraps rush down the hallway, shouting about strip poker.

An inch of tension eases from her shoulders at my invite. She scrambles into the room at the same time a guy nearly cartwheels into her. I quickly shut the door behind us.

I open my desk drawer, searching for my car keys, and she shuffles farther into the room.

"Where did I put them?" I mutter in frustration, shoving a few notebooks and cards to the side.

I'm organized. Everything has a place, and it's returned to that place after use. My keys always go in this drawer.

Essie drops onto River's messy bed. "Is, uh … everything o-kay?" A hiccup interrupts her last word.

I slide my hand along the bottom of the drawer. "Can't find my keys."

"It's okay." She attempts to mask the doubt in her tone.

She for sure thinks I'm lying about losing my keys to get out of driving her home. As if I were playing the *good guy* act, but it was fake.

I sit on my bed in defeat.

Her ash-colored hair is a wild mess of strands, and she isn't wearing any makeup.

There's something so euphoric about seeing someone when they're at their most vulnerable. And, *fuck*, please tell me that doesn't make me sound like a serial killer. But I love imperfection, seeing raw emotion and witnessing someone when not perfectly put together.

Love seeing it on other people.

Hate them seeing it on me.

World's biggest hypocrite right here.

She studies me, hesitating, trying to decide whether I'm trustworthy, and kicks off her boots. "Do you ever feel like your past is suffocating you, dragging you down and refusing to let you go?"

I nod as if in understanding.

But that nod is a lie.

Even though I grew up without a father, I can say that my life has been pretty good. Despite having an emotionally detached mother, I consider myself lucky. I tutored kids in high school and saw firsthand how hard life could be.

I'll take an isolated yet strict parent over an abusive one.

A deceased father instead of one abandoning me willingly.

I run my hand over my bottom lip. "Do you know the best defense against your past?"

"What?"

"You burn it down."

She bolts across the bed, her back smacking into the wall, as if my words were a physical blow.

I expected my response to appear more philosophical.

Not terrifying.

She inhales raspy breaths.

"What I mean is …" I stand, scrambling for better words, and lower myself onto River's bed while keeping a decent distance between us. My voice is low and even. "If you don't let go of your past and the pain it brings, it will ruin the rest of your life. The only way to break free from the past is by releasing yourself from it first."

My abuela once told my mother that.

I was only four or five years old when I woke up to my mother crying. I got out of bed and peeked around the corner into the kitchen to find her curled up on the floor. My abuela sat beside her, stroking her cheek, and spoke those words to her.

The thing is, I've had a good life.

One free from heartache, loss, and struggle.

But my mother hasn't.

"No one said you can't put yourself back together, child," my abuela told her. "But you're the only one who can fix you. If you don't find happiness, if you don't find a way to release your pain, you'll rebuild yourself just as broken as you are now."

Her words have stayed with me for some reason.

"You can crash here, in River's bed, if you want?" I suggest without fully considering my words.

She goes still, mid-hugging her knees, my offer surprising her as much as it does me. "Are you sure?" Her gaze shifts to the papers and laptop scattered on my bed and the two empty coffee cups on my nightstand. "I don't want to interrupt you."

I smile warmly. "No, not at all."

"What are you studying for?"

I shrug. "Just an exam on Monday."

"For what class?"

"Political science."

"Course?"

"Latin American Politics."

"Do you need help?"

"I'm not sure if this is one you can help with."

She lifts forward and rams her palm into my shoulder, and I grunt.

"Excuse me? Is that because I'm a girl?"

"No, it's law school shit. So, unless you plan on going into law—"

She cuts me off, "Which I am."

My body stiffens at the realization of how stupid my

comment was. I deserve another jab to my shoulder. It's not that I doubted her ability to help, but very few freshmen take the course.

"Sorry," I sputter. "River never told me."

She nods, an acceptance of my apology, and sweeps a chunk of hair away from her face. "Although, sometimes, I think about changing my major."

"I can relate to that." My eyes meet hers. "What route would you go instead?"

She picks off a loose thread from River's comforter. "Drop out. Learn to knit. Become a chef." She taps her finger on the corner of her mouth. "I'd have to take some serious classes to accomplish cooking, though."

"My mother would kill me if I switched majors."

"I don't know what my parents would do." She chews on her lower lip. "They're usually supportive of our decisions. They never told me to go into law or follow in their footsteps. Luckily, they allowed River and me to choose our futures."

My mother chose my future before I left the womb.

A step-by-step plan for the perfect son.

Born. Potty-trained early. Law school. Work at a prestigious firm. Marry after thirty. Babies no earlier than thirty-five so she isn't a young grandmother.

My face turns sullen, but I snap myself out of it, not wanting her to pick up on my jealousy of her having supportive parents.

I spring off the bed. "You thirsty?"

"Uh ... sure."

I open the mini fridge under River's desk. "Your options are water, cold coffee, Sprite, or these weird drinks called ..." I slowly read off the name of an apple cider vinegar drink.

"I'll take that, please." She scoots to the edge of the bed.

I grab a grape-flavored one, hold it up for her approval, and pass it to her after she nods. "So, you're the reason River buys those?"

They've been sitting in the fridge all year.

When I asked why he hadn't tossed them, he said, "They're gross, but you can try one," and then returned his attention to Netflix.

I tried an orange flavor.

And it tasted like cat piss.

At least what I imagined cat piss would taste like.

She nods. "He hates them, but I pretty much live on these and vanilla lattes."

I grab a cold coffee for myself. Coffee is what I live on.

Essie sits cross-legged on the bed, pops open the can, and straightens her posture, as if ready to get to business. "What can I do to help you study?"

"You're upset," I say. "I'm sure studying is the last thing you want to do."

"Actually, it'd help." She settles her can on River's nightstand, pulls a hair tie from her wrist, and scoops her hair up into a ponytail before securing it.

Studying relaxes her.

A remedy to her sorrow.

I understand it because I use studying to forget my problems.

As our eyes meet, I wonder how long that suffering has been there.

"Why are you upset?" I unscrew the cap to my coffee and collapse onto my bed. "Is it a guy?" My head spins as the next thought comes to mind. "No one hurt you, did they?"

"No one hurt me." A grave expression flashes across her face. "At least not in a physical sense." She gets up from the bed and snatches a book off my desk. "Now, what can I help with?"

I resist the urge to ask more questions.

If studying together will help ease her sadness, I'm happy to do it.

I pat the space next to me on my bed. She grabs her drink before plopping down. The next three hours are a mix of her quizzing me, offering suggestions on my paper, and small talk.

Even though I'm not as productive, having Essie here is nice. She also gives me great tips. Worry that I'll fail my exam creeps in, but right now, being with her feels right. Her company is better than any test score.

"I like this," she comments around a yawn. "A future attorney helping a fellow future attorney." She rubs at her tired eyes. "I've heard so many horror stories of how competitive and dark this profession is."

"Oh yeah, I've heard all about asshole attorneys from my mother." I power off my laptop.

"Ugh." She throws her head back. "I hope that never happens to me … that the selfish law bug doesn't bite me."

I hold out my hand. "To never becoming an asshole attorney."

She shakes her head and lifts her pinky finger. "I seal my promises with a pinky swear."

We laugh as our pinkies intertwine.

She goes back to River's bed, so we can get some sleep.

The following morning, Essie is gone.

But she left a note, wishing me good luck on my exam.

I carefully fold the note, stick it in my coat pocket, and bring it to class on Monday. My thoughts about Essie are even more intense than before.

I can't stop thinking about her.

About the laughs we shared.

About how she'd lean across me, point at the computer screen, and share all her tips and tricks. I threw my head back in laughter when she called them Essie's Law School Lowdown.

I consider asking River for her number, but then I remember the power of the internet. I'll avoid the risk of him saying no and warning me to stay away from her. He doesn't strike me as the type to spout off *bro code*, but you never know.

I unlock my phone and open Instagram. I'm not one for social media. In fact, I've been inactive for six months. I find

River's profile and search his pictures until I find one with Essie. He tagged her in a birthday post.

Essie's profile is public, so I immediately follow her and look through her photos. Our feeds are completely the opposite. I have just a few pictures, mostly of my dog and a couple from my high school graduation. Essie has hundreds—selfies, photos with friends and family, and studying pictures with the hashtag #shouldidropoutoflawschool. No evidence of a boyfriend.

A notification pops up on my screen.

Essie followed me back.

I grin, as if on top of the world, and immediately DM her.

> Me: I passed my exam. I think the good-luck note did it.

It takes less than a second for her to reply.

> Essie: I told you Essie's Law School Lowdown works ... and the candy! That and caffeine never fail me.

While studying, Essie asked if I had snacks. I crawled across my bed and opened a care package from my abuela. Care package meaning junk food, fast-food gift cards, and a picture of my dog with a toy that resembled me in his mouth. I offered her the opened box, and she grabbed a bag of Skittles. Whenever I gave a correct answer, she threw a Skittle into my mouth.

> Me: What's your favorite candy?

I collapse onto my back in bed and hold the phone up to my face.

> Essie: There's no better candy than Skittles. Your grandmother chose well.

> Me: I beg to differ. M&M's are where it's at.

> Essie: And now, I shall block you.

I frantically type, fearing she actually will. I don't one hundred percent know Essie's humor yet.

> Me: Just kidding.

> Essie: You weren't kidding, but that's okay. It means I know you won't steal all my Skittles.

We stay up all night, messaging each other.

And for the next three months, not a day goes by when we don't talk.

We build a friendship, studying for exams and video-chatting. Essie becomes my support system, as we always wish each other good luck before exams and share law school memes.

Then, one day, I take a deep breath of courage and message her.

> Me: Can I come see you?

There's no delay in her response.

> Essie: Yes.

Two nights later, I drive to Essie's college.

The closer I get to her, the faster my pulse races. It's wild how excited I am. I usually spend my drive time listening to audiobooks or podcasts. But not today. I turn up the music, sing along, and tap my hand against the steering wheel. You'd think I was a man who'd hit the lottery.

I text her when I arrive at her dorm. As I wait for her to come out, my excitement turns into anxiousness.

How will she react to us hanging out in person?

We hung out at the dorm, but it was unexpected and unplanned. This time, it's by choice.

During the two-hour drive, I'd rehearsed what I'll say to her.

Unfortunately, that plan goes out the window, and a simple, "Hi," falls from my lips when she gets into my car.

Essie playfully smacks my shoulder. "Don't make this awkward."

"Sorry." I nervously plow a hand through my hair.

"It's just us. Essie and Adrian." Her voice is chipper. "There's no difference between this and when we FaceTime."

She directs me toward her favorite diner on campus. While driving, I reach for her hand and hold it in mine. She doesn't flinch or move it, like it's where it belongs perfectly.

The server guides us to a booth at the back of the crowded diner. We order dinner, dessert, and then another round of dessert *to share*. This is just as comfortable as our calls. The awkwardness we started with has dissipated.

After midnight, we leave the diner just as it closes. As we make our way through the lit parking lot to my car, Essie stops suddenly.

"Did you book a hotel?" she asks. "Or do you plan to drive back tonight?"

We never discussed what we'd do or how long I'd stay during my visit.

I twirl my keys in my hand. "I plan to drive back."

She wrinkles her nose. "This late?"

"I'm a guy who burns the midnight oil studying. A drive is nothing."

She nods, but it's clear she dislikes my answer.

I don't expect Essie to invite me up to her room.

Would I go if she offered? Hell yes.

But sleeping with Essie isn't why I came.

When we get back to her dorm and park, she doesn't get out. She locks the door and lowers her seat.

"Let's sit in here and talk longer." She casually drapes herself across the center console and rests her head on my shoulder. "Even though I love texting and talking on the phone, doing it in person is *sooo* much better."

I bite down on a smile and lower my head until it meets hers.

There's no late-night drive for me because we stay in my car, talking until sunrise. Then, we fall asleep until someone smacks on the hood of my car. I kiss her goodbye on the cheek, and she wraps her arms around my neck, hugging me tightly.

On the drive home, I feel a crick in my neck and pain shooting up my shoulder, but the uncomfortableness is worth it.

That night becomes a pattern for us.

When I visit Essie, we select a quiet spot to spend time together, whether it's a diner, library, or park. Sometimes, we take blankets to the park and lie under the stars, whispering our dreams until we fall asleep. Sometimes we study. Our conversations are endless, and when there is silence, it's easy.

Familiar.

Never an awkward moment.

Scratch that.

There have been *a few* awkward moments.

Those times our eyes lock, dripping with tension, but we're too scared to make a move.

When we're sitting close in a cramped booth, sharing a milkshake, and our lips *just barely* miss each other as we lean in for a sip.

So many slipups have happened that would change our relationship. Our chemistry is impossible to deny.

If we were reckless, we'd have already crossed that line.

I'd have already kissed her, touched her, and confessed how hard I was falling for her.

Neither of us is one to make irrational decisions, though.

Sometimes I wish we were.

Everything we're doing could be considered dating.

Except for sex, but that isn't so uncommon.

Plenty of people wait to have sex.

Nights I lie beside her, I wonder if we'll ever have that shift.

The *friends-to-lovers* term you hear so much.

One day, I want Essie to be mine.

Lord knows, I'd do anything to be hers.

I'm falling in love with this girl.

"My friends and I are visiting my brother this weekend," Essie tells me while I FaceTime her from inside my car.

She hasn't returned to my campus since the night she showed up at our dorm unannounced. Every time we've hung out, I've gone to her. Which I have no problem with since we now have *our spots* where we hang out when I'm there.

"Have you told River we're hanging out?" I scratch my cheek. "That we ..." My words trail off. Even after all this time, I have no idea what to call us.

She shakes her head. "I mean, we can tell him we're friends."

I've never winced harder.

My throat tightens, stopping me from telling her we're much more than friends. I hate our sneaking around, and guilt creeps in when I see River without telling him. He mentions Essie to me, and when they're FaceTiming, he'll often point the phone at me and tell her to say hi.

I decide to change the *friends* subject because it always puts me in a funk. "Are you staying in our dorm room?"

It'd be a tight fit, and people would have to sleep on the floor, but I don't mind. I'd much rather run off and sleep somewhere private with Essie. We have plenty of parks here.

"No." She sips her latte while sitting outside her favorite coffee shop. "We rented a hotel room, but I'm sure I'll see you."

"You're *sure* you'll see me?" I dramatically massage my neck and deepen my voice. "Esmeralda, I'd *better* see you."

She rolls her eyes in fake annoyance at my use of her legal name. I didn't know Essie was a nickname until she dropped her school ID from her bag while we were studying in the library.

"I'd never go there and not see you, Adrian," she says matter-of-factly.

"That's my girl." I attempt to sound lighthearted, but I feel anything but. "You won't act like I'm a stranger, will you?"

"Absolutely not." She suddenly stills. "Why'd you even think something like that?"

"I'm sorry." I blow out a noisy breath. "I've just never had a secret friendship with someone."

"First off, we don't have a *secret friendship*."

"How many people know you spend nearly all your free time with me?"

"I don't have a great history with boys I've hung out with." She fingers her necklace with an *E* charm hanging from it. "I enjoy having you to myself."

"When our lives aren't so crazy, you're going to officially be my girlfriend. Promise me that someday you'll be mine."

"Promise." She raises her pinky.

I do the same, and we pretend to cross them through our screens.

17

Essie

Present Day

Puking is the worst.

I'd rather get stung by a dozen bees—granted, I'm not allergic—than vomit.

"Why me?" I groan into the office trash can.

Nausea churns in my stomach as sweat drips from my forehead. After rushing to my bathroom to vomit this morning, I thought this stomach bug would pass, and I'd be okay to work.

Wrong.

Last night, after taking Brielle home, I thought about calling Adrian but chickened out. Maybe my heart is mad at me for that and is taking it out on my stomach today.

I almost fall out of my chair and over the trash can when the door chimes. Out of all the times for someone to come here, it would be when I'm puking. It doesn't help that I'm at the reception desk, so there's no hiding from them.

I rest my head on my arm, too weak to raise it to see who's here.

"Yikes. You don't look so good."

My breathing falters when Adrian kneels in front of me.

I'd do anything to melt into this trash can.

"Thank you for stating the obvious," I grumble.

Dizziness washes through me, and I grip the desk to lift myself. I stop when another wave of nausea hits me. Adrian hurriedly clasps my hair in his hand, holding it back while I vomit again.

"Come on," he says when I finish, his voice gentle. "I'll drive you home."

I shake my head but allow him to help me up. Even when I'm balanced, he doesn't release me.

"You need to rest, Essie," he adds. "You can't work if you're vomiting all over your paperwork."

I bow my head, swallowing leftover vomit. "Hard pass on you knowing where I live." My response is rude, but I'd rather he leave me in my misery than see me sick.

"Either I sit here with you or take you home."

I somehow gain the strength to raise my chin and glare at him. "Why are you here?"

"I wanted to finish last night's conversation, but now, I want to get you home to rest. Now, come on. It's pointless to stay here, miserable, and you won't get any work done anyway." He cradles my arm and walks me outside to his car.

His car smells like fresh oranges and his cologne.

Surprisingly, it doesn't create more nausea.

It actually puts my stomach more at ease.

"Don't save that," I say after rambling off my address and watching him key it into his car's GPS.

Adrian's body brushes mine when he leans across me to buckle my seat belt. "You sure don't have good manners toward someone helping you."

"Your help has ulterior motives."

He snorts while buckling himself. "And what are my ulterior motives, Essie?"

I chew on my bottom lip.

Adrian shifts the car into drive. "I've never had ulterior motives with you. All I've ever wanted to do was help."

I slap a hand over my mouth, and Adrian brakes when I tap the console. He swerves to the road's shoulder. I throw open the door and vomit.

A kid on the sidewalk brakes on his bike and yells, "Ew!" before riding off.

Adrian opens the glove compartment, drags out a handful of napkins, and hands me one.

"Thank you," I whisper, wiping my face.

When I'm sure I'm all puked out, I fall back into the seat. Adrian holds out a bottle of water for me.

"Thank you," I say again. I swish the water in my mouth and spit it outside. Very ladylike, thank you very much. I do it two more times until my mouth feels as clean as it'll get.

Adrian silently waits until I shut the door and sag into the seat.

"You good?" He rests his hand on my thigh.

I nod and don't push him away.

We don't say another word as he drives.

"This is your house?" Adrian asks when we arrive at the gate.

You wouldn't think a Tuscan-inspired-slash-modern home would be aesthetically pleasing, but my parents somehow did that. They took each other's styles and made them work together. There are stone walls that match the walkway as it leads up to the front door and more windows than I can count.

It's on the outskirts of town, sitting on fifteen acres, and the landscaping is made up of bright colors and century-old trees.

"Technically, it's my parents'," I say.

"I never took you as someone who would still live at home."

"River and I each have a cottage in the back." I open the door and peer at Adrian over my shoulder.

Adrian steps out of the car. Since I'm moving at a snail's pace, he's at my door and ready to help me before I even stand.

My body hurts, and I'm lightheaded, so I don't pull away when he helps me toward the walkway that leads to the pool.

I wave at the pool cleaner while unlocking the door, and Adrian follows me inside. I'm still in his hold as I turn to face him, slipping him a guarded look. No matter how much Adrian has helped, there will always be a sense of distrust with him now.

But I do appreciate him driving me home.

"Thank you," I whisper again.

He cups my face in his palm. "You never have to thank me for helping you."

This right here reminds me of our first night in his dorm room.

I search for words so I don't get lost in his eyes. "I need to brush my teeth. *Like bad.*"

"You go do that." He chuckles and slowly releases me.

I go into the bathroom, shut the door, and brush my teeth four times. The taste of mint lingers in my mouth when I step out.

I stop when I find Adrian in the kitchen, grabbing a cup from the cabinet. "What are you doing?"

"Helping you." He smiles and fills the cup with water.

"What if I'm contagious?" I sit down on the couch.

"Then, you'll have to come over and take care of me, huh?" He hands me the water, then grabs a throw blanket and drapes it over me.

"Seriously? This is so unnecessary. I can take care of myself." I take a sip of water.

"It sure looked like you needed help."

"I'll call a friend, my parents, River."

"Your place is very you." He sits down on a chair and looks around. "I like it."

I yawn, which I learn *is* contagious since his starts right as mine ends.

He sticks a pillow under his arm and makes himself comfortable. "I'd also like to add that since I've already been exposed to your sickness, it's better if you're only around me. Don't want to get anyone else sick, do we?"

"It's a stomach bug."

"You have a law degree. Not a medical one."

"Suit yourself." I yawn again, this one longer, and wrap the blanket tighter around my body. "Pretty sure I'm about to crash out and will make for poor company."

"You never make for poor company, Essie. In fact, you've always been my favorite company."

As much as I want to argue, my eyes are too heavy.

Right before they shut, I catch Adrian watching me intently.

18

Adrian

A pillow hitting my head wakes me up.

"Ouch," I hiss, rubbing the spot it hit.

"You're drooling on my pillow," Essie says from the couch.

"I wasn't drooling." I wipe my mouth to check and smile. "But tell me, is it worse to drool or snore? Because, babe, you snore like no other."

She tosses another pillow at me. "I don't snore."

I didn't plan to fall asleep, but I didn't get much last night. Thoughts of Essie wouldn't leave my mind.

"How are you feeling?" I ask her.

Well enough to throw things, it seems.

"Like I was hit by a truck." She rubs her tired eyes. "It must be the Adrian Annoyance Flu."

I chuckle. "Or the Adrian Lovebug."

She rolls her eyes. "You're so cheesy."

"Do you feel okay to talk?"

This isn't the best timing, but I need to let it out. If I don't, I swear I'll explode. Every day we don't have this talk, regret eats at me deeper. We both deserve for her to hear my truth.

She rolls her neck and shoulders, avoiding eye contact. "Talk about what?"

"Why I disappeared."

"What if"—she picks at a loose thread on the throw pillow —"I don't want to know?"

"Why wouldn't someone want to know why they were ghosted?"

"You admit it, then? You ghosted me?"

Shit, wrong word to use.

And who the fuck says ghosted anymore?

I'm not some teenager on Snapchat.

The air is heavy as we stare at each other.

She waits for me to speak.

"I found something out that made me question everything I'd thought growing up," I start.

Tension rolls up my neck.

This is it.

What I've wanted to say all these years.

I open my mouth, but a loud knock on the door interrupts us.

I groan, turning to glare at the door.

The worst damn timing ever.

Neither of us makes a move.

Another bang on the door, this one louder.

"Essie!" someone yells on the other side. "It's me!"

"Come in," she finally shouts.

The door swings open. River and Easton walk inside. I've never seen River look so serious, even when his mother showed up early in the morning and he had a girl in his bed in college.

"What's up, Adrian?" River asks, his gaze suspicious as he glances from Essie to me. This time, he's not cracking jokes.

"He found me puking in my office and drove me home," Essie hurriedly explains.

The air is tense.

My body stiffens as no one says a word.

I'm not wanted here.

"What's wrong?" Essie finally asks.

Whatever it is, they don't want to say it in front of me.

"Thanks for the help, man. I have it from here," River tells me.

He's trying not to be rude, but he definitely wants my ass gone.

My phone vibrates with a text. All eyes are on me as I dig it out of my pants.

Mom blinks on the screen.

I feel guilty when I silence my phone, but I'll call her back.

If it's important, she'll text.

And seconds later, she does.

Mom: Call me, please.

My legs feel weak as I rise and peer at Essie. "I'll check on you later."

She nods, a weak smile on her lips. "Thank you for today."

"See you, man," River says, patting my back as I pass him.

Easton nods while opening the door.

Whatever the reason they're here, it's not good.

19

Essie

I used to call bullshit on twin telepathy.

    I was a twin and never experienced it.

Until today.

One look at my brother, and I know something is wrong.

The vomiting must've been a forewarning that something bad was coming.

"You didn't hear, did you?" River asks as soon as Adrian leaves.

I haven't seen him this serious since the accident when he said he'd murder everyone involved.

I gulp. "Hear what?"

River starts pacing, and Easton sits in Adrian's abandoned chair.

"The Prison Exoneration Program picked up Earl's case," River bites out.

You know that phrase, *getting the wind knocked out of you?*

That's exactly what happens.

The nausea I experienced earlier creeps up my stomach. I jump off the couch and dash to the bathroom. I don't bother flipping on the light before dropping to my knees at the toilet. What little I didn't puke out earlier comes up.

When I'm positive there's nothing left to vomit, I sink onto the floor and rest my back against the wall. Dread is taking over every inch of me.

I pull my knees to my chest and rest my forehead on them. I'm not sure how much time I sit there before River sits down next to me. I raise my head to rest it on his shoulder.

"Who'd believe he was innocent?" I cry. "The evidence was as clear as day."

"I don't know, but I'll hack into the system to find out." He attempts to make his voice as comforting as possible. "You know I'm always here for you. So are Mom and Dad."

I sit there and sob.

Memories of that night consume me.

I still have nightmares about it.

I'll fight Earl's release.

Not only for me, but for Ethan too.

When I was in the hospital after the accident, all my friends wrote me a letter.

They signed each one with, *You're not alone.*

I'll never forget that.

When I dove out of the Jeep, the fire hit my stomach and upper thighs.

Somehow, I remembered to *stop, drop, and roll* as soon as I hit the ground. The doctors claimed I was extremely lucky.

They did skin grafts but couldn't fix the scars.

I've tried to love my new skin—I really have.

The problem is, I can't forget how normal it was before.

The PEP taking Earl's case might not change anything. The prosecutors had a mountain of evidence against him. They said there was no doubt he'd caused the accident.

I pull my wet hair into a ponytail after showering and walk

out to my living room, filled with my friends. My parents are out of town and supposed to be gone for the week, but River said they booked a flight home as soon as they heard the news.

"We're by your side, no matter what," Callie says as everyone jumps up to hug me.

I don't doubt that.

"Maybe I should …" I slowly twirl my wrist and stare at it. "Maybe I should visit Earl and ask him to complete his sentence for his crime."

River stands and shakes his head furiously. "Fuck no. If anyone visits him, it'll be me."

I focus on my twin. "Do you remember the last time you saw Earl? The cops arrested you for trying to fight him."

He throws out his arms. "And?"

My phone vibrates in my hand, and a text from Adrian pops up on the screen.

> Adrian: How are you feeling?

I ignore his text and sit between Ava and Amelia on the couch. They instantly snuggle in closer, like they're my bodyguards.

I stare at my phone. There's an urge to google Earl.

To email the PEP and explain the hell they'll put me through if they attempt to set him free.

Amelia wraps her arm around me and drags me in for a side hug. "Let me be here for you, like you were me."

I lower my chin and nod. "Give me tonight, okay?"

Right now, I want to be alone because I know when my parents arrive tomorrow, all hell will break loose. They'll call the attorneys and attempt to fight Earl and the PEP.

I need a moment of peace before my life is changed again.

And I need to figure out how to push Adrian away so he doesn't ever see the real me.

20

Adrian

"Hi, Adrian," my mother greets when I enter her office. I called her on my drive home from Essie's, and she insisted I come to her office. She's only invited me to the Prison Exoneration Program's headquarters once before, so whatever she needs, it's important.

I stare over her shoulder at the framed pictures on the windowsill.

Her and my father in front of the Grand Canyon.

Her, my grandmother, and me in Puerto Rico.

The three of us again when I graduated from law school.

I always have to do a double take at pictures with my father. We're almost spitting images of each other. The genetic gods did everything they could to form me into a memory of him.

Other than those photos and her degrees, there's no other personalization here.

"How are you?" I ask, sitting in the white leather chair before her desk.

She reaches to her left, collects a thick manila folder, and leans forward to drop it on the space in front of me. "I need something from you."

I slide the folder off the desk, settle it on my lap, and flip through the top three pages. "What's this?"

"A man from Blue Beech requested our services. We did our research and accepted his case. And since you apparently live there now," she says with annoyance, "I'm asking you to help me. My caseload is full, but I'm ninety-nine percent sure he's innocent."

Ninety-nine percent sure is huge for my mother. As someone who called it blasphemous to ever state you were one hundred percent about anything, it's a rarity to even hear ninety-nine.

I flip back to the first page. "Reckless driving and felony manslaughter."

"Prosecutors claimed he purposely hit a vehicle head-on with two teenagers and killed one. The entire town loved the kids and hated the man. He was the easy fall guy, and other than hearsay, the information doesn't match up."

"There are photos of his wrecked truck."

"The man was drunk that night and had an alibi, and they never looked into anyone else."

I close the folder. "I'll look into it. Ask around."

"An innocent man is behind bars, Adrian. I'm asking you to make this a priority." She grabs her coffee mug, the PEP logo on it, and takes a drink. "I arranged for you to meet with him at the prison tomorrow. I'll text you the details."

"I'll be there." It's not like I have a choice, but if an innocent man is in prison and I have the means to help, I will.

"Thank you." She trades her cup for her phone and unlocks the screen. "I'm working late and ordering Chinese. Do you want to stay and eat?"

I close the folder and tuck it beneath my armpit before standing. "I can't, but rain check?"

She nods. "Rain check."

When I return to my car, I text Essie. She still hasn't replied by the time I'm back in Blue Beech. On the drive to my mother's office, I called and asked my abuela to make her infamous sopa de fideo—we call it the medicine soup. Anytime we get sick, she brings it over. It's a miracle worker.

"Knock, knock," I say, walking into her home without actually knocking.

She's in the kitchen with Terrance. He's washing dishes while she's in front of the stove, stirring the soup. She drops the spoon on the counter and marches up to me, smacking her hand against my forehead to check my temperature.

"You're not sick," she says.

I shrug. "I had a craving for it."

"What did I tell you about fibbing?" She swipes her oven mitt from the counter and whacks me on the side of the head with it. "If you're taking this to someone else, don't fib about it." She retreats a step and returns the mitt from where she took it. "But one rule."

Terrance laughs in the background while turning off the faucet.

I shut one eye and massage my head. "What's that?"

"Don't you dare take credit for making it." She shakes her head, as if running out of patience with me. "No way will I allow a woman to start a relationship with a man she believes will cook for her, only to be disappointed later." She skeptically stares at me. "And unless you plan to spend time with me in the kitchen, she'll definitely be disappointed, my dear."

I cross my arms and fake offense. "Well, that's rude."

She smiles brightly and pats my chest. "Rude but honest."

"How do you know it's for a girl?"

"Because I know everything."

I kiss her cheek, not even bothering to argue.

She's always had an intuition like that.

"Thank you," I say. "I promise to tell her you're the brains behind the soup."

I never planned to take credit for the soup. I'd look more like an idiot by faking I could cook rather than telling her my expertise was in ordering pizza or blending a protein shake.

"That's my good boy," she says in the tone as when she tells my dog the same thing.

I open the soup lid, inhale the scent, and turn off the burner.

I steal a cookie, shove it into my mouth, and grip the pot while telling them, "Thank you."

When I'm in my car, I secure the seat belt around the pot and text Essie again.

No reply.

I go back and forth on what I should do.

On the one hand, I don't want to overwhelm her.

On the other, I know whatever River went there to tell her was bad.

I want to be there for her, and if I have to use the excuse of not letting good soup go to waste, I'll use that excuse.

When I get there, none of the lights are on in the main house. I grip the soup pot while strolling down the lit walkway that leads to the back. The sounds of crickets chirping and the rock waterfall cascading into the pool echo through the night.

"Not a good time, my man." River's voice startles me.

I stretch my neck to find him slumped on a pool chair, inches from Essie's door. He must have dragged it across the concrete from the row of others to the door.

"She's sick." He leans back and takes a hit of a joint.

I awkwardly hold up the pot. "I brought soup."

He stares at me, untrusting. "Did my sister ever tell you what happened to her?"

I'm clueless about how to answer, and I scramble for words.

My lack of response confirms I have no idea what he's referring to. That takes away any luck of River saying a word to me about Essie's past. It was a test, and I failed.

We're interrupted by a beam of light when Essie's front door opens. River hurriedly snubs out his joint and jumps to his feet when she walks outside.

"River," she says in a weak voice, "can you *please* tell Mom I'll talk to her in the morning—"

She freezes when she sees me. "Adrian, what are you doing here?"

I carefully walk closer to them, like an unwanted door-to-door salesman. "I, uh … brought you soup."

My heart twists when I see Essie's face. It's red and splotchy. I can tell she's been crying.

She stares at me distantly, her eyes cold and empty. You'd think I was a stranger to her.

Essie isn't only dealing with a stomach bug now.

No, now, she has the weight of something stronger.

"It's my grandmother's recipe," I continue before she asks me to leave. "Guaranteed to make you feel better."

I feel like a clown for those last words.

Soup. A Band-Aid. Winning the lottery.

Nothing will help her right now.

River, taking the hint, collects the pot from me.

"Thank you," Essie finally says, bowing her head to conceal her face from me.

"Will you text me tonight?" I'm pressing my luck. "If you need anything or want to talk."

I've never rambled in front of someone so much in my life. Not even during my first court case, when my client told me I was a disgrace to attorneys worldwide because no matter how hard I tried, I couldn't come up with a legal reason to elude the charges from him hiring hookers on his wife's company credit card.

Essie keeps her chin tucked while nodding. "Good night, Adrian."

I stand there, my spine stiff, while she retreats into her house.

"It might be best to give her space," River tells me apologetically. "She's going through a tough time."

"Why?" I call out when he follows her.

"It's not my place to tell others' stories." He holds up the pot. "Thank you for this."

I turn away but then stop. "Wait."

River pauses and furrows his brows.

I dig the Skittles bag from my pocket that I forgot about. "Give her these for me."

He tilts his head, curious how I know her favorite candy, but then shakes off the thought like it's the least of his worries. As he walks through Essie's doorway, I hear him mutter, "Fucking Prison Exoneration Program," before shutting the door behind him.

Darkness engulfs me as I drive through the thickets of trees to go home. At night, it's eerie as fuck out here.

If I permanently move to Blue Beech, it'll be closer to town. There have been too many strange noises for me to feel at ease here.

Tucker hops off the couch as soon as I walk in.

"Hey, boy," I say, petting him.

He walks next to me and licks my cheek when I kneel to grab his food bowl. I feed him, and while he devours his dinner, I open the folder at the kitchen table and sit.

The wind whistles through the thin window as I stare at the man's decade-old mug shot. His face, pale and boxy, is weathered and wrinkled. His dark eyes have a hardness as he glares at the camera. The description under his photo says he has a glass eye and a single tattoo. I flip to the tattoo photo, and it's a smiley face on his right arm.

I continue reading through Earl's file.

A decade ago, the courts charged Earl McGrey with reckless driving, driving under the influence, and manslaughter. He was sentenced to forty years in prison. The evidence against him is strong, and there are no other signs of wrongful convictions in the court file.

A witness reportedly matched the make and model to the truck they saw speeding down a rural highway. Paint on the truck's hood matched the victim's car. The truck was not only in Earl's name but also parked in his driveway when the police arrived to question him.

The address they arrived at?

The one where I'm currently staying.

Earl lived here.

He was also so drunk that night that he could hardly stand when they arrested him.

Tucker nestles against my side as I speed-read through the rest of Earl's file, knowing I'll reread it a hundred times. I'll have every sentence nearly memorized by morning.

Ethan Leonard, eighteen years young and the school's quarterback, died in the accident.

The underage victim was only sixteen, a junior in high school. She suffered severe wounds but survived the accident.

And that girl was Essie.

21

Adrian

The Past
College

E ssie is coming today.

I wipe a sweaty hand over my pants.

Why am I so nervous?

We've secretly hung out for months. But this time, we'll be with her friends and River.

I already hear voices drifting from the dorm room when I reach it. I tuck a bag of Skittles into my pocket and walk inside.

Everyone stops and turns in my direction. My gaze immediately anchors on Essie. A rush of air escapes me as we stare at each other. Her eyes sparkle, and a smile twitches on her lips.

"Dude," River says, interrupting our moment, "quit creepily staring at my sister."

"Relax," Essie tells River. "I *was* the one doing the staring."

"She's right." I wink at Essie. "She was doing all the creepy staring."

"So, this is the roommate?" a dark-haired girl asks, eyeing me. She extends her arm toward me. "I'm Amelia."

An introduction isn't necessary.

I recognize Amelia from Essie's Instagram and photos she's shown me.

To not make that obvious, I still shake Amelia's hand. "Adrian."

Ava introduces herself next.

"You're right," the strawberry blonde beside Essie says, elbowing her. "He is cute." She lifts her fingers in a wave. "I'm Callie."

I return the wave and smile at Essie, whose cheeks are now red. "Oh, you said I was cute, huh?"

"It was my way of convincing them to visit River," she explains. "Ava was adamant she didn't want to hang out in his smelly dorm."

River rolls his eyes. "Ava's behavior has proven otherwise."

Ava flips him off.

"Help me convince Essie we should all go to a frat party tonight," Amelia says.

"I'd suggest *not* going to a frat party tonight," I say.

River nods in agreement. "Frat parties are lame."

"Too bad." Amelia crosses her arms. "We can't go alone, so you two are chaperones." She claps her hands. "We'll be here at nine. Be ready."

River scoffs. "Doubt Adrian will go."

"Why's that?" Callie asks.

River smirks at me. "He prefers to stay in every night, talking to his secret girlfriend."

"The cute ones always have a girlfriend," Ava mutters.

River mimics her in the background, and she springs across the room to push him back onto the bed. He drags her onto it as he falls.

"Nah, I'll go." I tuck my hand into my pocket and play with the Skittles. "Nine o'clock. Got it."

A frat party sounds like a nightmare, but I'll do it to spend time with Essie.

It might give us time to sneak away too.

It's confirmed. I'm not a *frat party* kind of guy.

I don't think one person in our group is a *frat party* type of person.

This is the first frat party I've attended since starting college, and unless Essie is there, it'll be the last.

The place is shoulder to shoulder with people.

I've never felt so claustrophobic.

Standing against the wall, I cross my arms, watching Essie dance with her friends. Every few moments, she glances in my direction.

When a buzz-cut guy holding a drink attempts to grind on her, she pushes him away. I can't stop myself from laughing.

She fans her hand in front of her face, like she's hot, and yells, "Be right back," to her friends.

I push myself off the wall and beeline toward her. "Water?"

She nods and sticks out her tongue. "Yes, please."

Fun fact: water is the hardest drink to find at a frat party.

Jungle juice. Beer. Cheap vodka shots. But no H_2O.

"Jesus, don't these guys hydrate?" I mutter while searching the cabinets.

"They hide all the water," a guy finally tells me. "So random people don't steal them."

"It's funny, isn't it?" the short girl beside him says. "They'll shove alcohol at us all day, but Lord forbid anyone touches their water."

"Come on," I tell Essie. "I have some in my car."

They rode with River to the party, and I drove separately.

Capturing Essie's hand, I lead her outside to the road lined with cars.

"You look beautiful," I finally say what I've wanted to all night.

We're normally dressed casually when we hang out. Tonight, she's wearing a loose floral dress and pink cowgirl boots.

Essie shyly pulls at the hem of her dress. "Thank you."

This isn't the first time I've told Essie she's beautiful, but we're out of our element here.

I unlock my car and grab a water from the storage basket in my back seat. I always keep extra drinks and snacks for when I visit Essie and we hang out in here.

She takes the water from me and drinks half the bottle in one gulp.

"Thank you," she says around a sigh.

She grins when I tug the bag of Skittles from my pocket. I waited for the perfect time to give them to her. When I hand them to her, she rips the corner of the bag open, spills a few into her hand, and pops them into her mouth.

I cross my arms and lean against my car.

She stands in front of me, shaking the bag in the air. "I ask a question. If you answer it correctly, I'll toss it into your mouth."

I throw my arms out. "Go for it, babe."

"Did you want to come to the party tonight?"

"Hell no." I catch the Skittle in my mouth when she throws it.

"But you came for me?"

"Yes."

I miss the Skittle she throws, and it bounces off my car window and drops onto the ground.

"Am I the girl River referred to as your secret girlfriend?"

"Yes." Another Skittle caught.

"Was I the only girl you watched on the dance floor?"

"You're the only girl I watch, *period*."

"Stalker style, or I'm just so beautiful that you can't look away?" Her voice is playful.

"I was staring because you're gorgeous, but some could say it was too much on the stalker side."

"Correct. But FYI, you're the only man I'll allow to stalk me without kneeing you in the nuts."

I slap my hand to my chest. "I'm so honored." I steal the bag from her. "My turn."

She performs a *have at it* gesture.

"How excited were you to see me?"

"A little full of ourselves, are we?" She laughs.

"Answer the question." I shake the bag in the air. "Or no Skittles for you."

"Fine." She drawls that word out. "I was super excited but nervous."

I cast a Skittle toward her, but she misses.

"Why nervous?"

"I don't know." She shrugs and circles on her toes, motioning toward the party. "Being out of our bubble."

"Being out of our bubble blows," I grumble.

"It absolutely does. Give me milkshakes at the diner and the smell of mothballs in the library over this."

"I've never heard a more correct answer." I toss the Skittle and yell, "Bam!" when she catches it. I rip the bag open farther to discover only one Skittle left. "Final question, Esmeralda."

She throws her arms out. "Go for it, Castillo."

I pause. "Final *two* questions."

"That's cheating."

"What if I tear the Skittle in half?"

"Oh my gosh, just ask them."

I hold up the Skittle as if it were an expensive diamond. "Question number one: will you sneak out with me tonight?"

She goes quiet for a minute.

I play with the Skittle in my hand, noticing red dye bleeding into my skin.

"I'll sneak out with you tonight," she says around a long breath before smiling wide.

I almost tell her to pinky promise on it, but she keeps talking.

"Now, tell me question two and give me my Skittle before it melts in your hand and gets all gross," she teases.

"Question two"—a slow smile builds on my face—"can I kiss you?"

22

Essie

The Past
College

"**Q**uestion two: can I kiss you?"

Adrian's question sends a flutter through my stomach. His eyes drink me up underneath the streetlight. I shuffle back a few steps and lean against his car to steady myself. I didn't expect us to have alone time tonight.

For so long, I dreamed of him kissing me, but fear always shatters through that fantasy.

What a joke I am.

I'm nineteen. A kiss shouldn't feel so serious.

You don't have to strip to kiss.

Albeit kissing sometimes leads to that.

All these thoughts circle my brain while Adrian waits for my response.

If I say yes, it's not that simple.

It'll change everything about our friendship.

You can't take back kisses.

Can't take back love.

Now or never, Essie.

My head spins, my surroundings swirling around me—all but the view of Adrian.

And so, as if it were a sign, I blurt out, "Yes! Please kiss me, Adrian," without a drop of regret.

He immediately steps to me, wraps his arm around my waist, and draws me in closer. As he stares down at me, my body burns for him. He fixates his eyes on my mouth, tracing them with his fingertip, and I inhale a deep breath.

His mouth hovers over mine, slightly brushing it. "You have no idea how long I've waited to do this."

And we finally kiss.

The kiss starts closed-mouthed until Adrian sneaks his tongue inside my lips. I brush my tongue against his, and we start making out. His lips are soft and perfect.

He groans, nudging my hips forward and curling his hand around my hips.

"Yes, girl! Get it!" a girl slurs out.

Adrian's lips break free from mine as a group walking down the road passes us.

"Yeah, man," a guy with them says, giving Adrian a thumbs-up.

Another makes a thrusting motion with his hips.

Mood ruined by drunk coeds.

Adrian blocks me from their view, and his phone rings.

He eases it from his pocket, holding it up to show me the screen. "River."

"Yeah," he says after answering and nods as he listens. "We ran to my car to get water. Cool. Meet you in five."

He ends the call, shoving the phone back into his pocket, and brushes a strand of hair away from my face. "Meet me later?"

There's no hesitation this time when I say, "Okay."

"You know, when I left for college, my parents gave me rules," Amelia says, lying on her stomach in the hotel room bed. "One of them was to never drink anything given to you at a frat party."

"Same." Ava plops down next to her, and our snacks on the bed spill. "Like they expected me to bring a bottle of vodka in my purse."

I snatch a few M&M's and pop them into my mouth. "Or they just didn't want you going to college parties."

Tonight was my first college party. When I'd first moved into my dorm, my roommate had invited me everywhere. After a month of declines, she started telling everyone I stayed in all night, talking to my secret boyfriend on the phone. She and River have a lot in common, it seems.

Amelia groans and tosses her phone onto the floor. "Jax and Christopher are hanging out tonight."

Callie fluffs her pillow. "When don't they hang out?"

"Jax will probably talk shit about me going to a frat party in an attempt to make Chris question our relationship," Amelia continues, chewing on her bright pink nail. "I swear, that boy wants us to be miserable."

"He doesn't want you to be miserable." I lean off the bed upside down and collect her phone before one of us steps on it. "He wants you to be his."

Amelia smiles while I hand over her phone. "Jax doesn't want his *best friend's girl*. That's against all *bro code* rules."

"There are no rules when it comes to love," Ava argues.

Amelia glares at her, then me, and then Callie, like each of us needs to know she dislikes Ava's comment. "Hand me those Funyuns, and you crazies shut your mouths."

Adrian left after we met up with River, and River took us to a local pizzeria to eat.

It takes us ten minutes to decide on a movie—*Legally Blonde*, of course. I wait until the others are asleep before texting Adrian.

Me: Ready whenever you are.

My phone vibrates seconds later.

Adrian: Be there in 5.

I double-check the girls are asleep, swipe the key card from the nightstand, and tiptoe out of the room. The clerk peers up from the reception desk as I leave.

Adrian waits for me at the entrance. I honestly wouldn't be surprised if he'd been hanging out in his car until I texted.

My nerves build with each step I take.

You've done this with Adrian dozens of times; you have no reason to be nervous.

He jumps out of the car to open the door for me. I blush when my body brushes his as I climb into the passenger seat. He makes sure I'm all the way inside before shutting the door and sliding behind the wheel.

"Simple Twist of Fate" flows from the car speakers, and he turns to look at me. A smile breaks out on his face, but it's different from usual.

Adrian's smiles are always friendly.

Like a warm hug.

But this time, there's more to it.

Friendly with a hint of flirtation.

The good boy with the wicked smile who's up to no good tonight.

My eyes stay on his lips.

Lips that were on mine earlier.

I grin back. I'm sure mine looks different too … giddier … *cheesier* than usual.

"Hi," he whispers.

I bite my lip like I can still taste him. "Hi."

Then, we burst out in laughter, realizing we're both acting weird.

"What do you want to do?" he asks, the mood turning somewhat normal while he drives through the hotel parking lot.

"Take me where you go to think." I already know where this is.

Burbota Park.

He's FaceTimed me from there plenty of times. Sometimes, he's in his car. Other times, he's walking alongside the stream or sitting under a tree.

I stare at Adrian as he drives.

I trust this man, and deep down, I know I love him.

"Did you go back to the dorms?" I ask.

He shakes his head. "I read until you texted."

I smile at him.

Maybe tonight, I'll tell him everything.

Just maybe.

The park is empty, and Adrian pulls up under the only illuminated light. He pops the trunk and collects a blanket in his arms as I step out.

It's our blanket.

The one we always use.

It's starting to unravel, and the color is fading.

But like a baby blanket, the age and use are what makes it special.

It's what makes you want to keep it forever and never let it go.

The blanket has heard us talk about our dreams, our futures, our fears.

Adrian drapes a sweatshirt over the blanket, and I follow him toward a secluded area. As soon as we got back to the hotel earlier, I changed into my pajamas. So I'm dressed in a plaid pink pj set and sneakers.

He spreads out the blanket. I sit, and he wraps the sweatshirt around my shoulders, knowing I'm almost always cold.

"Well …" I drawl when he sits next to me. "What do you want to do?"

He taps his cheek, fake thinking. "I wouldn't mind kissing you again."

"Then, do it."

He drops his head, and his lips smash into mine.

This kiss isn't as careful as the last one.

It's more rushed, like he planned for this moment the entire time he waited in the car. We kiss and kiss and kiss. I lower onto my back as he climbs over me.

We've never had the sex talk.

He doesn't know I've only had sex once, and I have no idea about his sexual history. I know he isn't a ladies' man, but he's dated.

He drags the sweatshirt off and flings it to the edge of the blanket as his lips trail from my ear down my neck. I moan and grip his shoulders.

Then, it happens.

He lifts my pajama shirt.

My reflexes kick in before my brain does, and I shove him away. He falls back on his ass. The lighting is limited, but I can see the shock on his face.

"I need to go," I say, my voice breaking.

I'm nervous, embarrassed, and scared. I can name a million other emotions flowing through me.

Adrian scoots closer but still keeps a comfortable distance. "What did I do wrong?"

"Nothing." I stand and pull my pajama shirt down so far that I'm surprised it doesn't rip. "I'll text Amelia and ask her to pick me up."

Amelia drove us to the university and is the only one with a car, other than River, who most definitely isn't getting a call from me.

"No way in hell am I leaving you out here alone." Adrian gathers the blanket in his arms when I step off it. "I'll take you back to the hotel. You don't have to say one word to me in the car."

I cross my arms.

Adrian might think I'm beautiful now, but that will change when he sees what I really look like. Whenever we hang out, I'm careful to make sure I'm always covered. It's become a habit I've mastered.

No bikinis, only one-pieces.

No crop tops.

My breathing halts, words dying in my throat. I don't know what to say to him without breaking down.

Adrian stares at me as if he wants to crack into my soul and get the answers I'm unwilling to give him. After all this time, he thought he knew the real me. But no one can ever know the real you until they know every burned inch of your skin.

He's anxious, his body shaking as he waits for my next move.

"I'm sorry, Essie." His voice cracks. Thinking he hurt me hurts him.

My pain is his.

I hate that he thinks he's the problem, that he pushed me too far.

I need to tell him the truth. Or at least that what's happening right now is my fault and my fault only.

"Please take me back to the hotel," I say.

"Okay," he replies.

Tears prick my eyes as I tread toward the car. It feels like the longest walk of my life. Adrian follows, keeping distance between us, as if he knows it's what I need.

When we return to the car, I close my eyes and rest my head against the seat. The same song plays on repeat in the background.

I attempt to swallow down the regret of how I'm treating him.

Of not giving him answers.

I'm a terrible person.

My sobs join the stupid song as we grow closer to the hotel.

He slowly brakes in front of the hotel entrance.

I swing open the door. "Good night," I rush out, holding my breath as I jump out of the car.

"Essie—" he yells, but I cut off his voice by slamming the door shut.

I dash inside the hotel.

"Is everything okay?" the receptionist asks.

"Yes," I say, proud of how level I keep my voice.

I take the stairs instead of the elevator and stop between floors to give myself a break. I grip the railing, dipping over the side, and scream into the silence.

I hate myself.

I should've never treated him like that.

When I get back to the hotel, everyone is still asleep. I lock myself in the bathroom and pull my phone from my pajama pocket. There's already a text from Adrian.

> Adrian: I'm sorry for whatever I did to upset you.

My hands tremble as I text back.

> Me: It wasn't you. It was me.

> Adrian: I hate that line.

Just as I'm trying to come up with a response, my phone vibrates with another text from him.

> Adrian: From now on, friends only. Got it. We'll never cross that line again.

No! I don't want that. I just need time.

> Me: I don't want to lose you. Please give me time.

> Adrian: I'll be patient with you because I love you.

My heart nearly bursts at his words.

Adrian: I'm sorry. I had to get that off my chest, especially if I'm losing you.

Me: Can we talk after finals? Maybe you can come to my dorm?

Adrian: I'll be there.

But that doesn't happen.

I never get to tell Adrian my truth or that I love him back because he stops talking to me three days later. At first, I blamed his lack of response on finals week.

But after two weeks, I know he's gone. River tells me he moved out of the dorm while he was away for the weekend. He deactivated his social media and changed his number.

It's as if my secret best friend, the man I was falling in love with, never existed.

23

Adrian

Present Day

I swerve into a parking spot and check my phone for what feels like the billionth time for any word from Essie.

Nothing.

I gulp down the last of my coffee and rub my tired eyes. I spent the entire night poring over Earl's file and combing through every online detail.

Holding my attorney badge, I walk toward the prison, the golden sunrise above me.

The officer at the front desk eats a muffin as I sign in as Earl's representation to speak with him. Guilt swirls in my stomach.

I should tell Essie I'm here.

But even if I tried, she's ignoring my calls.

And this isn't something I can text.

A guard leads me into a room that reeks of mildew and sweat. Since I specialize in family law, interviewing incarcerated clients is uncharted territory for me.

Two guards escort Earl into the room. His hands and ankles are shackled. As he sits across from me, I blink at him. He's aged since his mug shot.

He settles his arms on the table and waits for me to speak.

"I'm Adrian with the Prison Exoneration Program," I introduce. "I'm here to help you with your case."

He stares at me with gratefulness. "I appreciate you coming, Adrian, and that the PEP is taking my case." There's a deep pain in his voice.

"Did you do it?"

It's a stupid question. He applied for the program's help, so why would he admit guilt? But it's one I need to ask for my own sake.

"Hell no, I didn't do it." This time, instead of pain, there's a slight twang in his voice. "I'm innocent."

"It's a question I had to look you in the eyes and ask." I stare at him while opening the folder. "Tell me your story."

"My story is that I'm innocent. Someone set me up."

I run my thumb along a paper clip. "Why would someone set you up?"

"I was the easiest to blame. I made a few mistakes, and everyone in Blue Beech automatically decided I was some creep. Who better to point your finger at?"

"Why would they think you're a creep?"

He sighs. "I was a custodian at the local high school. The kids, they liked to sneak around and hook up. I always ratted them out to the principal. Then, one night, I found them drinking and partying at the football field. I ran them off, called the cops, and reported it to the principal. After that, the popular kids decided I was enemy number one. They made my life a living hell, said I only found them because I was a stalker, and pulled a stupid prank on me that got me fired."

"What kind of prank?"

"A student told me she couldn't get her locker unlocked. I had a master key and unlocked it for her. She asked me to grab a bag from the top shelf since she couldn't reach it. I did, and something fell out of it. On instinct, I bent down to pick it up, and before I even recognized what it was, the kids came out from around the corner. They took pictures of me standing next to this high school girl with her panties in my hand. I was fired the next day and investigated by the police."

"They couldn't check the cameras?"

"For some reason, they claimed they weren't working that day."

I adjust my glasses. "What does that have to do with you being set up for hitting two kids head-on and killing one?"

"I don't know, man. All I can think of is they wanted to ruin my life. I went to work at the theater—that was my new job since I'd lost the one at the school. They messed with me there too. I have an alibi. I was picked up from the bar and taken home, and then I passed out. The next thing I know, the cops were at my home, saying I'd run some kids off the road and killed one."

"There was damage on your truck."

"I don't know how that damage got there. My grandmother drove my truck home. Neither one of us drove after that. Someone must've taken my truck."

"So, you think someone stole your truck, hit them, and then blamed you for it because you'd tattled on them?"

"I know it seems a little messed up, but yeah."

"They were high school kids, Earl. The boy who died, he was friends with the kids you say could be involved."

"I never said they were to blame. You asked why someone would want to blame me, and that's why."

"Anyone else?"

"There was this couple who kept trying to buy my grand-mother's property. They've been on my possible suspect list."

"What was going on with the property?"

"After my grandfather died, he left the property to my grandmother and me. We struggled to afford it. This couple, they kept telling my grandmother to sell it to them, and she wouldn't because I was able to keep us afloat. They kept offering her money, the amount going up each time—more money than it was worth."

"Who was this couple?"

"Pete and Agnes White."

I nearly drop my pen.

I thought moving to Blue Beech would be calm, no crime.

Boy, was I wrong.

There are too many dots to try connecting.

But I need to do it.

Earl and I talk for an hour before a guard comes in and tells us, "Time's up."

I spend another thirty minutes in my car gathering my thoughts.

My mother has always said to listen to your gut, and I am. I can't put my finger on it, but something tells me Earl is innocent.

That, or he's a damn good liar.

If he's being truthful, then whoever did it is out there.

I need to find them.

If he is, he deserves to be free.

And Essie deserves justice for who actually committed the crime.

I'll figure it out, but first, I need to talk to her.

When I get home and start on my next round of Earl research, I finally get a text from Essie.

Essie: Thank you again for the soup.

24

Essie

Brielle and Rhett's court date is today.

Other than my text thanking him for the soup, and emails regarding Rhett and Brielle's divorce, Adrian and I haven't spoken.

The county courthouse is a thirty-minute drive out of Blue Beech, and when I pull into the parking lot, I see an old Volvo stopping at the entrance.

Adrian steps out of the passenger side. I park, waiting until he's in the courthouse, and then walk inside to find him sitting on a bench.

When he sees me, he stands and offers a gentle smile. Our smiles connect like long-lost friends.

"Did something happen to your car?" I ask when I reach him.

"Punctured tire," he explains. "I must've run over something. That's what I get for staying in the middle of nowhere."

"Where are you staying?"

"I want to get this shit over with," Rhett shouts.

I turn to find him barreling in our direction, waving papers in the air.

"I signed," he yells. "It's done."

Brielle chases behind him. "The bastard wants to marry his mistress," she explains, crossing her arms.

Rhett thrusts the papers in our direction. "I've signed them, granting her what she wants as long as she signs *to-fuck-ing-day.*" He snaps his fingers. "Right damn now so this is over with."

I smile.

First case won.

Eek, yay!

Brielle shrugs, grins, and collects the papers from him. "Works for me. Does anyone have a pen?"

I hurriedly grab one from my bag and hand it to her.

Adrian smiles in satisfaction and slips his hands into his pockets.

Technically, his client didn't get the deal he'd wanted.

Isn't he supposed to be disgruntled about that?

He's dressed in another one of his black suits that fits his frame perfectly. I can't stop myself from roaming my gaze down his body.

Brielle clicks the pen open, presses the papers against the wall, and flips through the pages, signing each red-tabbed line. When she's finished, she hands them to me.

"Thank the lords. Now, I'm taking the kids out for ice cream." Brielle blows Rhett a kiss. "Pleasure divorcing you." She squeezes me tight in a hug. "Thank you, Essie. I knew I could count on you."

I watch her and her mom leave the courthouse, arm in arm.

"Fucking bitch," Rhett mutters, scuffing his shoe against the floor.

I roll my eyes at him and move in the opposite direction as he and Adrian huddle in a corner, talking.

They shake hands, and as soon as Adrian walks away from him, Rhett is on the phone, telling someone, "*I fucking got rid of her.*"

"Essie."

I whip around at the sound of my name to find Robert Sullivan coming toward me.

"I thought that was you," he says, concern on his face.

Robert has aged some, but I'll never forget how kindly he treated me—the teenager forced to give multiple interviews about the worst night of my life. He was one of the prosecutors in Earl's trial. He pleaded with me to testify, but I refused. They did use my videos as evidence, though.

Robert rubs his chubby chin. "I heard about the Prison Exoneration Program taking Earl's case. I'm sorry, Essie."

I weakly smile at him. "You had enough evidence to put him behind bars. That should be enough to keep him there."

Earl will be a free man one day—I know this. I just thought I'd have more time to prepare myself for it.

"Stay strong. I'll do everything I can to keep him where he is." He gently squeezes my shoulder and walks away.

"I'll get there as soon as I can, okay?"

Adrian's panicked voice grabs my attention. He's pacing in front of the restroom, talking on the phone. I inch closer to eavesdrop.

"It's not your fault," he says. "Take him to the animal hospital."

"Is everything okay?" I ask when he ends the call.

He swings around to look at me, his face as pale as a ghost. "A car hit my dog." He stops to text on his phone. "I'm trying to find a ride, but the downside about small towns is that there are no Ubers."

"I'll drive you."

He keeps texting. "You don't need to do that."

"Adrian, I'm already driving to Blue Beech." I jerk my head toward the double doors and start walking. "Come on."

"Are you sure?" he calls out.

"Let's go to your furbaby."

The second we get into my car, he's back on his phone. "I'll be there soon, Abuela. Where are you taking him?" There's a slight pause, and he looks at me. "Blue Beech Animal Hospital."

I exit the parking lot.

"Tell the vet to do whatever they have to do," Adrian says. "I don't care how much it costs." He nods, listening to what she says on the other end.

As soon as we get to the animal hospital, I park my car, and we run inside. A few animals and their owners are in the waiting room, but thankfully, there's no line.

Adrian rushes toward the receptionist's desk, nearly colliding with it. "They brought my dog, Tucker, in."

"Hit by a car?" The receptionist stands.

"Yes."

She opens a door and motions for us to follow. "Right this way."

She leads us into a small exam room, where a woman—who I recognize as his grandmother—and Terrance are waiting.

His grandmother jumps up from her chair. "I'm so sorry! Tucker saw a squirrel and got loose." She wipes tears from her cheeks.

Adrian wraps her in a hug, rubbing her back. "It was an accident. Don't blame yourself."

"Here, Essie," Terrance says, standing to offer me his chair.

"Oh, no," I say, stopping him. "Thank you, but it's all yours."

"Essie, this is my abuela, Valeria," Adrian says when they separate. "Abuela, this is Essie."

Valeria is an elegant woman with tan skin, black hair, and a tenderhearted gaze.

A warm smile graces her lips as she looks at me. "Ah, the pretty girl from the pub."

Pretty girl from the pub?

I don't ask why I'm referred to as that.

It's not the time.

Instead, I return her smile.

"You're so kind to give him a ride," she says.

Adrian loosens his blazer. "I'll be here for a while. You guys can go home."

"You don't have a car, honey," Valeria argues. "You also don't need to sit here all alone."

"I can stay with him," I volunteer before thinking about what a horrible idea it is.

Everyone's eyes shoot straight to me.

"Are you sure?" Adrian asks.

"Of course," I say softly.

Adrian hugs Valeria goodbye, and surprisingly, she hugs me next.

"You take good care of my boy, sweetie," she whispers.

Adrian drapes his blazer over the back of a chair and sags back in the seat. I sit beside him, and as we wait, he taps his foot against the floor.

Over and over.

Louder and louder.

Reaching out, I grab his hand.

When he calms, I start pulling away, but he holds on to it like a lifeline.

"Thank you for being here," he says lowly.

I squeeze his hand. "You were there for me when I was sick."

His hand in mine feels like a missed comfort.

Like when someone who's been gone from a long trip finally comes home.

The exam room is chilly with bright white walls. Posters, educating about heartworm and the importance of flea medicine for pets, decorate the walls.

"He's an old dog," Adrian rasps. "What if he doesn't make it, Essie?"

"From the stories you've told me, Tucker's a fighter. He'll pull through this and be home soon."

Foster walks in, interrupting us. "Tucker suffered a hip fracture, and we're prepping him for surgery. We're always cautious when administrating anesthesia to dogs his age, but I promise, he's in good hands."

I trust Foster. He received recognition as one of the top veterinary surgeons in the state this year. His uncle, on his mom's side, owns the animal hospital and the one in Anchor Ridge. Foster alternates between the two.

"Can I see him before?" Adrian asks.

Foster smiles. "Of course."

Foster leads us to a surgical room, where the vet techs are preparing Tucker for surgery.

He's sedated, lying peacefully on the table. The vet techs move back a step, giving us space. Adrian blows out a series of breaths, and his eyes are wet.

"You'll be okay, boy," he soothingly tells Tucker. "And when you get home, I'll give you all the treats you want." He strokes Tucker's head before giving it a kiss.

I pet Tucker, feeling his heavy breath against my palm.

"I'll take good care of him." Foster clasps Adrian on the back.

A blonde vet tech escorts us back to the exam room, and we sit there quietly for a few minutes.

Minutes that feel like hours, honestly.

Adrian slumps forward. "Tucker was my father's dog's puppy. I saw him as a piece of my father I never had. Now, I might lose him too." His voice breaking crushes my heart.

He sits back, and I kick off my heels, making myself comfortable.

"Will you tell me about your father?"

"My mom said he was the funniest person she knew, but he lost all his humor when he got sick. I guess that's to be expected." He sighs. "She said she prayed every night that he'd live long enough to meet me, to have at least one day as a father. He died two days before I was born."

"Even if you didn't get to meet in person, he loved you."

"No, he didn't."

I flinch, waiting for him to explain.

He doesn't.

I want to ask more questions, but don't.

He can choose which scars to bleed open for me.

I, too, have a habit of hiding mine.

Lowering my head, I rest it on his shoulder.

Adrian clears his throat. "Do you remember the night we studied in my car for twelve straight hours, drinking only coffee and eating snacks?"

I smile at the memory. "Even though we technically didn't need each other to study, you being there was a comfort."

"I feel that same way right now. You're my comfort. Thank you for this."

We spend the next ten minutes in silence.

"Do you want me to read to you?" I ask when he grows fidgety.

In college, when he couldn't sleep, he'd ask me to read to him either in the car or over the phone. He never cared what I read. Hearing my voice relaxed him.

He squeezes my knee. "I'd love for you to read to me, Essie."

I raise my head, take my phone from my bag, and choose one of his favorites. He wraps his arm around my shoulders, drawing me closer, and we make ourselves comfortable as I read.

This is us.

Because it doesn't matter where we are or what we're doing, we've always been the other's comfort.

Sometime during my reading, we fell asleep.

Foster knocking and entering the room wakes us. "The surgery went well. Tucker did great, but he's groggy from the anesthesia. I'd like to keep him here for the night to monitor him."

Adrian stands. "Thank you, Foster."

"Would you like to see him before you leave?" Foster gestures toward the doorway.

"I'd love that."

Adrian offers me his hand and helps me to my feet. Our hands stay clasped as we follow Foster out of the room to the surgical recovery area.

"Hey there, buddy," Adrian says in a whisper, as if he doesn't want to wake Tucker. "You're having a sleepover with Foster tonight, and then you'll come home tomorrow, okay?"

I run my fingers through Tucker's thick fur, careful to avoid his stitches.

Adrian lowers his head to kiss Tucker's head before stepping away to thank Foster again.

They shake hands, and then Foster hugs me.

The sky is black when we walk outside to my car.

"I'm sorry I kept you out so late," Adrian says.

"Don't you dare apologize." I snuggle into his side. "I offered because I wanted to stay."

He helps me into my car.

"Do you want me to take you home?" I ask when he's inside.

He rubs his tired eyes. "I've never gone home to an empty house without Tucker before."

"Do you want to come to mine, then?"

25

Adrian

E ssie's invite reminds me of the first time I visited her in college.

She doesn't know how much this means to me.

I want to wrap her in my arms and never let her go.

The music plays low on the drive to her place. Two other cars are in the driveway as she parks. Her heels click against the concrete as I follow her to the cottage.

"Would you like something to drink?" she asks when we're inside. "Water? Tea?"

There's an urge to say vodka, whiskey, something strong to help me get through the night. Tucker is fine now, but post-surgery complications are always possible.

"No, I'm okay," I reply.

She fills a glass of water for herself. I stand to the side as she moves into the living room, places her glass on a coaster, and kicks off her heels.

"Essie, I need to explain myself," I say.

I'm fucking exhausted, but this might be the only chance I have to talk to her.

She needs to know why I did what I did—how I had to face my personal battles before I could be there for anyone else.

I want to tell her why I disappeared, joined Adaway and Williams, and then followed her to Blue Beech.

"Adrian," she whispers, "it's been a long day for you. You don't have to do this now."

I drop into the chair I sat in when she was sick. "You need to know this. Ten minutes after you were fired at Adaway and Williams—"

"You mean after I quit," she corrects.

I can't help but chuckle. "Yes, right after you quit."

I hunch forward, resting my elbows on my knees. "I was shocked when they called me into the boardroom and congratulated me on the promotion. I had no idea about it. The only reason I was at Adaway and Williams was to make amends with you. Which didn't work out as planned since you pretty much gave me the *fuck you*."

"Can you blame me? Did you expect me to welcome you with open arms?" Her voice softens. "You hadn't given me a goodbye, not an *I'm sorry, I just don't like you anymore*. You moved and completely cut off contact, as if our relationship meant nothing."

"You've always been my everything, Essie." I massage my temples. "It wasn't just you I was running from. I ran away from everyone and everything."

"Why?"

Here goes.

I'm ready to rip open this wound.

26

Adrian

The Past
College

"I found some of your father's old stuff when cleaning the attic," my abuela says, dropping a box at my feet. "I thought you'd enjoy having this."

She came to visit today, and we went out for lunch.

"Thank you," I reply, and she kisses me on the head before leaving my dorm.

I settle on the edge of my bed and open the box marked *Daniel's Things*.

A beat-up flip phone rests on a pile of clothing and old Polaroid pictures. I open the flip phone, and it's completely dead. I search the box and find a charger at the bottom.

Growing up without a father was tough. My mom did everything she could to make me feel close to him. She took me out to dinner on Father's Day, shared stories about him, and always signed his name on my cards with a halo above it.

After plugging the phone into the charger, I hit the power button again. It takes a second to come on.

This could be considered an invasion of privacy, but curiosity gets the better of me. The phone is bare-bones, not like the smartphones we have now. I scroll through the options and select Texts. I browse through the messages until one stands out to me.

It's a conversation between my mother and father.

> Daniel: You'll have a bastard kid, Paula.

Dread washes over me.

I'm an only child.

The text is about me.

Clutching the phone tight, I fight with myself on whether to keep reading.

Unfortunately, I do.

> Daniel: I told you I didn't want a kid. I'm dying, for fuck's sake. And this is what you do?

I go through text after text, reading their exchange.

> Paula: I told you I wanted a son. He'll be a part of you I can hold on to. Please don't be upset with me.

> Daniel: Why? A kid doesn't deserve to grow up without a dad. I did, and it wasn't fun. We discussed this. You need to get an abortion. I don't want this. I don't want him.

I was unwanted.

I fling the phone across the room.

A satisfying crack echoes as it hits the wall.

It breaks.

Good.

I wish it'd caught the fuck on fire.

I slide down to the floor, leaning back against the bed frame, and bury my head between my knees.

Unwanted.

Essie pushed me away at the park a few days ago, and now this?

I feel like I'm suddenly losing everything.

A tightness forms in my chest at the thought of her.

I've texted her a few times, but she hasn't replied.

What did I do wrong?

I'd thought she was okay with what we were doing.

I've always respected her when we're together. I'd never want to force myself on her.

My phone vibrates, a call from my mother lighting up the screen.

I ignore it.

She calls again.

Ignore.

For hours, I sit there, not speaking, not moving, thankful River is gone for the weekend.

When I finally check my phone again to turn it off, I find a text from Essie.

> Essie: Hi. I'm sorry we haven't talked much. I'm really struggling to find the words to explain myself. Please don't be upset with me.

Please don't be upset with me.

Is that a prologue to rejection?

I feel like I'm breaking down, and if I read a message from Essie that's bad, it'll completely crush me. I drop my phone on the floor, stand, and smash it with my foot.

Then, I do it again.

Again.

Again.

Until it's nothing but fragments.

I pack my bags and drop out of college.

Delete all my social media.

I sleep in my car for a few nights. That's hard because it has so many memories of Essie.

A couple of days later, a friend from Cali sends out a mass email that he's looking for a roommate. So, I move there and work for his father's construction company.

I avoid my mother.

She sees me as a substitute for something she lost.

Eventually, she and my abuela find me. That's when my mother shows me a letter my dad wrote to her before he died. In the letter, he apologized for treating her so horribly when he found out she was pregnant. He confessed his fears of being judged as a bad father for bringing a child into the world, knowing he was terminally ill and couldn't raise him.

I feel sorry for him after reading the letter … until I find out he left my mother pregnant and alone for eight months. She didn't see him again until his funeral.

After going through his things, she found he'd saved all my ultrasounds she'd mailed to him while pregnant. Each one had *My son* and a smiley face written on them.

I'll always wonder if his love was real or if he wrote that in guilt. But my mother has always worked hard to keep his good name and convince me he loved me.

A week later, I decide I need to go back to who I was.

I enroll in a school in California, start therapy, and graduate from law school.

Essie is always on my mind, but I'm scared of rejection.

I regret smashing my phone after reading her text.

It takes two years before I finally search her out.

She declines my friend request and blocks me.

She wants nothing to do with me.

I spend six months working for a California law firm before moving back to Iowa. I shamelessly stalk Essie online and find out where she's working. I apply to the firm, not expecting a response, but a week later, their call feels like fate. Charles went to law school with a partner at my old law firm, and he gave me a strong recommendation.

California became my healing haven after I left Iowa.

But that healing cost me the one thing I wanted.

It cost me the girl I loved.

27

Essie

Present Day

"Why didn't you tell me?" I ask Adrian, tears in my eyes. "I'd have been there for you in a heartbeat."

He massages the back of his neck. "I thought we were done, and it'd be another rejection."

"We agreed to meet after finals, but you just disappeared. I went to your dorm, but it was like you never existed. Like you were a figment of my imagination."

His gaze connects with mine. "Essie, will you tell me what happened in the park that night?"

I shiver, clutching myself. "I was afraid."

He puts a hand over his heart and whispers, "Afraid *of me*?"

"No, I've never been afraid of you."

"Then, what was it?"

Taking a deep breath, I stand.

It suddenly feels like everything is happening in slow motion.

I take small steps toward him.

When I reach him, he sits up straighter.

My hands shake as I free my shirt from my skirt, and I use

his hand to raise it. I gulp, my eyes on his hand as it touches my skin.

My heart beats so fast in my chest that it aches.

I've never felt so exposed.

"I was scared of you seeing the real me," I tell him. "I didn't want you to see my imperfections."

Adrian doesn't flinch as he stares at my scarred skin.

He looks at my scars with a tenderness I wish I had when looking at myself in the mirror.

A gentle plea is in his eyes, as if asking for permission when he raises his gaze to mine.

I nod.

A shiver runs down my spine when he brushes his hand over my skin.

His eyes stay on mine when he reaches his free hand to my shirt buttons. I nod again, and he slowly starts unbuttoning it. The cool air hits my skin as my shirt slides off my shoulders.

I'm on full display for him.

Like an open book revealing my past.

He traces the path of my scars with his thumb, stroking them before tenderly kissing one.

"Essie," he murmurs, "you embody perfection in every sense of the word. I've been in love with every part of you for years."

I believe him.

And regret washes over me like a wave.

I should've been honest with him in the park.

He'd have been just as accepting as he is now.

My cheeks are wet with tears, the salty taste on my lips. I take a step back when he stands. He peers down at me, cradling my cheek in his large hand, and brushes away my tears.

Adrian has finally seen the true me.

I feel so free.

"Thank you," he mutters.

"For what?" I whisper.

"For finally trusting me."

I rise on my toes and kiss him.

He hesitates for a moment, like he didn't expect it. His gaze drops, colliding with mine, and I nod. He circles his arm around my waist, pulling me close, and kisses me.

It takes only seconds for our kiss to deepen.

He slips his tongue into my mouth, dancing it with mine.

He tastes like cinnamon.

His breathing is ragged when I break away from him, grab his hand, and lead him to my bedroom. I flick on the light and toy with my skirt zipper while walking backward. He doesn't take his eyes off me as I wriggle out of my skirt and kick it aside.

As if he can't hold himself back any longer, he takes two long strides to me. He slips his hand into my panties and cups my pussy. Gripping his shoulders, I moan as he caresses my clit with his palm.

"Adrian," I whimper, craving more.

I shimmy out of my panties, and he licks his lips.

"Let me see all of you, Essie," he says in a hushed tone.

I choke back a breath before unhooking my bra, freeing my breasts. My nipples pucker when his tongue smooths along his bottom lip in approval.

"Get on the bed," he says, unbuttoning his shirt. It falls to the floor.

I do as he said, watching as he unbuckles and unzips his pants. But he doesn't pull them down. They hang loose around his waist as he comes closer and kneels between my legs.

Goose bumps spread over my skin as he kisses my thigh, trails his tongue along my slit, and plants a kiss on the other thigh. I lean back and rest my hands on the bed to steady myself.

I haven't been with anyone since high school.

And that was only a few times with a high school boyfriend who had no idea what he was doing.

But no one's face has ever been this close to my pussy.

Adrian grips my thighs, lifting me off the bed, and settles my legs on his shoulders.

"I told you, every inch of you is beautiful," he states, staring between my legs like it holds the key to all his desires.

I tremble when he spreads my folds with his fingers and leans down to suck on my clit. But unfortunately, it's only brief.

"Crawl up the bed," he instructs. "I want to worship your body better."

He follows me, and for the next I don't know how long, he does just that.

He places gentle kisses on each of my stomach scars before working his way up my body. He cups my breast with his hand while sucking on the other nipple. Every nerve ending in my body buzzes.

When he moves back down my body, my legs shake. He buries his face between my legs and groans, sending a vibration through me.

My body is on fire as he uses his fingers and tongue to hit every angle until he finds my G-spot.

"Come on my tongue, Essie," he says. "You let me see you. Now, let me taste you, baby."

My legs tighten, my clit is throbbing, and—

Oh my God, I'm so close.

The only other times I've orgasmed were compliments of yours truly.

A moan escapes me, followed by a loud, "Yessssss."

I crumble under his weight, and my head wildly thrashes from side to side. If I wasn't taking a trip to orgasm heaven, I'd be absolutely horrified and embarrassed.

Adrian draws back and sucks on his bottom lip.

"Fuck, you taste so good," he groans before pushing his finger back inside me, covering it with my juices. He pulls out his finger and sucks on it. His eyes stay on me the entire time, and he groans again.

"Adrian," I pant, "I need you."

He freezes. "Are … are you sure?"

"Positive."

He pauses for a moment, then another, giving me the chance to change my mind.

"Please," I beg. "Give me what I wanted so many times when we were in college."

He doesn't look away while getting off the bed or when he fishes for a condom from his wallet. His erection springs forward, and—

Oh my fucking God.

He's huge.

Bigger than my ex.

Bigger than any porn I've watched.

His cock twitches when he rolls the condom down his cock. Kneeling on the bed, he positions himself between my legs.

Which immediately lock up.

He stops. "We can wait, Essie."

"No," I rush out, shaking my head. "It's just been a while. But I want this, want *you*."

He grips the base of his cock and strokes it. "You tell me if you want to stop or do something different, okay? Promise me."

I bite my lip. "I promise."

"I can't wait to make you feel so fucking good from the inside out."

I lean forward to grip his ass and draw him closer.

Then, with patience, he slowly eases his cock inside me.

My breath catches in my throat, my back curves, and my hands reach for his arms. I sink my nails into his skin while adjusting to his size.

"Is this okay, baby?" he asks.

"It's perfect," I whisper.

"You're so tight."

"And you're fucking huge."

He chuckles. "I'm giving you an extra orgasm for that."

He slowly starts moving inside me.

I feel myself growing wetter and wetter with each stroke, needing more.

My pussy walls pulsate against his cock.

I watch him bite his lip, fighting back restraint not to speed up.

"Do it," I say, my voice strained. "Don't hold back. *Fuck me, Adrian.*"

He stops mid-stroke, taking a second to process my words, and then lifts my legs back over his shoulders.

And he gives me exactly what I asked for.

Him, in my bed, inside me, with no restraints.

Okay, well, I'm pretty sure he is showing a little restraint.

But that's my Adrian—so selfless.

We move together as one.

Meeting each other stroke for stroke, like we've done this for years.

There's no awkwardness with him.

No fumbling around.

He licks up my neck and kisses me while circling his strokes.

"That's my good girl," he says, tilting my hips up for a better angle.

He makes me feel like the most important person in the world as he thrusts in and out of me.

As I get closer, he drops my legs and presses his body harder against mine, nearly pushing me through the mattress.

He traces a kiss along my neck and whispers, "Absolutely beautiful everywhere, baby."

His words ignite my orgasm, and his lips are on mine as I lose control of my body. I fall apart, crying out his name, and close my eyes before suddenly opening them back up.

I want to watch him.

See him get off inside me.

"Give me one more," Adrian says, quickening his movements. "Give it to me, Essie."

"I … I can't." My words definitely sound muffled.

"I told you, your comment granted you another orgasm. Give it to me."

He continues fucking me. His hand finds my clit until another orgasm takes over my body.

As my body goes back into pure bliss, I'm unable to form words.

My orgasm brain doesn't work as well as my normal one.

As I come down from my high, I watch him again.

Sweat beads on his chest.

His face tightens.

"I'm coming," he breathes out. "I'm about to come so hard for you, Essie."

My love for Adrian is so deep that even my heartbreak couldn't crush it.

He understands me.

Doesn't judge me.

And tonight, I've learned he also knows how to fuck me.

And here I thought, him moving to Blue Beech was a bad idea.

My *ten out of ten* orgasm says otherwise.

28

Essie

I wake up to Adrian lying next to me.

His body heat against mine is a comforting weight I never knew I needed. This is my first time waking up to someone in bed after having sex with them.

In college, we'd sometimes doze off in his car after late-night conversations, but I never felt this refreshed when I woke up. The days after would always include a stiff neck and exhaustion.

Why was I so scared of him seeing my scars?

He's always accepted me for who I am.

Neither of us knew it then, but he was there for me during my darkest time. The accident happened only two years before we met.

I lost my sense of self.

That's why I attended a different college than River. I needed space to learn to love myself again. I hid my emotional suffering from everyone.

But Adrian, unknowingly, ended up helping me with that.

He made my dark days feel brighter.

He was comfort without making me feel broken.

His arm is draped over my waist, and his slow breathing fills the room, creating a soothing effect.

I break away from him and fall on my back. The cool air hits my skin as the sheet slides down, exposing my stomach. I instinctively cover it with my arms.

"Don't, baby," Adrian grumbles, his voice sleepy.

I cast a timid glance in his direction.

"Never hide yourself from me," he says, lifting onto his elbow and pulling my arms away, splaying them out on each side of my body.

"It's habit." I blow out a breath and fight the urge to re-cover myself.

Stop it, Essie.

This is Adrian.

Your Adrian.

With his eyes locked on mine, he slowly moves the sheet down farther.

My heart pounds when he brushes his hand over my scarred skin, so similar to how he did last night. As he lowers it between my legs, I bite my lip. When it slips beneath my panties I'd put on before we went to sleep last night, all traces of my insecurities vanish.

"You're soaked," he whispers, dragging a finger through my wetness.

Rising to his knees, he positions himself between my thighs. He smiles up at me, dragging my panties down, and lowers his mouth to my clit. He gently sucks on it, and my knees buckle.

As his fingers slip inside me, my eyes flutter shut, and my head rolls back in pleasure. I feel him slide farther down the bed on his stomach, and he pulls my thighs over his shoulders.

A charge of excitement I've never felt speeds through me as he starts fingering and eating me out.

"You make me feel so good," I moan.

That causes him to finger me faster.

His slow pace is gone, and he fingers me harder while groaning against my core.

My heels press into his back as I fight to hold back my body's pleasure. I want this to last forever.

"Let go, baby," he says, his words hardly audible.

Ecstasy courses through me as I shout his name.

As I come down from my high, he keeps licking and gently stroking me. He carefully lowers my legs from his shoulders. They fall slack against the bed, as if I've lost all control over them.

My body has never felt so tired yet full of life.

Adrian pretty much ate all the energy out of me this morning.

Goose bumps prick my skin as he moves up my body and presses his face against my neck.

He softly sucks on my skin and whispers, "I can't count how many times I've thought of you as the most beautiful person on this planet. And now that I've seen all of you, I know I was right. You're perfection, Essie."

29

Adrian

"Thank you, Foster." I end the call with him and stroll into the kitchen where Essie fusses with her espresso machine.

She's dressed in a loose tank top and shorts that barely cover her ass.

Shorts that are officially my favorite pair in the world.

I could sit here for hours and watch her ass jiggle in them.

Biting into my lip, I feel on top of the world from last night.

I'm fucking in love with this woman.

I told her in college, but that feels like centuries ago.

Even though I think the feeling is mutual, I'm afraid of scaring her off.

It could be too much, too soon.

Turning around, she picks up a mug shaped like a cowboy boot. "How's our boy?"

"He's recovering well." I drop my phone on the table and walk toward her, wearing only my unbuttoned slacks. "Foster wants to keep him one more night."

My shoulders slump in disappointment. I hoped to have him back today.

"We'll have to throw him a *welcome home* party." She takes a sip of her latte.

I grin, loving that she cares about Tucker enough to do that. "Now, I know you gave me *plenty* of favors last night, but can I ask for one more?" I form my hands into a pleading motion. "I need a ride to the auto repair shop to pick up my car."

She dramatically squishes her face. "I *guess* it's the least I can do after last night."

I wrap my arms around her waist and draw her closer. "If you still need convincing, I have another hour until I need to go."

"Unfortunately, I must take a rain check on that. I have a busy day today."

"What's on your agenda, Ms. Lane?"

"I have an interview with a paralegal candidate in an hour. And tonight, Mia is throwing Callie a surprise birthday party. Want to come?"

Even though I want to jump for joy at her invite, I keep my cool.

Essie has gone from repeatedly telling me to get my ass out of town to inviting me to parties.

I like this version much better.

"I'd love to come." I push a strand of her hair behind her ear. "And thank you for showing me all of you last night."

"I'm sorry for taking so long." Her gaze drops to the floor, avoiding eye contact with me.

I place a finger under her chin, lifting it until our eyes meet. "Don't apologize. You needed time, and I respect that."

She clears her throat, slowly walks to the table, and sits. "My burn scars are from a car accident when I was in high school." She holds up a hand. "It wasn't an accident. My friend and I were purposely hit. My friend died. I survived, but that didn't mean I got out untouched."

"What do you mean, purposely hit?"

"He meant to hit us."

"Why would someone do that?"

"It was our school custodian who'd been fired. He blamed

his firing on the students and decided to take it out on us. He started with me and Ethan, a friend I tutored. We were in his Jeep when a truck came toward us in the wrong lane with its bright lights on. Ethan kept trying to swerve out of the way, but the truck kept following us."

Her lip trembles, and she covers her mouth as a sob leaves her.

I grab her hand, giving it a squeeze, and massage my thumb along her skin.

She clears her throat and sniffles before going on, "He finally hit us. Ethan was killed on impact. The Jeep caught on fire, and as I crawled out of the car, debris hit my stomach, going through my shirt. I rolled on the grass, trying to get rid of the burns and put them out. But I still suffered third-degree burns and these ... scars." She sighs. "The man is in prison now." A tear slips down her cheek. "But he might be free soon."

Free because of my mother's organization.

My breathing slows.

Tell her, Adrian.

Tell her, goddamn it.

I'm such a chickenshit.

Instead of confessing I know the story, I decide to console her.

"I'm so sorry, baby," I whisper, stretching across the table to wipe away her tear, hating myself for not saying more.

"Have you ever heard of the Prison Exoneration Program?"

A tightness forms in my chest as I nod, hating myself for not saying more.

"They took his case. That's why River was so upset the day you were here."

I scratch the back of my neck, positive that every person who cares about Essie will want to kick my ass if they find out I talked to Earl.

Tell her, Adrian.

Fucking tell her.

Essie and I are finally in a good place.

I don't want to fuck this up, but I'm damned if I do, damned if I don't.

If I tell her now, I'll fuck it up.

If I tell her later, I'll fuck it up.

But right now, I'm going to give myself time.

Time before everything blows up in my face.

I'll tell my mother I don't want to be involved in Earl's case and to give it to another attorney. I refuse to betray Essie and cross that line even further.

I lost her once.

I won't survive losing her again.

"Top of the morning to ya," a shirtless River greets me with a grin when I step out of Essie's cottage.

He sprawls back in a patio chair and takes a long drag off his joint. Smoke curls around his face.

"Morning." I run a hand through my hair and look back at the door.

Essie was right behind me but suddenly stopped. She said she had forgotten something and would meet me outside. Considering she somewhat lives at home, I should've known there was a chance of running into someone. Better River than her parents seeing me.

River snubs his joint out in the ashtray. "Don't worry; I won't give you a hard time about your walk of shame. I love my sister and want her to be happy, and you seem to help with that. She's going through some shit right now, so don't you dare fucking hurt her—you hear me?"

"I care about your sister." I slip my hands into my pockets. "I'd never hurt her."

He nods, as if accepting my response. "You coming to Callie's party tonight?"

"I'll be there."

He salutes me. "See you tonight then."

Ava walks out of River's cottage, interrupting us, and I raise a brow.

She's wearing baggy sweatpants and a sweatshirt that nearly hits her knees. I'm positive both belong to River.

She gathers her tangled hair into a messy ponytail and smiles at me. "Oh, hi, Adrian. I came by to visit Essie but needed a bathroom break. I couldn't hold it, so I stopped by River's to pee."

"Oh, come on," River says, wearing the widest smirk I've ever seen. "Do you expect him to believe that?"

She flips him off.

River laughs and gives her a playful smack on the ass as she turns to leave. "Shouldn't you go *that way* if you're visiting my sister?" He points in the opposite direction.

"I changed my mind." Ava rolls her eyes at him before checking her nonexistent watch. "I have a few errands to run. See you tonight."

Everyone turns when Essie's door opens, and she steps out.

"Good morning, sis," River says. "Can you please tell your friend to stop breaking into my place and stealing my clothes?" He cocks his head toward an annoyed Ava. "I'm officially hiring you as my attorney to stop this sweatshirt thief."

"Don't worry," Ava says, flicking her hand in the air. "I'll burn the evidence when I get home."

River scoffs. "I have countless pics of you wearing my clothes. I'll definitely win the case."

"Then, I'll destroy all said clothes and pics for funsies." Ava pulls at the hoodie's drawstrings.

"Don't forget, I have a key to your place," River warns.

Ava rolls her eyes. "I told you, I want that back."

River shakes his head. "Nah, I like having access to you at all times."

"Oh my God." Essie cries, covering her eyes, as if blocking out the sun. "I'm not even going to bother questioning what's going on between you two right now."

Ava shrugs. "That makes you a better person than me because I'm about to ask all the questions about your little sleep-over date."

There's no hiding my smile when all eyes turn to Essie.

"Tough shit," she says, grabbing my hand and pulling me away from them. "People who make poor choices with my brother don't get any tea this morning."

River stands and looks at Ava. "Trust me, babe, bad decisions with me are much better than gossip." He grabs Ava around the waist and throws her over his shoulder. "Question her later tonight. I'll make you breakfast in exchange for my hoodie."

"I'll be asking all the questions tonight, Essie!" Ava shouts, kicking her feet and doing a poor job of pretending to break out of River's hold. "And you, mister! You're making me breakfast in exchange for me not stabbing you in your sleep."

River laughs. "We can play doctor, and you can stitch me up after. I keep begging you to role-play with me."

"Swear to God, I'm poisoning your eggs," Ava mutters.

They continue arguing, but their words are drowned out as we get farther away. Seconds later, I hear River's door slam shut.

The morning air is chilly, and birds are splashing in the bird-bath next to the gate that leads to the driveway where cars are parked. A few gardeners are pulling weeds, and Essie waves at them.

"Ava and River are a thing?" I ask when we get into her car.

I noticed sexual tension between the two at the brewery opening, but I thought maybe they were just two friends who bickered.

"No one knows what River and Ava are." She buckles her

seat belt. "They're two people with busy careers who don't have time for relationships. I guess that's something they bond over."

"That's what they do? *Bond*?"

She whacks me in the head with her bag while putting it in the back seat. "I don't say anything to him about who comes and goes from his place, and he gives me the same respect."

River *did* say something, but it could've been worse.

He could've tried to fight me or some shit.

A situation like that happened to my old roommate in Cali. He'd hooked up with a girl, and her older brother came home early. He snatched my friend by the neck and threw him out the window, naked, which resulted in two broken bones. After that, he was strictly a *you come over* guy.

"Wait," I say, blinking. "Who comes and goes from *your* place?"

"You." She starts counting out her answers on her fingers. "Yummy Arrangements delivery person. Amazon. While my brother's visitors are of the opposite sex—" She stops and holds up her hand. "Well, actually, his opposite-sex visitor always goes by the name of Ava. Mine tend to arrive in USPS or FedEx uniforms."

"Yummy Arrangements?" I ask.

She nods. "Blue Beech's version of Edible Arrangements."

"I'm learning this town has quite a lot of their own versions of things."

"All things are better when they come with a small-town flair." She smiles and ruffles her hand through my hair. "You'll never want to go back once you're comfortable here."

"Trust me," I mutter under my breath, "that's my plan."

30

Essie

"Congratulations! You're hired!" I hold out my hand toward Lainey. "Welcome to the team."

Team of one, but, hey, still a team.

Small teams are the best anyway.

You get to know everyone better.

Lainey is twenty-three and has only had her paralegal degree for a few months, so she'll need training. But I know she'll be a great fit. We clicked during her interview. Both of us are obsessed with steamy romances, overpriced coffees, and vampire TV shows. Her mom used to work on the town paper with my aunt Chloe.

Lainey dances in place. "When do I get started? I can now if you need me."

I smile at her. While I appreciate her offer, I'm about to end my day. We need to start decorating for Callie's party.

"How's Monday?" I ask.

"Sounds great." She adjusts her purple skirt. "That'll give me time to shop for some cute office clothes. What is the skirt-length rule here?"

I laugh. "You just dress as cute as you want to."

She drags me in for a hug.

If anyone had tried pulling something like this at Adaway and Williams, they'd have been fired immediately. But I like that Lainey is comfortable with me.

New office—check.

Win first case—check.

Hire paralegal—check.

I'm crushing this attorney thing.

"Thank you for coming," I tell Adrian as he walks toward me inside Callie's Bake Shop, right on time, like the responsible man I've always known him to be.

Whenever he visited me in college, he was never a minute late.

We love us a punctual man. He even brought a gift.

Foster trails him. Adrian texted me earlier and said Foster was riding with him. I like that he and Foster have become friends. Foster has always been a stand-up guy.

"Who the hell invited him?" River shouts, throwing his arm out toward Foster.

Ava comes up behind him, ruffles her fingers through his hair, and grins. "I did, obvi."

River crosses his arms and glares at Foster. "Since when are you in our circle of friends?"

"*Circle of friends*?" I say, mocking my brother. "Please, as a grown man, never say that again."

"Yes, it sounds very high school," Mia adds. "Not a good look if you're trying to impress Ava, a woman who legit has surgeons begging her for dates." She grins, knowing that'll further press River's jealousy button.

Foster signals back and forth between River and Ava before stopping his finger on River. "When will you start dating her, bro, so you can stop thinking I'm in love with her?"

River knows Ava and Foster aren't in love.

He just enjoys giving them shit.

Ava dramatically gasps at Foster. "You're breaking my heart over here, Foster."

Foster shrugs. "I'd prefer not to have a video game character named after me who'll most likely get killed."

River snaps his fingers and points at Foster. "Thanks for the idea." He taps the side of his head. "I'm mentally noting that now."

"As you can tell, my friends are very mature," I tell Adrian.

"They're fun." He kisses my forehead. "I enjoy spending time with them. When you told me stories about them and growing up here, I always tried to imagine it. Now, I can, and I enjoy it. Thank you for including me in this, Essie."

"I like that you're here. I'm happy you stood your ground and didn't let me run you out of town."

There will never be enough words to express to Adrian how grateful I am that he stayed here. When I found out Earl's case might reopen, I wasn't sure how deep I'd fall into the hole of sadness. But Adrian being here has kept me standing.

"Trust me, it'd take a lot more than you throwing your attitude—which I find sexy as fuck, by the way—to convince me to mess this up with you again," he tells me.

I perk up even more. "Does that mean you're staying?"

"That means, as long as you're okay with it, consider me Blue Beech's newest resident."

He presses a kiss to my lips, and I can feel eyes on us.

The questions will commence in *three ... two ... one.*

Ava walks away from River when he and Foster start having a civilized conversation that doesn't revolve around arguing about her.

"You can save your questions for girls' night," I tell her as she moves in our direction.

She slumps her shoulders. "Geesh, you're no fun tonight."

Adrian laughs, looking around. "This place has its own character. I feel like I'm in some modern version of a Barbie Dreamhouse."

"Your comment definitely shows you never had a sister. This is *far* from a Barbie Dreamhouse."

Callie's Bake Shop is like stepping inside a magical storybook.

The decor is exactly what you'd imagine for happily ever after's number-one fan. The bake shop's walls are rose pink, and a few months ago, Easton helped her install floral panels to three of them, bringing an even more romantic setting. Sparkling crystal chandeliers hang from the ceiling, and pink suede sitting couches create entertaining spaces. Rose-gold tablecloths cover the tables, and the chairs are pink.

The space would make even the most anti-love person wish for their Prince—or Princess—Charming.

Well, besides Mia. There's no changing her mind when it comes to love.

It'd been Callie's dream to open her own cake shop, and five years ago, she made it happen. I love that my friends are creating their happiness here.

Jax and Amelia have the brewery.

Callie has the bake shop.

I have the law firm.

Ava is an ER surgeon at the closest hospital.

Mia is a product manager for her mother's clothing and skincare line, and personal stylist.

We're all settling down here.

The bake shop is a town favorite, serving brunch and hosting birthday and wedding parties. The schedule is always booked, and it's not uncommon for people to drive here from other towns.

Fortunately, River hacked into the reservation site and blocked tonight's availability. Kendra, Callie's assistant baker, told her she'd cover the event so Callie could enjoy her birthday dinner with her parents. Considering Callie is the queen of micromanaging, I'm shocked we were able to pull this off.

Aunt Chloe texted Mia five minutes ago and told her they were on their way after dinner.

Headlights shine through the parking lot window, and we shout, "Surprise," as soon as Callie walks in with her parents.

Callie stops in her tracks and slaps a hand over her mouth. "Oh my God!" she shrieks under it.

If the word *surprise* had a picture next to it in the dictionary, it most certainly wouldn't be of Callie's reaction. No, hers would definitely be next to *fakest surprise look in history*.

"All right," Mia groans, looking around the crowd, "which one of you ratted us out?"

"The reservation was booked under Ace Ventura," Callie says. "You didn't think that'd stand out to me?"

Mia throws her arms out toward River. "Really? You couldn't come up with a better name?"

"You asked me to hack into the software. Creating an alias was never included in your demand," River replies.

"Super surprised or not, thank you for this," Callie says in her sweet voice.

We spend the next five minutes all taking our turns hugging and wishing Callie a happy birthday. When she sees Adrian behind me, she gives me a pointed look before thanking him for coming.

She then mouths, *I can't wait for this story later*, to me.

I grab a fresh glass of rosé—Callie's drink of choice—and Adrian opts for a bottle of water when I hear Mia say, "You've got to be kidding me."

I follow the path of her glare to find it pinned on my older cousin, Trey, who just walked in. Standing tall, he shoves his hands into his black pants pockets while taking in the room, his face unreadable. Everyone pauses for a moment, as if they might be imagining him.

Trey rarely comes home.

Not that I blame him. This town hasn't been kind to everyone.

In fact, it was cruel to Trey more than it was nice.

He's seventeen years older than me, so I've only met him a few times, when we traveled to either LA or New York. He has million-dollar homes in both cities.

But I guess if any party could bring him home, it'd be one for Callie. They're extremely close, and she knows him better than any of us.

Callie squeals—this one definitely not fake—and dashes over to hug him.

He squeezes her tight. "Happy birthday."

She pulls away. "God, I can't believe you're here."

Trey's backstory is complicated.

He's my, River's, and Callie's cousin.

He's *also* Callie's uncle.

Grab your pencils because I'm about to explain a wild ancestral tree.

The girl my grandfather had an affair with was Chloe's older sister, and she had Trey. Chloe's family took hush money from him for fifteen years.

Chloe didn't feel guilty about keeping the secret since she hated Kyle in high school after a prank. Years later, when they were grown, they became neighbors and started dating.

When the truth came out, it was a shit show. Everyone learned Trey wasn't only Chloe's nephew but also Kyle's younger brother.

People called Trey a bastard child, and it was hard on him. As soon as he graduated from high school, he left Blue Beech. He became a huge name in tech and recently sold his start-up for over a billion dollars.

Mia snags a glass of rosé and downs it.

She grabs another and does the same.

Mia typically isn't a huge drinker. She's very type A, and she made sure everything about the party was perfect.

"Who's he?" Adrian asks, pointing toward Trey with his water.

"My cousin."

He tips his head down, lowering his voice. "And why does Mia look like she wants to murder him?"

"Oh, they've never been fans of each other." I grab a mini cupcake and drop it into my mouth.

Adrian leans forward, wipes frosting off my lips, and licks it off his finger. "Why?"

"You know what? I actually have no idea."

"Hmm," he murmurs.

"What does your *hmm* mean?"

"It means, I'm pretty sure there's more there than just hate."

"It's normal for people in this group to want to kill each other sometimes. It's because we're all stubborn pains in the ass. It must be something that runs in the water here." I tip my head to motion toward Jax and Amelia cuddled up in a corner. "Those two wanted to kill each other for half our lives."

"And what are they now?"

I chew on my nail. "Fair point."

While we all knew Jax was secretly in love with Amelia, maybe whatever history Mia has with Trey has slipped under the radar. But as far as I know, they haven't seen each other since Trey's last visit when Callie graduated from high school.

I laugh. "Look at you, already involving yourself in the drama and love lives here."

He smirks. "It seems the small-town life is rubbing off on me."

As the night grows later, more people show up.

I make my rounds, saying hello and introducing everyone to Adrian. Most people have already met him or heard about him in town. I saw the surprise when they realized we were there together, though.

When my parents arrive, they tell Callie happy birthday

before moving straight to me. I've been their number one concern as of late.

"Mom, Dad, do you remember Adrian?" I ask after hugging them both.

My mom smiles at him. "Of course I do."

Adrian holds out his hand, as if in complete *meet the parents* mode.

It's so similar to how he acted when he saw them at the brewery.

He clearly wants to win them over.

Listen, a man who wants to impress your parents is a green flag.

Adrian shakes my mom's hand, then my dad's, and then he compliments him on his latest video game.

"I've played all your games, but I have to say, this one is by far the best."

I blink at him.

Since when did he turn into a video game fan?

When he starts going into specifics, it's clear he either played or researched this so he could have the conversation with my dad.

We sit at a table, and Adrian spends the next hour getting to know my parents.

Impressing them.

Impressing me.

I've had one boyfriend come around my parents, and that was in high school. They weren't fans, and we didn't stay together long. They threatened to take away my car if I kept sneaking out with him. When I look back on it, it was a crappy relationship. I'm glad it didn't work out.

Because now, I get to share my heart with Adrian.

I'm not a freak by any means.

It's hard to be when you don't feel comfortable in your own skin.

That's why I'm shocked when I tell Adrian we're not going home after the party. He peers over at me with curiosity every few moments as I give him directions to a secluded park.

I don't know if it could even be considered a park.

It's not popular in Blue Beech.

In fact, the grass is overgrown, the benches are rusting, and there are no streetlights.

But I had to pick somewhere secluded, where I knew no one would be.

"This is like old times," I tell Adrian as he parks at the end of the dead-end road. "Us hanging out in your car."

Those were some of my favorite nights.

While Adrian doesn't have the same car as in college—it's a new model—the memory is still fresh.

Somehow, the leather seat feels the same.

The air smells the same.

The comfort is still there.

As badly as I want to redo what we started in the park that night in college, the last thing I need is for someone to see us having sex in public.

Okay, technically, we're in public-ish, but we have the privacy of his car.

I've dreamed about having sex in his car for as long as I can remember.

I'd sit in my dorm room, hand between my legs, my fingers sliding through my folds as I imagined myself riding him in the driver's seat.

During the party, I watched Adrian interact with everyone, as if they'd all been friends for years. Even when I wasn't with him and talking with someone else, there was no awkwardness between him and the others.

He belongs in Blue Beech.

Belongs here *with me*.

Before we even left the party, I knew I wanted this to happen tonight.

I turn down the radio, unbuckle my seat belt, and situate myself on my knees, facing him. The only light source shines from the dashboard and radio lights.

He shifts, focusing his soothing eyes on mine the best he can in the dark.

Thrill charges through my body when I reach over the console and unzip his pants.

"Holy shit," Adrian hisses, his hips bucking forward.

I grin, feeling seductive for the first time in my life.

The multiple glasses of rosé I consumed are also helping to create this Openly Sexual Essie.

"Shh," I whisper, running my finger along the outline of his cock, which is growing harder by the second. It jerks under my palm, and I peer up at him, grinning.

Getting the hint, he presses the button to recline his seat.

He waits to see where I'm going with this.

I roll my hair tie on my wrist down my hand and secure my hair into a ponytail at the top of my head. His body tenses when I touch him again, running my hand over his cock.

"Help me take it out," I say softly.

He nods, lifting his hips to lower his pants until they're down his waist. Grabbing my hand, he uses it to pull his cock free. My heart drums in my chest when he opens my palm, spits in it, and guides it to his erection.

He's throbbing, his cock jerking under my hold.

As I stroke him, his head lolls back.

He slips down the seat farther, giving me a better angle, and I rise higher on my knees. He thrusts his hips forward as I jerk him off. His groans fill the car, but they grow more frantic when I lower my head and lick the head of his cock.

I suck gently before slowly pulling back.

Slobber falls from my mouth onto his cock.

I fight with myself on whether to tell him I've never done this before.

I mean, it could give me a decent excuse if I give him a sucky blow job.

Jesus, Essie. Get out of your head.

It's a blow job.

It's not like I need a damn degree to know the basics of sucking cock.

Mia once told me that men don't care about the quality of the blow job most of the time. All that's on their mind is that there's a mouth on their cock.

"Please, Essie," he begs, his voice strained, "keep going."

His plea is all the encouragement that I need.

I lick my lips before taking his entire length in my mouth. He's so large that the tip rams against the back of my throat.

Don't gag.

Don't gag.

Thankfully, I don't.

I climb closer and suck him.

He collects my ponytail in his fist. Jerking his hips forward, he feeds me his cock. I gag a few times, but he doesn't seem to care.

"Fuck," he groans. "You suck me so good, baby. Stroke it as you suck."

I do that and suck him at the same time.

He moans when I deep-throat him and grip the base of his cock.

"Can I come in your mouth?" he asks.

I stop. "If you do that, will you be done for the night?"

He smirks at my awkward wording. "Do you mean, will I be able to fuck you as well?"

I nod.

"Baby, I will absolutely be fucking you tonight."

"Then, yes, come in my mouth." I start sucking him again.

His movements become more frantic, choking me a few

more times, and he pulls my ponytail. His entire body shakes, and his dick spasms in my mouth before I get the first taste of him.

I keep my mouth on his cock, sucking, so I can taste every drop of him.

When I finally pull away, his breathing is wild. He crooks his finger, directing me to come his way. As soon as my face is close enough, he grabs me around the back of my neck and pulls my lips to his.

"Now, it's your turn, baby." He lowers his hand and starts stroking himself.

It doesn't take long for his cock to get hard again.

I grab my bag and find the condom that I asked Ava for earlier. When I asked her to *borrow one*, she asked me if I planned to give it back or something. I'm sure that'll be an inside joke between us for the rest of our lives.

I rip open the wrapper, and Adrian's eyes are wild as he stares at me.

Luckily, I made the smart decision to wear a dress. I shove it up my waist and start climbing over his lap. He stops me, placing a hand on my stomach before lowering it between my legs. The sound of him ripping my panties echoes through the car.

"Those would've been a problem," he says, clenching them tight in his grip. He shoves them against his face and smells them. "You're soaked for me. I want to remember this smell for the rest of my life, so I'm keeping these."

"But they're ripped." I shyly bite my lower lip.

"I don't intend to wear them, baby. I'm keeping them so I never forget this fantasy of you."

"Someone sure has an obsession with how I smell."

"No, it's more of an obsession with you, *period*. Your smell, your taste, everything about you—I'm completely obsessed. Now, climb up here and ride my cock."

I smile and lift a shoulder. "Since you said it so sweetly."

He guides me onto his lap and gives me time to make myself comfortable. It's a tight fit, and the steering wheel jams into my back. Gripping my hips, he lifts and then carefully lowers me onto his cock.

I drop my head forward and dig my nails into his shoulders.

With his hands still on my hips, he bucks me forward.

I ride him, slow and easy at first.

Then faster and faster.

The closer I get, the wilder I ride him.

God, this is perfection.

The best feeling in the world.

I feel the wetness between our legs.

On our thighs as we slide against each other.

I feel everything I've ever wanted to feel with Adrian.

And I want to do this again and again and again.

My hips slap against his, and I lose control of myself as I grow closer.

My need for him is everywhere.

In my blood.

My bones.

I never want us to end.

My entire body is flying high, and so many emotions are flowing through me that I can't keep up until I fall apart.

I fall limp against Adrian, but he isn't done with me yet.

His hands dig into my skin as he pounds into me.

I'm completely spent, no longer in control of my body.

My head hits the ceiling a few times. Adrian stops, but I tell him to keep going.

"I want to watch you come while I'm on top of you," I whisper.

My words undo him.

His body trembles beneath me.

He squeezes his eyes shut while muttering my name.

It takes us a few seconds to calm down, and when his eyes open, I smile down at him.

"Essie," he says when he fully catches his breath, "I love you." He brushes back my messy hair. "I'm in love with you."

My body feels at ease yet enthralled.

My heart pounds like wildfire yet feels composed.

I rest my forehead against his. "Good thing."

He cocks his head to the side as I pull back, waiting for me to elaborate.

"Because I'm also in love with you."

31

Adrian

Morning number two of waking up beside Essie is heaven.

I could grow used to this, yet I'll never take for granted.

God, please let it be our future.

Before leaving for Callie's party, I packed an overnight bag, *just in case*. Luckily, Essie invited me to stay over. After what happened in my car, if she hadn't, I'd have been damn heartbroken.

I finally told her I loved her.

I didn't care if the feeling was mutual.

The three words needed to leave my mouth.

Essie needs to know how damn obsessed I am with her.

Scrubbing a hand over my face, I grin.

But then that grin drops when a pang of guilt hits me.

I roll over to look at her sleeping on her back.

I need to tell her about my visiting Earl and my mother's connection with the PEP. She'll be upset with me, but the longer I keep it from her, the worse it'll be.

But, fuck, I'm terrified of losing her.

I made a mistake by not telling her in the beginning. The moment she showed me her scars, I should've fessed up and told her I already knew what had happened. I sat there and let her tell me about Earl, knowing he'd already told me his side of the story.

Tonight, I'll do what's right and tell her.

"I love waking up with you here," she whispers.

Her words snap me back into reality, and she turns on her side to peer at me.

Grabbing her hand, I weave my fingers through hers. "This, right here, is something I've dreamed about." I raise our laced hands and kiss the top of hers.

She smiles up at me and runs her free hand along my cheek. "I wish we'd done this in college. For years, this could've been our morning routine."

"From now on, this *will* be our morning routine."

"Damn straight." She strokes my cheek.

"What are your plans for today?"

"First, I need to shower. Care to join me?"

"Baby, you never have to ask me that twice."

"Grab a condom."

I slide out of bed and help her out of it. She collects my hand in hers and leads me to the bathroom. It's one you'd find in a luxury suite in a five-star hotel. It has a claw-foot tub, a shower with four showerheads, and a vanity that runs along the entire wall.

Another perk: the damn floor is heated.

I turn on the water while she tosses two towels in the towel warmer. As the water runs, she wiggles out of her boy shorts, and I drop my boxers. I lick my lower lip as I admire her naked body.

Everything is so perfect about her.

Hands that perfectly fit into mine.

Thick curves and a plump ass.

Since college, she's been my personal wet dream.

But now, that dream is my reality.

The water doesn't take long to warm, and as soon as we're

under the showerheads, my mouth is on hers. I feel so alive as I run my hands down her wet body and back her up against the shower wall.

Neither of us worries about even attempting to pretend to wash ourselves.

Our bodies instantly meet, our mouths on each other's, and she moans when my tongue massages hers. I rip open the condom, drop the wrapper on the tiled floor, and slide it onto my erection. She lowers her hand to my cock, slowly stroking me, and I hiss through my teeth.

When I slip two fingers inside her pussy and stroke her, her hand falls, and her back straightens against the wall.

"Oh my God," she moans, gripping on to my shoulders as I finger her.

My cock is throbbing as it slides against her leg, but I want to get her off with my fingers first.

With how hard my heart is pounding, I know as soon as I get inside her, my dick is going to be ready to bust.

Essie wraps her arms around my neck. "Don't be gentle with me, Adrian. Fuck me against this wall *hard*."

"All right then, baby," I say, smiling against her lips while pulling my fingers from her pussy.

A second later, I kneel to line my cock up with her entrance, and she groans when I stand, pushing my cock inside her. I give her a second to adjust to my size, and she tightens her hold on me, dragging me closer.

I pick her up, wrapping both her legs around my waist, and slap a hand against the wall to keep us steady. Her wet hair drips on my face as I pound inside her.

Over and over and over.

She meets my grunts with her moans.

I know we're both going to be sore after this.

Knowing I'm close, I have to get her off before I do. I rotate my hips, trying to hit every angle I can inside her.

"Right there, right there," she says when I hit the spot.

I stay there and thrust my hips forward, shoving my face into her neck and sucking on it. A few strokes later, her nails bite into my neck. I hold her body tighter as it goes slack, losing all muscle power. A burst of pleasure shoots through me as I move faster.

I groan her name as I fill the condom with my release.

It takes us a second to gain our composure, and I help her down to her feet.

"Well," she says, drawing out the word, "shower sex is definitely fun ... and dangerous."

"We'll do it a few more times." I smack a peck on her lips. "You and I can perfect everything, baby."

After we're showered and drying off, Essie's phone beeps.

She picks it up and reads the text. "My mom asked if we want to come over for breakfast. Either she noticed your car here or River told them about our sleepover."

I pull my shirt over my head. "I'm always up for a good morning meal, *especially* after you exhausted me." I stop for a second before grabbing my pants. "They're cool with me staying over, right?"

"That sounds way too high school for my liking," she jokes. "But my parents know we're adults. Plus, after last night, I'm positive they're Adrian fans."

I playfully drag my hand over my forehead in a *phew* gesture.

We dress, leave her cottage, and find Essie's mom, Carolina in the kitchen when we walk into the main house. The smell of biscuits and cinnamon wafts through the air.

She turns off a stove burner and smiles at us. "Good morning."

"Morning," Essie sings out as I shut the door behind us.

"Good morning, Mrs. Lane," I add.

"Oh, no, call me Carolina." She waves her hand through the air. "The only people who call me that are my students." She pauses as if a thought suddenly hit her. "Though I think they also call me by my first name."

"All right then." I nod toward her. "Carolina, it is."

"Can I help with something?" Essie asks.

Carolina shakes her head. "Everything is almost finished."

"Mom tries to get everything finished before I can come in and possibly help," Essie explains. "That way, I don't mess anything up."

"Not true. I did leave you the job of drinks," Carolina argues.

"Now, that's a very difficult job," I say with a laugh.

"Yes, collecting juices is very complicated," Essie comments.

"What can I help with?" I ask.

"You grab the juices. I'll grab the glasses." Essie points at the fridge.

I open the fridge, seeing a large selection of juices.

"Just bring them all," Essie says.

Carolina takes out a plate of French toast and pancakes from the oven warmer. As it cools, she stirs the sausage gravy on the stove.

I set the juices on the counter at the same time the patio door opens. River walks in, yawning and stretching.

"Well, good morning, sunshine," Essie says.

He yawns again. His eyes scan from Carolina, to Essie, to me, and then he does a do-over to make sure he's seeing everyone correctly.

"And here I was, running my late-night houseguest off this morning," he murmurs, smirking at his sister.

Essie rolls her eyes. "No, it looks like your hand is still intact."

"Essie!" Carolina scolds, swatting her with a towel.

River chuckles. "I'm glad to see my sarcastic, pain-in-the-ass sister has returned. She's my favorite. But joking, no house guest."

"Ava had a shift at the hospital, so of course, you didn't," Essie fires back.

River ignores her and jerks his chin toward me. I return the gesture.

He walks behind Carolina and kisses her cheek. "Everything smells delicious."

"That I'll agree with," Essie's father, Rex, says, coming into view. "River and I were up all night, brainstorming ideas for a new game." His gaze swings to me. "Hi, Adrian."

None of them seems bothered by my presence.

Even with me being an adult, I'm sure my mom would give me hell if I had a sleepover.

My abuela? Not so much. She'd be the opposite and probably serve us breakfast in bed.

We all gather the food and juices to set the table. My stomach growls as we take our seats, and Carolina sets the massive spread of food in front of us.

There's no conversation for a good ten minutes as everyone eats.

Carolina's breakfast might be better than some expensive restaurants I've dined in.

"So, Adrian," Rex asks, "how are you liking Blue Beech?"

I wipe my mouth before replying, "I'm really enjoying it here."

"Where did you live before?" Carolina asks.

"Des Moines, then LA, and then back to Des Moines." I take a sip of orange juice.

"Oh, wow, this really is your first small-town experience," Carolina comments.

"I like how peaceful and laid-back everyone is. They seem to always want to help each other out. When Terrance invited me to Blue Beech, I had no idea if I'd like it. I'm glad that it's really growing on me."

"What made you decide to come here?" River asks with a sly smirk.

The asshole is really trying to give me shit.

"For me, obvi," Essie says, slapping my shoulder.

"A job," I explain with a smirk.

"I call bullshit," River says.

Rex holds up his hand. "I second it."

Essie rests her elbow on the table. "I third it."

Carolina drops her fork and sighs. "I guess I need to be the fourth to do it then." The corners of her mouth turn up into a smile. "I'm happy you're here, Adrian."

River relaxes in his chair. "I'm also happy that you two are running competitive businesses, and I get to watch how it plays out."

"Hey, River, how's Ava doing?" Essie asks him sarcastically.

"I don't know. Why don't you go to my place and ask her?"

"What?" Carolina shrieks. "If Ava is in there, you tell her to come eat—" She stands as if ready to find Ava.

"I'm joking," River replies, drawing the last word out. "Do you think she'd ever skip out on your breakfast?"

Rex scratches his head. "She might not be at his place, but River sure had to take plenty of breaks to text her back all night."

"It was for research purposes," River says. "For the game."

"Ava is a doctor. What research could she provide for that?" Essie takes a bite of bacon.

"People die in the game. I want to know how to make them alive again."

"Uh, hit the Try Again option when it says Game Over," Essie says before taking a sip of orange juice.

I sit back and listen to their breakfast banter.

I've always wanted a family like this.

And while I didn't get it, growing up, I'm glad Essie did.

I also hope that I can experience more meals like this and get to know her family better because I *also* want to be her family. And someday, I want us to have a little family of our own.

I spend the next two hours with Essie and her family. River and Rex show me the new beta of their video game, and we hang out in the family room.

And right before we leave, Rex stops me at the door. "Thank you, Adrian."

"For what?" I ask.

"For making my daughter smile again."

32

Adrian

"I'm so happy Tucker is okay," my abuela says over the phone. "Is he feeling well enough to come over and see us? I'm having dinner, and I would love to see my granddog."

Tucker is stretched out in the back seat and biting at the cone around his head. Foster put it on so Tucker wouldn't bite his stitches.

"Gee, thanks," I say around a chuckle. "What about your grand*son*?"

"Well, of course, you too, honey. But let's not be a selfish dog dad. You weren't the one who just spent days in the animal hospital."

"Fair point." I scratch my head as I cast a glance toward Essie in my passenger seat. "Can I bring someone?"

"Is this someone Essie, the pretty girl from the pub and vet?"

I can't see my abuela, but I know she's wearing a giant smirk on her face. In high school, I didn't bring many girls home. Sure, I went to a few school dances and had study partners, but nothing like what I have with Essie.

I crack a smile, my eyes still glued on Essie. "Yes, the pretty girl from the pub and vet."

"Of course you can bring her!" she bursts out. "Any girl who's a crush of my grandson's is a friend of mine."

I shake my head, thankful I didn't put her on speaker.

That's a known rule with her, though.

Never put Abuela on speaker when in public.

You never know what'll leave her mouth.

Though I know there's no muting her when we're at dinner.

You game? I mouth to Essie.

I'm game, she mouths back.

"We'll be there."

"Great! See you soon." She makes a kissy sound and ends the call.

Tucker starts wagging his tail and barks, like he senses what we're saying.

"You calm down, mister," Essie says, gesturing for him to lie down. "Foster said you need rest."

Tucker nuzzles his cone against the seat before lying back down.

I peer at Essie. "Whatever my abuela says, only believe half of it."

Essie throws her head back. "Oh, I'm believing every little thing. She could tell me you wet the bed for your first sixteen years, and I'd believe her."

"It was only until fifteen, thank you very much."

"Remind me to put an extra mattress cover on my bed tonight."

"Does that mean I'm invited over for another sleepover?"

She chews on the edge of her lip. "Possibly."

"Tucker too? Because we come as a package deal."

"Tucker is a definite yes. You? We'll have to see what many secrets I hear about you today."

"My abuela likes you. I have faith she'll want you to stick around, so she'll take it easy on me."

The aroma of pineapples, essential oils, and mixed spices welcomes us when we walk through the front door. Essie holds it open wider, allowing me extra space to carry Tucker inside.

He's already up to his old ways. As soon as I opened the car door minutes ago, he spotted a squirrel and attempted to chase it. Luckily, I stopped him.

We'll be having a serious *no chasing squirrels* conversation later.

Essie helps me settle Tucker on the couch, and then we follow the sound of laughter to the kitchen. My abuela is at the stove, and Terrance is washing dishes.

I'm grateful my abuela found Terrance.

Anytime he's at home, he's always helping her.

Teamwork is important in relationships, and sometimes, it's one of the first things overlooked.

"There you are!" She rests her spoon on the counter, wipes her hands on a towel, and circles the island. "I'm making your favorite—carne guisada." She smacks a kiss on my cheek, hugs Essie, and then glances behind me.

"He's on the couch, resting," I reply, reading her mind.

"Be right back," she sings out. "My poor guy needs some grandma love."

"I'm surprised she hasn't dognapped him from me," I comment to Terrance.

Terrance turns off the water and waves us over. "I'm buying her a dog next week." He places his finger to his lips in a *shh* gesture.

"She'll love that. Though, heads-up, she'll probably have it sleeping in bed with you two."

He pushes his glasses up his nose. "That's why I'm getting her a small one—a teacup. One of those she can carry around in that big ole purse of hers."

I can already picture her doing that now.

We stop our conversation when my abuela returns to the kitchen.

"I just love that little guy," she comments.

"What can I help with?" Essie asks.

My abuela peers at me. "How about you open a bottle of wine for us?" Her attention moves to Essie. "And you just relax."

I open the wine cooler and pull out a deep red.

"Hello," Foster calls from the living room. He says something to Tucker about napping and resting before coming into the kitchen.

Terrance collects glasses from the cabinet. I open the wine and start pouring our drinks.

"Everyone is almost here," my abuela says, removing a tray of biscuits from the oven. "Fingers crossed your mom is on time."

I jerk forward, spilling wine on the counter. Essie hurriedly grabs a towel to help clean it up.

If my mother brings up Earl's case at dinner, I'm so fucked.

33

Essie

Adrian doesn't want me to meet his mom.

That much is clear.

After spilling the wine, he knocks over a glass. Terrance catches it before it falls to the floor.

From the way Adrian keeps peeking at the doorway every few moments, it's obvious he's mentally searching for an excuse for us to leave.

It doesn't make sense.

I know his mom was always hard on him growing up, but why would she dislike me?

Because we're competing law firms?

His mother hasn't arrived by the time we sit at the table for dinner.

Maybe she'll be a no-show, and Adrian will stop being a bundle of worry.

"Now, Essie," Valeria says as we start moving food around the table, serving ourselves, "what's your backstory with my grandson here? While I love him being in Blue Beech, I have a feeling a large reason for that is because you're here. He was uncertain about Terrance's job offer until he learned where the firm was."

"I'm not sure. We became friends in college, and maybe he wanted to catch up." I take a sip of wine, choosing not to tell her about Adaway and Williams.

If I could, I'd erase my time in hell there from my brain.

"Sorry I'm late," a woman says, rushing into the room and sliding her black blazer off at the same time. "I always forget how long the drive here is from the city."

"Essie," Adrian says, "this is my mother, Paula. Mom, this is Essie."

I see the resemblance between them. They share a similar height. I wonder if his father was tall too. Paula's hair is thick and wavy, and her bangs hit her brow.

Paula's lips turn into a smile. "The girl from the pub."

"I'll forever be known as the girl from the pub," I mutter.

Adrian stays stone-faced, not even cracking a smile at my comment. He definitely would've if we weren't with his mother.

"It's nice to meet you," Paula says, taking her seat beside Valeria.

Adrian downs the rest of his wine and refills his glass.

"Adrian," Valeria says, peering at me, "how's the case you're helping your mom out with for the Prison Exoneration Program? Isn't the man from Blue Beech? She said you visited him at the prison. I bet that was an experience." She clasps her hands together. "I love you two working together."

Adrian curses under his breath and runs a hand over his forehead.

Paula pays me a glance before whipping her attention back to Valeria. "I don't think we want to talk about work right now. How is everything going with you?"

"Wait," I say, not going with Paula's suggestion. It takes me a moment to find my words. "You work for the PEP?"

"Essie," Adrian whispers.

Terrance shifts in his chair, looking at me with concern, and whispers, "Oh, this isn't good."

Paula is quiet for a moment.

I'm unsure if it's because she's trying to find the right response or waiting for Adrian to answer the question.

"I do," Paula finally says with a gentle smile. "I started the program."

"And ..." My voice is hoarse. "The case ... the man from Blue Beech. Is his name Earl?"

Paula's gaze shifts to Adrian, who's not saying a word.

He slowly lowers his head, turning it, and looks at me. "If you'd let me explain."

I sit there, but he doesn't mutter a word.

No one does.

At first, it's hard for me to move.

It's like I'm frozen to this chair.

"Explain," I whisper.

He doesn't.

I hurriedly stand.

Adrian does the same.

Valeria looks from person to person at the table, forehead wrinkling in confusion.

He knew.

Adrian sat in my kitchen and listened to me relive my hell. He watched me dig into my chest, break myself apart, and tell him about my scars. All the while, he'd already known my story. I mean, damn, he could've at least stopped me and said he already knew it.

He definitely should've told me his mother worked at the PEP and was working for Earl.

"What's going on?" Valeria asks, her gaze bouncing to each of us at the table.

"Earl is in prison for a crime committed against Essie," Terrance finally explains.

And that's when I politely thank Valeria for dinner and race out of the house.

Tears are in my eyes before I even make it out the front door.

34

Essie

As I walk down Valeria's drive, I tug my phone from my pocket.

I trusted him.

"Essie," Adrian calls out to my back.

My hand shakes when I hold my phone to my face to unlock it. I walk faster down the driveway and send a voice message to River, asking him to pick me up.

"Let me explain," Adrian shouts, chasing me.

"Stay away from me," I yell over my shoulder. "Please tell everyone I had a family emergency and had to leave. River is picking me up."

Adrian jogs until he's in front of me. He walks backward, facing me while I make my way down the sidewalk.

I shake my head, tears burning in my eyes. "How long did you know about Earl and my car accident before I told you? You even visited him in prison. That man ruined my life, scarred me, and now, you're helping him?"

Adrian continues walking backward. "I looked over his case and met with him *once*. All before—"

"Exactly!" I cut him off. "*Before*. You should've told me the moment you knew I was involved."

"I won't work with him."

"You think this is about you working with him? You lied to me!"

The distrust is rooted there now.

It can't be pulled.

"Essie," he pleads.

I hold up my hand when he attempts to come closer. "Don't. I need to process this."

Adrian slumps his shoulders. "Let me take you home at least."

I check my phone when it vibrates.

> River: I'm at Down Home. Checked your location on your phone. Be there in 3 min.

Everyone in our circle has location share on our phones.

"River is on his way," I tell Adrian, walking in the direction of downtown. The faster I get to River, the faster I get out of continuing this conversation.

"I don't want to lose you again," Adrian says, smacking his hand across his chest. "I *can't* lose you again."

"The trust is gone. Years ago, you disappeared on me." I stop walking, as if letting these words out need my full attention. "Now, you hide this. You're just not honest."

"You can always trust me. *Please*, let me drive you home, and we can talk."

With perfect timing, River pulls up next to us in his black BMW.

I immediately open the door, peer at Adrian for a moment, and get in.

Adrian turns, facing us, and his pained eyes are on mine as we drive away.

"What happened?" River asks.

"If I tell you, promise you won't turn around and do something stupid?"

He only stares at me with curiosity, not promising anything.

Knowing my brother, I figure he won't agree to that promise.

I blow out a long breath. "Adrian's mom works at the Prison Exoneration Program."

"Shit," River hisses through suddenly clenched teeth.

"And she asked Adrian to help with his case."

"To which Adrian said no?" He brakes at a stop sign.

I shake my head. "He looked at the case and visited Earl."

"What are you going to do?" He keeps driving. "What's *he* going to do?"

"He said he'd tell his mom he didn't want to help, but he'd already involved himself. I told him what happened, and he sat there, acting like he had no idea." I cross my arms, a pang in my chest. "Other than a therapist, he's the only person I've told who didn't know from the beginning."

River switches his hands on the steering wheel to settle one on my shoulder. "I'm sorry, Sis. I really am." He peers down at his lap and shakes his head. "Fuck, I wish this'd never happened to you."

"It was a reality check that I need to prepare myself in case Earl is released."

My phone vibrates.

A text from Adrian.

It vibrates with another text.

I don't open them.

Instead, I turn off my phone.

When I get home, I pour myself a glass of wine and make a bowl of popcorn.

It's sad I never got the chance to finish Valeria's dinner.

I feel my stomach grumble, just thinking of it.

When we got home, River asked me if I wanted company, but I told him no. I need time to clear my head and decide what to say to Adrian. I can't ignore him, but I also can't forget what he did.

Some might not think it's a big deal, but it is to me.

I turn on my Heartbreak playlist and drink one, then two, then three glasses of red wine and eat half a bowl of popcorn. Then, in slow movements, I grab my phone, turn it on, and read Adrian's texts.

> Adrian: I'm so sorry. Let me explain myself.

> Adrian: Pls hear me out.

> Adrian: What I did was messed up. I should've told you.

> Adrian: 5 minutes. Give me 5 minutes.

I hit the Reply button.

> Me: 5 minutes. You can come here.

There.

That's me being the responsible adult.

I chug the rest of my wine and pour myself another.

Adrian knocks on the door. I inch back my curtain, seeing him shift from one foot to the other on my welcome mat that says *Cute shoes.*

My heart pounds as I open the door.

He raises his head and stands there, waiting for an invite in.

I backtrack a step, allowing him space, and he shuts the door behind him.

Music continues to play in the background, and the song changes to "Someone You Loved" by Lewis Capaldi.

Great, way to set the depressing mood.

The last time we fell apart was different.

It was created by missed calls and texts.

Nothing face-to-face.

He follows me into the living room. I take the couch, and he sits in the chair.

"Essie, I fucked up," he says, scrubbing a hand over his face. His eyes are watery when he stares back at me. "I should've told you from the beginning, but we were finally in a good place, somewhere I'd dreamed we'd be for years. I was scared to ruin it."

I feel my pulse running wild. "You didn't think I'd eventually find out?"

"I knew you would. I just ..." A stressed breath leaves him. "I didn't think it'd happen how it did."

"Do you remember the night I went to River's dorm? The first night we hung out."

He nods.

"I suffered from flashbacks of the accident, but they'd come and go. The night I came to your dorm, they'd returned, and I hadn't slept in days. I came looking for my brother, but that search led me to you. Our relationship and late-night conversations became my peace. I never thought you'd end up helping the person who'd stolen it to begin with."

Adrian flinches at my last sentence. "I'm sorry, Essie. I messed up. I'll completely clear myself from the case," he says in a low tone, bowing his head.

We're both quiet for a moment.

I frown. "You can't pick and choose when to be honest, Adrian. Trust in a relationship is all or nothing with me."

He raises his chin, meeting my eyes in anguish. "Please—"

"The damage is done," I say, talking over him and shaking my head.

"Essie," he pleads again, pain in his eyes. He stands, drops to his knees in front of me, and takes my hand in his. "Give me another chance."

He weaves our hands together and rests his head in my lap. The cords stand out in his neck, and his Adam's apple bobs.

I slowly pull away from him, finger by finger. "I don't trust you."

"Let me prove it to you."

"I need time," I whisper. "And I need for you to please leave."

He nods, his shoulders slumping as he stands. "Take your time. I'm not going anywhere. I'll become a better man for you, Essie. I swear it."

I don't say a word as he leaves.

River answers his door on my first knock.

"You ready to get whooped?" I ask, holding up my bedazzled controller.

He opens up the door wider and gestures for me to come in. "Don't forget who's the pro here, Sis."

We haven't gamed together for years.

It used to be a regular thing for us, but then college and law school happened. I lost myself to studies and then working at the firm.

River's pool house—he refuses to call it a cottage—smells like incense and cedar. The layout is like mine, but that's where the similarities end. The vibe of his is what you'd see if you searched for homes with a Silicon Valley—slash—gaming aesthetic.

Movie and game posters hang on the walls. A bookcase is filled with high-end controllers and different gaming systems. A long desk along the wall has four computer screens.

A sectional is in the middle of the living room, but two gaming chairs are settled in front of us, closer to the TVs. Yes, he has two, side by side.

Gaming isn't only River's job. It's also his passion.

He'd code and game even if he wasn't paid for it.

Like me, he can afford to move into his own place, but he's stayed here.

Some might say it's time for us to cut the umbilical cord, but free rent in this economy? Who'd say no to that?

He shuts the door and strolls toward the fridge. "You want something to drink?"

I plop down on a gaming chair. "What do you have that'll make me feel nothing?"

"Beer, whiskey, vodka if you want something to make you forget your problems. I have some CBD drinks or gummies if you want to relax."

"I'll take *forget my problems* for a hundred, please."

"Got it." He salutes me, opens a cabinet, and pours us Cherry Coke and vanilla vodkas.

I snatch the remote.

He snags a bag of Cheetos from the counter, gripping them in his teeth, and delivers our drinks to the table between the two gaming chairs.

"What game do you want to play?" He plops down on a gaming chair and opens the Cheetos.

"You pick." I wrinkle my nose. "I don't even know what's popular anymore."

"Want to try our new game? It's still the beta version, but so far, I'd say it's near goddamn perfect."

"Sounds good to me." I sip my drink and pinch my lips as the alcohol slips down my throat.

He spends the next ten minutes explaining the game before pouring us refills.

I've never been good at drunk gaming.

But at this rate, it's not my goal to win.

My goal is to forget about Adrian.

River, on the other hand, can win, even when practically passed out.

I study the remote as he starts the game.

"Sooo …" He draws out the word like an entire sentence.

"Are we back to hating Adrian? I need you to send me updated alerts on who we do and don't like."

"We're back to not liking him," I declare, side-eyeing him. "*Obviously*, considering I told you his mother works at the program that's helping Earl."

He blows out a long breath and lays the remote on his lap. "I don't get why people have such a hard time with just being honest. Lies and secrets will always catch up to you."

"Cowardness," I mutter, slumping in my chair.

"The downfall of many."

"Why are men so dumb?"

He scoots his chair closer to mine to wrap me in his arms. "I wish I could answer that for you, but unfortunately, as a man, I fit into the dumb category."

I sniffle before laughing. "I can't believe you just called yourself dumb."

"Nah, it's a fact. Ava showed me reports about it." He kisses the top of my head. "Now, that's not to say it's an excuse for Adrian's dumbass mistake. He needs to be held responsible for that."

"I'm glad I came over tonight," I murmur as he pulls away.

"Me too. I might be too dumb to give advice—because of the whole *being a guy* thing—but I'll always be here to make you laugh." He stops to show his muscles. "Or fight, if you decide you want me to kick Adrian's ass."

I grab a Cheeto from the bag and toss it at him. "You only want to punch him so you can break your hand, go to the hospital, and have Ava treat you."

"How the hell did you come up with that conclusion?"

"You're my twin. I know you too well."

He takes the Cheeto I threw at him from his lap and eats it.

We play video games for the rest of the night.

It's nice, video-gaming with my brother and forgetting boys exist … at least temporarily.

35

Adrian

I slump down in the kitchen table chair. "I messed up."

"Make it right then." My abuela delivers a bowl of reheated carne guisada to me.

She apologized repeatedly for bringing up the case the entire time she reheated it for me. I don't blame her—or anyone—for the shit show that was tonight. It was my own damn fault.

"Easier said than done," I grumble, picking up my spoon.

If *making it right* were such an easy task, Essie would've been mine a long time ago. I've been figuring out the best way to *make it right* with her for years. But this time, I won't give up and disappear from her.

She settles a teacup on the table and sits across from me. "The best things in life are never easy, honey. That's what makes them so special." She balls her hands up and thrusts them forward. "Nothing easy is worth having anymore, really. You don't take for granted what you had to work hard for."

I stir my food, not bothering to take a bite. "When Essie and I were in college, it felt so easy between us. If I hadn't stupidly run off, maybe we'd have been together all these years."

"From what you've told me, you both were broken souls then. Two damaged pieces from different vases will never make one whole. You must find and repair your vase first. And often, doing so takes time. This could all be a part of your fate, your love story, with Essie."

"Abuela, you know fate isn't real, right?"

"Fate is as real as the moon. A destiny each one of us is born with and dies with. But unlike the moon, fate gives you the chance to change her, despite what some say. The reality is we have one life, one sun, one moon, but *many* fates. Some you control. Some you don't. Honey, I can promise you, your fate with Essie is love. But it's your job to make it your true destiny." She reaches across the table. "Do that, and you'll live a happy life."

I rub my forehead. "It might be too late."

"It's never too late." She plays with the string on her tea bag. "It might be *harder*, yes. But not too late. Saying it's too late is saying you're giving up, and we didn't raise you to be a man who gives up on what he loves. Essie might need time, but don't walk away from her."

Time.

What Essie asked for.

Not for me to leave her alone or go to hell.

Time.

It's what I needed when I read those texts from my dad on his phone.

So, I'll give her those seconds, hours, days, whatever she needs.

And during that time, I'll devise the perfect groveling plan to get my girl back and regain her trust in me.

Sleep was nonexistent for me last night.

I didn't hear anything from Essie.

Dread rips through me when I pull up to the PEP's building.

Terrance gave me the morning off, but staying in Blue Beech might not be my future if Essie doesn't forgive me.

It'd pain us both if I stayed there.

My mother called and texted a few times, but I haven't gotten back to her yet.

Luckily, she's in her office.

I watch her through the glass door, sitting behind her desk and talking on the phone.

"I need to call you back," she says when she notices me and ends the call.

She gestures for me to take the chair directly across from her.

She looks at me with sadness. "Honey, you didn't tell Essie about Earl. Why?"

"I planned to," I say around a stressed breath. "I was just waiting for the right time."

"The *right time* was when you opened the file and saw she was involved."

"Did you know she was involved?"

"No, I only thought she was the girl from the pub until you introduced her by name. Now that I look back at it, Terrance had mentioned her name, but I never thought too much about it."

"I can't help you with Earl's case."

Her shoulders sag. "What if he's innocent, Adrian?"

"Or—hear me out—what if he's guilty and playing you and everyone else here? Essie said it was Earl. She was there."

"Essie never saw the person behind the wheel. She saw Earl's *truck*."

"A truck he only had access to."

"Is that a fact?" She sighs, softening her voice. "Do you want to keep Essie safe?"

"Until the day I die."

"Then, let's find out who really hurt her."

"Terrance, you lived here when the accident with Essie happened, right?"

Terrance sets his coffee mug down. "I did."

I motion toward a maroon diamond-patterned chair in his office.

He nods, waving me inside.

If I stay in Blue Beech, this office will be mine one day. It smells like dust. Books and awards line the wooden shelves. His beat-up desk shows wear of hard work, and his paperwork lies on his desk, organized into three even stacks.

I made copies of all the files from Earl's case before returning them to my mother. I'm not stupid enough to just hand them back, especially if Earl is guilty and we have to fight to keep him behind bars.

"Did anything seem off to you about the case?" I ask, making myself comfortable. "In your honest opinion, do you think Earl committed the crime?"

He straightens his back in his chair. "Earl had a public defender. An inexperienced young man who'd had maybe four or five cases. Sometimes, when he was in town, he'd stop in and ask me questions. But my wife eventually asked me not to involve myself. She didn't want to get on anyone's bad side in town."

"Was that common? Did people blame him out of fear of retaliation or because they wanted to agree with the rest of the town?"

"The accident killed a young man the town loved. People were mad. There were no other suspects. Earl looked and fit the part."

"Do *you* believe he did it?" I stress.

Terrance has done this a long time, and I've already learned so much from him. I value his input.

"It doesn't matter what I believe," he replies. "A group of his peers did and convicted him."

Most of the time, it's no fun speaking with attorneys.

We all share the same mentality.

I leave the office to find River waiting for me under a dark sky.

His car is next to mine. He's leaning against the door, arms crossed, like a high school bully from an '80s movie.

"He's guilty," he spits when I reach him. "Earl's fucking guilty, and you're an asshole for protecting him behind her back."

I raise my hand, palm facing him. "I'm not protecting him. Let me explain myself."

"Explain fast."

"Let's talk over a beer." I rub my forehead, fighting exhaustion.

He scoffs. "Essie will kill me in my sleep if she finds out I had a beer with you."

"One beer. And you can tell her you threatened to kill me."

"I am threatening to kill you."

I spread my arms wide. "We're not lying, then."

He nods toward his BMW. "Let's go, then."

A cover of "Sweet Caroline" plays in the background while the server delivers our drinks to our table. We're in the back, away from the noise, and Jax is tending the bar.

While I've been sticking to Down Home ale lately, tonight, I need something stronger. And that's gin. Gin has helped me through many late nights of working on cases.

"Listen, I'll give you the benefit of the doubt since you weren't here when the accident happened," River starts. "I'm sure you've read the case, but those files don't include every detail."

I scratch my chin, taking a second to answer so I can filter out sounding like a sarcastic ass. "The case file has all the evidence used in his prosecution."

The file has more information than even River and his parents know.

He takes a sip of beer. "Before we get into the case, I want you to do something for me."

I raise a brow. "What's that?"

"Look me in the eye and tell me you didn't come to Blue Beech to get information about Earl from Essie." He leans in closer. "Tell me you weren't using my sister to help him."

I grimace.

Oh fuck.

I never considered that Essie might look at it like that.

That I was using her.

"I give you my word, I didn't," I reply. "I found out the same day you went to Essie's and told her. I had no idea about Essie's past until my mom handed me Earl's file."

"Why'd you hide it from her?"

"When we were in college, I made a mistake and fucked it up with her. I was scared of losing her again." I swipe a hand across my face. "I planned to tell her everything."

He scoffs, picking up his beer. "Eventually, you'd have had to. It was better now than seeing you at Earl's side, defending him in court."

"I'm not defending him."

"Tell your mom to withdraw from his case. He's guilty. End of story."

"That's not in my power."

"What's in your power, then?"

"Deciding whether I help the PEP."

"Help by convincing them of his guilt. In fact, I have no problem helping you with that."

"Does that mean you'll work with me?"

"I'm not an attorney, but I'll fucking become one if it means protecting my sister."

"Cool. Let's get to brainstorming, then." I'm not wasting a moment of this.

He rubs his hands. "Let's get this done."

"What makes you so certain he committed the crime?"

"All the evidence was there in black and white."

The details are fresh in my mind since I reread them repeatedly last night.

I drain my drink. "Earl's night began here, at Down Home."

He nods.

"He realized he was too drunk to drive and called his grandmother, Esther, for a ride. Esther had a friend drive her to the pub so she could drive Earl and his truck home. Earl was so intoxicated that he needed help getting out of the pub and into the truck."

River nods again.

"Earl lived with his grandmother. In her statement, she said they went home and Earl didn't leave for the rest of the night."

"She could have been covering for him, or he'd snuck out, and she didn't know." He makes a *simple as that* motion.

"This man, who couldn't even walk out of a bar, somehow drove from their home in the middle-of-Blue-Beech nowhere, tracked down Essie and Ethan, waited until no other cars were around, and then played a traffic game with them?"

River shuts his eyes.

I can tell he's playing out the scene in his head.

"The grandmother also said she hid the keys," I continue. "They were still in the place she'd hidden them when the police arrived less than an hour after the accident. It took them over twenty minutes to wake Earl up."

"They found a spare key under the truck's floor mat," River argues.

"Earl's prints weren't on that key, and the grandmother, who drove his truck regularly, said she'd never seen it before."

"That doesn't mean he didn't use it."

"There was a logo on the key from the machine where it was copied. The PEP reviewed Earl's bank and credit card statements. They couldn't find a charge for it."

"Cash." River snaps his fingers and slams his hand on the table.

"The machine doesn't accept cash. Only credit. There was nothing on the grandmother's bank statements either."

"He could've found another way. A prepaid card. Paid someone to make a copy for him. The key isn't a deal-breaker on the case." He signals the server for another round of drinks. Instead of a beer for him this time, he orders a whiskey shot.

"All right, moving on from the key. Why would he target Ethan or Essie? Neither of them was involved in the prank."

"Ethan was at the party on the football field." River pulls at his jacket collar, as if he's suddenly burning up.

"With twenty other students."

River works his jaw, focused on my every word.

"Why Ethan?" I go on to really drive my point home. "Why not retaliate against one of the kids who played the prank that cost Earl his job?"

As soon as the server drops off our drinks, River downs his shot. "Maybe Earl thought Ethan was one of them. There's no disputing that the truck that hit Ethan's Jeep was Earl's."

"In her statement, Essie said the truck followed Ethan every time he tried to move out of the way. Do you think a man who was carried out of a bar less than an hour before had the motor skills to do that?"

He glares at me. "And here you were, trying to convince me you weren't fighting for Earl."

"I'm fighting for the truth, River, and you said you'd help

me. I won't work with Earl, but I also can't forget this case until I know the truth. Blame it on the attorney part of me *and* the part of me who wants to keep Essie safe."

"Fine, let's say we rule out Earl. Then, who did it?"

My gut knots. "That's the million-dollar question."

"If you're thinking it was high school kids, there's no way they could have pulled off a crime like that in revenge. Hell, half the kids were happy they had been suspended and got days off school."

"It could be them or the family who wanted his property." My mouth goes dry, and I pray that it wasn't Pete and Agnes. I still can't bring myself to ask them about it.

River cracks his neck from side to side. "Let's figure it out, then."

36

Essie

The past week has gone by in a blur.
I've been living on autopilot.
Eat, sleep, work.

"I can't wait to eat here," Lainey says as we settle at our four-top table at Callie's Bake Shop. "My friend told me to try the carrot cake. Another suggested I go with the red velvet. I'll probably order both … oh, and a double chocolate."

We're having lunch to celebrate Lainey finishing her first week of training. I'm also using it to distract myself from constantly thinking about Adrian.

After ordering a peach lemonade, I take a restroom break.

As I'm washing my hands, another stall door opens. A cold dread washes over me when Jenna, a girl I went to high school with, walks out. Our eyes meet in the mirror, and she shrinks back a step.

"Oh, hi, Essie," she says, startled.

I turn off the faucet. "Hi."

Jenna and Ethan were close friends. Rumor had it they hooked up at a party once. When I asked Ethan about it, he told me he didn't kiss and tell.

Jenna, her boyfriend, and their friends blamed me for

Ethan's death. I'd gone through hell and suffered in the hospital for almost a month, only to return to school and have them taunt me almost daily.

They spread rumors that I had been in the car with Ethan because we were secretly hooking up. The guy I'd been dating dumped me because he believed what they'd said.

They claimed Ethan wouldn't have died if he hadn't had to drive me home. Ethan liked to study at his house, and since I hated driving at night, he would take me back and forth.

It wasn't only them either. The entire football team held me responsible for his death. Half the kids at school wouldn't even talk to me.

"How have you been?" she asks, staring into the mirror. She fixes her blonde hair and then starts washing her hands.

"All right." I dry mine on a soft white towel with the bake shop's logo embroidered on it.

"I heard they're reopening Earl's case. Is that true?"

I edge back when she grabs a towel. "It seems so."

"I'm sorry," she murmurs. "Are you going to fight it?"

"I'm not sure what I'm going to do," I quickly say, wanting to get out of here.

I've seen Jenna around town a few times, but we always do our best to avoid each other. Years might have passed, and we might have grown up, but she's had so many opportunities to apologize for how they treated me.

Mia told her to leave me alone. My parents even reached out to the principal, which only resulted in them bullying me more. River punched Jenna's boyfriend in the face for it once, resulting in him getting in trouble with the school and my parents.

I start to leave, but she calls my name, stopping me.

"I'm really sorry for the way we treated you," she says, averting her eyes.

"You had to blame someone." I shrug, staring at her blankly, pretending their bullying didn't make me want to die sometimes. "You chose me instead of the man who actually did it."

"Everyone knew it was Earl." She raises her head to look me in the eyes, then lowers her voice when someone joins us in the restroom. She waits until they're in their stall before continuing. "You can't let them release Earl from prison. It wouldn't be fair to Ethan."

"I have no say in what the PEP does."

"But aren't you an attorney?" She raises her brows. "You were also a victim in the accident. That's reason enough for you to fight to keep him there, right?"

"I'm not sure."

From the research I've done, the PEP has a history of winning cases. Their website reports a ninety percent success rate. For that, I'm bracing myself for Earl's possible release. I just pray he doesn't return to Blue Beech.

Jenna picks at her nails. "If Earl is free, does that mean he didn't do it?"

"Not necessarily. They could've found a weak spot in the case."

She holds up her hand, intersecting two fingers. "Fingers crossed he stays where he belongs."

"Yeah," I mutter, "fingers crossed."

I don't match her gesture.

I simply turn around and leave the restroom.

Lainey stops shimmying her shoulders to a Sabrina Carpenter song and sets down her lemonade when she sees me.

"Are you okay, Essie?" she asks in concern.

"I'm fine." I sit and nervously wipe my sweaty palms down my dress.

Her blue eyes meet mine from across the table. "You don't look fine."

I gulp. "I'm just feeling a little under the weather, I guess."

"Let's go, then." She tosses her wallet and phone in her bag that's hanging on her chair and starts to stand.

I catch her hand to stop her. "I don't want to ruin your lunch."

"We can come another day. Plus, I probably don't need the carrot cake. The lemonade and three strawberry Pop-Tarts I had earlier already have my sugar levels soaring."

I sigh and spread my napkin across my lap. "Carrot cake and mimosas are just what I need right now."

She gives me a sly look. "I'm willing to make that sacrifice with you, if it helps."

When the server returns, we order two mimosas.

As soon as I take my first sip, I hear someone yell my name.

I lift my gaze to find Valeria walking toward us.

"I thought that was you!"

Adrian is right on her heels.

I want to sink into my chair and disappear.

"My apologies for the other night," Valeria says, joining us. "To make it up to you, lunch is my treat." She quickly pulls out a chair and sits between Lainey and me without waiting for an answer.

Adrian rudely does the same.

I smile at Valeria and then glare at Adrian.

Lainey extends her hand to Valeria. "I'm Lainey." Her eyes drift to Adrian, a smile gracing her lips. "It's nice seeing you again." Her tone isn't flirtatious. It's more friendly.

I motion between them. "You two know each other?"

"Adrian posted a paralegal ad," Lainey explains. "I interviewed with him before I did you. He didn't hire me, but said I'd make a better fit working for you. I thought he was blowing me off because he wasn't interested in hiring me. As it so happens, you and I were a better match."

My gaze travels to Adrian. "You did that?"

He scratches his cheek and nods. "Terrance put out the ad, thinking maybe we'd need another paralegal with me joining the firm. We already had one, so you needed her more than we did."

Valeria clasps her hands together. "Aw, how sweet."

"Definitely sweet," Lainey agrees. She motions between Adrian and me like I did with them moments ago. "I didn't know you two had a little thing going on."

A little thing?

Adrian chuckles at her comment.

"We most definitely do not have a *thing*," I argue.

"We most definitely *do* have a thing," Adrian corrects, leaning back in his chair and smiling innocently. "She's keeping it from you to stay professional, her being your boss and all."

I'm going to kill him.

Though I'm not too proud to admit *internally* that it was nice of him to send Lainey to me. But as a certified grudge holder, I'd appreciate it if he continued behaving badly, not doing good deeds like that.

Tell me my favorite reality show is trash.

Hide my Oreos.

Don't be sweet.

"A rival romance," Lainey says, perking up in her chair. "I've seen so many rom-coms about this. Let me tell you, they always end in a happily ever after."

My mimosa threatens its way up.

Valeria grins from ear to ear.

When the server comes to take their drink order, I ask for another mimosa. Valeria does the same, and Adrian sticks with a water.

I sit there, awkward and quiet, while Lainey and Valeria discuss the menu. Every so often, I do offer my input on my favorites.

"Essie," Valeria cheerfully says, "did my Adrian ever tell you he stole a car?"

"No, he didn't," I say, drawing my response out in curiosity.

Adrian grabs his water and stares at Valeria in confusion.

"When he was twelve, he stole my car while visiting me during his winter break. I had come down with the flu. While I was napping, he took my keys and drove to the pharmacy to get me medicine and a stuffed animal. He was just a block away from getting back when an officer pulled him over."

Covering his face, Adrian shakes his head. "Really?" he asks, his hand slightly muffling his word.

"What?" Valeria shrugs and then raises her glass toward him. "The judge sentenced him to twenty hours of community service. He volunteered at the nursing home, but after he finished his hours, he kept going there." The smile on her face builds. "I'd find him playing Monopoly, knitting, and even taking tango lessons with them there."

I trace the rim of my glass, fighting the urge to look at him. "That's nice."

"Oh, he was the sweetest boy," Valeria goes on. "He always tried mowing my yard in the summers. He was too short to see over the mower and not great, but he really wanted to help. He'd even pause to flex his muscles." Her sincere gaze flits to Adrian. "His heart is so big, but sometimes, it bites him in the butt. My grandson sometimes holds back the truth to spare people's feelings."

I finally turn in my chair to look at Adrian.

Apology is on his face as he leans toward me to whisper, "Sorry."

What is he apologizing for?

Hiding that he was working with PEP?

Crashing lunch?

Breaking my heart again?

"We love us a man who does chores," Lainey comments.

Dear God.

From the way they're bragging about him, you'd think they were starting a fan club.

Adrian either paid them or has blackmail against them.

Valeria spends the rest of lunch telling us stories about Adrian's generosity. He started an after-school study program and bought pizzas with his allowance to motivate kids to come. He made his mother breakfast every weekend and walked dogs at the local animal shelter.

Lainey adds her approval to the stories.

They praise him as if he single-handedly united iPhone and Android users.

Adrian rests his elbow on the table, eyes fixed on me, clearly enjoying this moment.

37

Adrian

Want to win your girl back? Have your abuela tell her all your embarrassing stories.

She spends the entire lunch doing just that.

Essie tries to look uninterested, but my abuela has her full attention. She also spends her time asking Essie questions about herself. Essie tells her she loves living in Blue Beech, and my abuela takes that opportunity to mention how much I've grown to like the town as well.

When the server drops off the check, my abuela grabs it faster than I can.

She then passes it straight to me.

"I know I said lunch was on me, but Adrian would never let me pay," she says with absolute certainty. "He's the definition of a true gentleman."

I nod, pulling out my wallet. "Never."

I'll happily spoil Essie every minute of every day.

My abuela looks at Lainey. "Didn't you mention needing a manicure?"

"I did," Lainey replies.

"How about we make a stop at the salon?" My abuela's gaze snaps to Essie. "Would you like to come?"

Essie holds up her hand to show off her pink nails. "I actually just got a fresh mani-pedi."

"Are you able to take Adrian home, then? I don't want the salon to close before we get there."

Essie's face reddens, and she bites into her lower lip.

There's no way she can say no to my abuela.

"Uh," she stutters.

The server returns, interrupting us. I hand her the bill and cash before telling her to keep the change.

If this were a normal situation, I'd tell my abuela not to put Essie on the spot with her question. But right now, I need this.

I need to talk to Essie.

Putting her on the spot be damned.

I'll make it up to her later.

"I actually walked," Essie starts.

"No, we drove," Lainey unknowingly corrects, scrunching her brows. She's not trying to throw her friend under the bus.

"I mean ..." Essie pauses, frazzled. "I was going to walk and get some fresh air."

"That's just perfect," my abuela says. "Adrian loves a good stroll after a meal. It helps with his digestion."

This time, I can't stop myself from groaning. "Abuela."

She stands, Lainey following her move, and they say their goodbyes and leave the table before Essie has the chance to say no.

"Okay," Essie drawls out, her eyes wide as she glances around, "what the hell just happened?"

"You were Valeria'd," I explain. "It's one of her many skills."

If my abuela wants something to happen, she'll make it happen.

"Yeah, well, joke's on you," she huffs. "You can walk."

She unwinds her purse strap from the chair, drops the bag onto her lap, and searches for her keys.

When she finds them, I immediately take them before she can stop me.

She attempts to grab them, but I jerk back.

I wiggle the keys in the air before shoving them into my pocket. "I like the idea of *us* walking. It doesn't have to be to my place, though. We can take a walk. Like my abuela said, it's good for digestion."

"It's also good for tripping you or throwing you off a bridge," she murmurs.

"I mean, if it gets you to take a walk with me, then trip me all you want." Standing, I hold my hand out toward her. "I'll choose that over the bridge, though. It's a little cold to swim this time of year."

She rolls her eyes, ignoring my hand, but rises from her chair. "You're insufferable." As she walks toward the exit, she says, "This was such a setup." Her ponytail swings through the air with every stride she takes.

"A setup I will definitely not complain about," I say to her back as she waves goodbye to the hostess, who then tells us to have a good day.

"Of course you aren't complaining." She opens the door and walks outside.

"In my defense, I had no idea of said setup."

I wish my abuela had told me, though, so I could've been better prepared. I'd have brought flowers and had one of those romantic apologetic speeches planned.

But not that I really need that shit. It's so easy to come up with reasons I want her to be mine, why I'm in love with her, and I have no problem admitting my wrongs. I'm perfectly okay with groveling.

She makes a right, not toward the parked cars but down the sidewalk toward her office.

"I miss you," I say to her back.

She keeps walking.

"Tell me what I have to do to make things right."

She doesn't stop.

I run my hand through my hair, and my voice almost sounds pained when I say, "Essie, my life is lost without you."

She whips around to face me, shock on her face.

I take a step toward her, and surprisingly, she doesn't pull or shove me away.

I'm pushing my limits as I grow closer and closer.

She stays in place. When I reach her, my movements are careful as I cup her face in my hand. Her lower lip trembles.

"You make me a better man, Essie. You make me feel like I have a life."

"Adrian," she whispers.

"I was so lost in my day-to-day routine, not living life, until you showed up and changed everything for me. When I went to bed, I couldn't wait until I got to talk to you in the morning. Even when I was sleeping, I dreamed of you. You consumed my every thought. My life is empty without you. I'm begging you, *please*, tell me how I can make this right."

All she has to do is tell me *what*.

I'll do it, no matter how hard.

Because nothing can be harder than knowing I lost her.

Abso-fucking-lutely nothing.

I moved to Blue Beech to win Essie back, but now, I want more.

I want us to build a life here.

To build happiness.

I don't care about being the best attorney, or a promotion, or *anything*. All I care about is spending my life with her.

A soreness forms in my throat.

I want to say more but also want to give her time to reply.

Though, from the sadness on her face, I'm unsure if she will.

Her eyes are downcast.

My hand falls from her face when she retreats a step.

When she takes another, a breath leaves me. I capture her hand to stop her and clutch it tight, like a lifeline, because she's mine.

And, goddamn, do I want to be hers.

I want to make her feel safe with me.

I want her to trust me.

"Adrian," she whispers.

Without a word, I tighten my hold on her hand and walk us to a bench a few feet away. Our steps are unhurried, and with each one, it's like she's contemplating whether to break away and make a run for it.

We sit on the bench at the same time, and I wrap my arm around her.

She doesn't snuggle into my side, but she does scoot somewhat closer.

Minutes pass, neither of us saying a word.

It's like right now, silence is what she wants.

What she needs.

Every move she makes is slow.

She rests her head on my shoulder and sighs.

She shuts her eyes and levels her breathing.

"I like this," she finally says, staring straight ahead as cars pass by.

"What?" I ask, peering down at her.

"Sitting here, saying nothing, being with you." She sighs. "It reminds me of our history—how, even without saying a word, you always calmed me."

I twirl a strand of her hair around my finger. "I'm here anytime you want me. Talking, silence, whatever."

I'm not sure how much time passes as we sit here.

I don't check my watch or phone.

The longer we're here, the more I notice the tension leaving Essie's body.

The same with mine.

Some people need a hot bath to relax.

Others, the gym or their favorite movie.

But Essie and me? We just need each other.

"All right, give the keys up," Essie says, breaking her silence.

Her voice is more playful than before.

A smile plays on my lips. "No, ma'am."

"Oh, look at you, getting the small-town manners down."

"I'd like to inform you that my abuela taught me those manners decades ago."

"Mm-hmm."

"If we're going with your reasoning, then it seems I was built for the small-town life here, then, huh?"

I frown when she ducks out of my arm and stands. Rising to my feet, I hold the keys in the air. It's childish, I know.

She crosses her arms, faking annoyance.

Deciding to play the game further, I walk toward a sidewalk trash can and pretend to *almost* drop them inside. She stalks toward me and makes another attempt to take her keys back.

I shake my head and teasingly jiggle the keys in front of her.

They're *just* out of her reach.

Smirking, I turn on my toes and head toward her office.

She does the same, and then we're walking side by side, the silence returning.

When we reach her office, the door is locked.

"How convenient that I have these," I say with a grin while unlocking the door.

"How convenient will it be when I call the cops and have you arrested for key theft and breaking and entering?" she fires back.

"Breaking and entering? No, babe. I'm simply letting myself in."

"Okay, you're over here, using the *serial killer* version of *letting yourself in.*"

The door opens, and as soon as we're inside, she tries swiping her keys *again.*

"Babe," I say with a laugh, "you're nearly four to zero."

She puckers her pink lips. "Aaliyah taught me that if at first you don't succeed, dust yourself off and try again."

"Try again. I don't mind you jumping all over me. In fact, I'm a fan."

This time, when she tries, I move away from her until she's chasing me. As she follows me around the office, laughter breaks out of her.

It's like this is what we needed to lift all the heaviness off our shoulders.

We're two people who have been serious for so long that we nearly forgot how refreshing not caring for a minute feels.

Without thinking, I turn on my toes, envelop her in my arms, and circle her around. She loses a breath, the laughter fading.

I halt, afraid I went too far.

But after a few seconds, a giggle leaves her. "Just like the silence, maybe this is also what I needed."

She doesn't pull away, and I feel like I'm on top of the damn world.

"Is this like one of the rom-coms Lainey was talking about?" I ask.

She squints, closing one eye as if in deep contemplation. "I think so, but since I haven't decided whether I forgive you yet, I don't want to say yes."

"How about we watch a rom-com together to see if it qualifies?"

With her arm out, she pulls back and does another twirl. "Don't you have a job?"

"I'm off for the rest of the day."

"That's not very professional."

"I'm not concerned about being professional at the moment."

"What are you concerned about?"

We're in the lobby, in front of a window, for people's eyes to see. I collect her hand in mine, take us to her office, and push her against the door as soon as I shut it.

My lips are instantly on hers, and she doesn't hesitate before kissing me back. Our kiss is slow-building and intimate, and I fucking love it.

Essie grips the back of my neck, sucking in breaths, and slips her tongue inside my mouth. I groan, grabbing her thigh and hooking it around my waist.

She moans my name at the same time my pocket vibrates.

The sound cuts us out of our *everything is okay between us* trance.

Reality cracks through us, and she lowers her leg from my waist.

I draw back a step, pulling my phone from my pocket, and without bothering to glance at the screen, I ignore the call.

Our moment is gone.

Silence returns, but this time, it isn't comfortable.

It's awkward and bursting with uncertainty.

I gulp, wishing we could time-travel back to only a few minutes ago.

Hell, if I had an actual time-traveling wish, I'd go back to before I was stupid in college.

She clears her throat. "I, uh … need to get back to work."

I rub my sweaty hands together. "Do you want me to walk you back to your car since it's still at the bake shop? I'm sure you could use the company."

"No," she says, her voice suddenly shaky.

It's like we were riding a high, and now, we're coming down *hard*.

And, dammit, just like an addict, I want to take another hit to bring us back to when my lips were on hers.

I nod, playing with the phone in my hand. "Before I go, will you promise me something?"

She flutters her lashes, halfway looking at me and the floor simultaneously. "What?"

"I'm sending you an email. Please read it."

"Nice work today," I say, fist-pumping my abuela when I slide into her Buick.

According to my GPS, the walk back to my place would have been an estimated hour.

Since my abuela was still at her nail appointment, I sat on the same bench Essie and I had been on earlier and waited until she was finished.

My abuela grins from ear to ear. "We make a good team, don't we?"

I nod. "Sure do."

"Now, I need you to do me a favor."

"Yeah?"

"Tomorrow is the town's fall festival. You're helping me in my booth."

I shrug, buckling my seat belt. "Works for me."

She shifts the car into drive. "I'll put my money on a pretty, dark-haired girl who sports cowboy boots and speaks legal jargon being in attendance as well."

A fall festival—whatever the hell it is—sounds like a nice way to spend my day, especially if I get to see Essie.

38

Essie

If you want unbiased advice, you go to Mia.

I swear, the girl should charge for her services.

We're sitting at her house in the sunroom. She lives on her parents' property, secluded from most of Blue Beech for privacy, so the view, almost forest-like, is breathtaking.

A lemon candle is lit. I've never been inside her home when it doesn't smell like something lemon-related.

"Your situation is tricky, babes." She sits on the sectional across from me. "Adrian hiding the Earl thing was shitty. He should've gone straight to you the moment he read the case, *but* I see where he was put in a rough spot." She raises a finger. "I'm in no way saying that's an excuse. If you think he's worthy of a possible second chance, hear him out and make it clear *no more secrets, period.*" She relaxes against the cushions. "If you didn't look the happiest I've seen you in years, I'd suggest you tell him to go fuck himself. But, Essie, the times I've seen you two together, a smile I haven't seen since before the accident graced your face. I missed seeing that."

I can't help but smile.

Is this the smile she's talking about?

"It's kind of that smile, but brighter," she says, as if reading my mind.

"Wait," I say before gasping dramatically. "Does this mean Mia secretly likes love?"

She's usually the most anti-love person I know.

It's wild because her mom, Stella, has starred in countless romance movies. Mia has attended movie premieres since she was young. A lot of people thought she'd follow in her mom's footsteps into entertainment, but she likes to stay far away from the spotlight.

Not that I blame her. I've heard the stories of stalkers, paparazzi, and the invasion of privacy Stella has had to deal with. Mia also has the fear that people only want to be around her *because* of her mother's stardom. She learned that the hard way when her first boyfriend accidentally texted her instead of a friend, pretty much saying those exact words.

Mia scrunches her nose, as if in disgust. "I hate love *for myself*, but it'd be selfish of me to deter others from it. On the few occasions I've found myself growing feelings for someone, I block their number and buy a new bag for myself instead." She gestures toward the black leather Prada bag on the chair. "They don't break hearts."

I nod in agreement. "Retail therapy can be as satisfying as a male-given orgasm at times."

Not that I know *too* much about that topic. My experience is limited to two guys.

"My best advice?" she goes on. "Read the email."

I bite my lower lip, thinking. "Do you want to read it to me?"

She climbs across the couch, snatches her MacBook, and places it on my lap. "Log in."

I open the MacBook and sign in to my email.

Adrian's email sits in my inbox with the subject: **Please read, Essie. I beg you.**

I exhale a deep breath and mutter, "Here goes," while opening the message before handing it to Mia.

She holds the MacBook in her lap as I watch her read the email. "It looks"—she pauses, continuing to read—"like a bunch of legal jargon regarding Earl's case."

Scooting back, she makes herself comfortable. She balances the MacBook on her lap as she reads the email. Minutes pass, and she doesn't say a word.

It's like she's lost in whatever this *legal jargon* says.

"Essie," she whispers, looking up at me through thick lashes, "I think you need to read this yourself. I never thought I'd say this, but Adrian might be right. Maybe they should open his case back up."

I sigh, my shoulders slumping. "I need a minute before I do that."

She shuts the MacBook. "I understand." She rests her hand over mine. "But read it, Essie. You're one of the smartest and strongest people I know. You're a great attorney, and you know this stuff better than anyone. Read it yourself and form your opinion."

"I need a break from talking about myself."

She grabs the remote and turns on the TV. "Fine with me. What's your show of choice?"

I snatch the remote and turn the TV off. "Nope, it's your turn."

"My turn to what? Pick a show?"

"Your turn to talk about *your* love life."

"We've already established my love life is as existent as a vampire's love for garlic."

"That is a terrible analogy," I say, laughing.

"Hey, no one said I was the jokester of the group."

No way am I letting her attempt to joke her way out of this.

I'm not only asking for my curiosity, but I'm almost positive Mia hasn't talked about this with anyone. Holding in your secrets, your hurt, alone, only makes the pain harder.

"What happened with you and Trey?" I ask.

"All right, time for you to go home."

She attempts to stand, but I grab her arm and pull her back onto the couch.

"Nice try," I say, scooting closer to pretend to hold her in place. "Spill it."

"There's nothing to spill." She gives me a stern look. "Trey and I have never gotten along. Everyone knows that."

"And *why* haven't you ever gotten along?"

"He's always thought of me as a spoiled brat and a bad influence on Callie."

I squint at her. "Really?"

"Yes, really. And considering he's an asshole, I've stopped trying to correct him."

I've always seen Mia as the opposite of a bad influence. As much as I love Callie, she can be naive. Her parents hid the darkness of the world away from her too much. Even my parents have said that.

Since they were kids, Mia has always looked out for Callie and kept her away from trouble.

Trey is dumb as shit if he thinks Mia is a bad influence.

That's just the excuse he's giving her.

But the excuse *for what*?

Yes, Mia grew up rich and spoiled.

And, yes, she's a little standoffish, but she'd kill someone for Callie. No joke.

"It's obvious *something* happened with you two," I go on.

"All right," she says with a groan. "I'm officially kicking you out of my home."

I repeat the same motion of when she tried to stand earlier. "Just answer one question. That's it."

She falls down and gives me her best dirty look.

"Does Callie know?"

"There's nothing to know."

"That means the answer is no."

"Again, because there's *nothing* to know."

"I'm letting you get away with that answer for now because when this gets out—and it will if Trey moves back—I can say I knew nothing about it."

A slight hint of a smile crosses her lips. "Good logic. New subject. What do you want for Christmas?"

"For Trey to move home so all of us get to find out your secrets."

She picks up a pillow and whacks my shoulder. "If he moves here, I'm moving away."

"If you ever try to move away from here again, I'm dragging you back myself," I say, referencing when she moved to New York for a while. "What did we say when we were kids? *We're never leaving Blue Beech.*"

"I think you're forgetting the part where I objected to that every single time," she fires back.

Before I can argue, my phone beeps with a text.

Adrian: Did you read the email?

"He's asking if I've read the email," I say, holding up my phone to show Mia the text.

Her face softens as she hands the MacBook back to me.

I lower my phone to the couch, take a deep breath, and read the PEP's argument for why they believe Earl might be innocent.

39

Adrian

I take out my phone and text Essie a picture of Tucker. I made sure to choose the one with the saddest puppy face I could find.

> Me: Tucker says he misses you and that all the stress of you being mad at his dad is stopping him from his recovery. He's sad he didn't get to see you at lunch, and he thinks he deserves time with you as well.

I haven't spoken to Essie since yesterday, when I asked if she'd read my email.

She replied with a simple, **Reading it now**, and I haven't heard back from her about it.

Since I don't want to be buggy about the email, I've decided to use the advantage of being a dog dad to good use. No one can say no to Tucker.

My phone beeps with a reply.

> Essie: Tell Tucker he can come over. His dad can drop him off at the door.

I laugh for a moment, seeing the irony of us acting like

divorced parents co-parenting, but then my smile drops when I remember the reason behind co-parenting—breakups.

Right now, I'm not sure if that's where Essie and I are.

Hell, I don't know if we were even in a relationship that could technically be broken up.

I immediately respond.

> Me: Hold on. I'll ask him.

I do, embarrassingly, look over at my dog and say, "You want to go see Essie?"

Then, I hurriedly tell him to calm down when he attempts to get up and rush toward the door.

As soon as he's situated again, I return to my conversation with Essie.

> Me: He said we're a package deal.

> Essie: You can wait outside while we hang out, then. The patio furniture is comfortable.

> Me: Tucker said that'd hurt his feelings, and since he already has hip pain, that's kind of evil to make him feel even more. Tsk, tsk, Essie.

> Essie: Fine, come over. But I'm only doing this for Tucker.

> Me: Tucker says thank you and see you soon. *bark*

I regret the *bark* comment after I hit Send.

I don't know what it is, but Essie brings out the cheesiness inside me.

As someone who grew up with a serious mindset, it's nice to joke around.

"Let's go," I say, going to help Tucker up.

I smile while helping him into my car's back seat.

Dogs are referred to as a man's best friend for many reasons.

One of them I've learned is that women love them.

Even if they're pissed at you, they'll always make time for your dog.

"Thank you for letting me come over," I say as soon as Essie answers her door.

She points at Tucker before lowering herself to one knee to pet him. "You'd better thank him."

"Oh, I gave him an extra treat and promised him pup-corn and a movie this week. He's a big fan of *Air Bud*."

A hint of a smile plays at her lips. "I loved that movie growing up." She rises to her feet but keeps her attention on Tucker. "You'd better hold him to that."

I shut the door, and Essie helps Tucker into the living room, where she has a dog bed, along with pillows, blankets, and toys.

"Whoa, did you recently get a dog?" I ask, looking around.

"No. I bought them for Tucker," she comments. "Joint custody means he needs belongings at both homes."

I scratch my cheek. "How long have you had all this?"

"I ordered them from Amazon." She shrugs, looking away from me and petting Tucker. "There was no point in sending them back."

"Does that mean Tucker is spending the night?"

"He needs to be comfortable while he's here." She kisses his head, and Tucker nuzzles his head against her knee. "The little man needs catered to."

I groan, suddenly pretending my leg is sore. "Did I tell you I had a little accident too?"

"Oh, yeah?" she asks with a low laugh, her arms crossing. "Were you also squirrel chasing?"

"It was a bear, actually." I shove my hands into my pockets and lean back on my heels. "I was rescuing a baby cub for the mama. Like my abuela said, I'm one of the good guys, always caring about others."

She laughs, smacking my shoulder. "Okay, take your ego back outside, mister. You can come back when it's hit a three."

I pretend to backtrack a few steps and slap said *ego* away from my face as she fills up a water bowl for Tucker. Tucker ignores it, opting to snuggle in his new bed and chew on a bone instead.

She sits on the couch, crossing her legs, and stares up at me. "I read the email."

Shit, she's diving straight in.

This is what I wanted, right?

I sit on the floor at her feet, making myself comfortable, and stare up at her. "And?"

Silence from her.

One of Tucker's toys squeaks in the background as he plays with it.

"I want to help you on Earl's case," she says in a quiet, even voice, shocking the hell out of me. "No, not *help*. I want to be in the loop. Everything you learn, you tell me."

"Are you sure?" I ask in a whisper, scooting closer.

"There were claims that could possibly support Earl's innocence, but there is still plenty of evidence against him. I'm asking you to find out the truth. I don't want you to do this for the PEP. I want you to do it *for me*."

"I'll do that," I say, rising to my feet and joining her on the couch. "I promise I'll find you the truth."

And I won't fucking stop until I do so.

I yawn, raising my arms into a stretch. "Tucker said he's too tired to drive home tonight."

Essie and I peer over at Tucker, who's snoring louder than the TV.

We watched *Air Bud* and then *Dog* and then *Beethoven*, keeping Tucker the theme of the night. Essie was adamant that no dog movies where a dog died were allowed. I had no disputes with that.

Essie dips her toes out of her blanket and wiggles them. "Good thing Tucker doesn't drive."

I chuckle, stretching my neck. "Tucker's dad is also too exhausted to drive." I attempt to force a yawn, but it ends up coming out as a real one, causing Essie to yawn right after.

I'm damn tired.

Sleep has been nearly nonexistent for me the past few days.

I'd do anything for Essie to let me sleep over.

Not for sex, but to just be around her.

To not have to leave and tell her good night.

Hell, I'll even sleep on Tucker's bed, if need be.

Just the presence of her puts me on top of the world.

Being in the same space as her is damn heaven.

Essie shakes her head. "You can pick Tucker up in the morning. I'll feed him breakfast."

I mimic Tucker's snoring. "It seems I'm in the same shape as him." I perform another fake snore, then gesture back and forth between him and me. "Plus, package deal. Remember?"

"Fine," Essie says around another yawn, and it doesn't stop as she keeps talking. "You can sleep in the living room with him." She raises a brow as if waiting for me to object to her terms.

I frown, hating that she thinks I would.

I'm not one of those assholes who only stays with women if it means sex.

I'd stay even if I knew she planned to egg me in my sleep or draw stupid shit on my forehead with a Sharpie.

"All right," I say, standing and then holding out my hand to Essie, helping her to her feet. "The living room it is."

She passes her blanket to me.

I cradle it in my arms, lowering my head to kiss her forehead. "Good night, Essie. Sweet dreams."

"You're really going to sleep on the couch?" She stares at me, eyes wide in disbelief.

"I'm grateful you're not kicking my ass out. So, you make the rules."

We've spent nights together without sex. That's not why I'm here. Sure, the sex is a plus, but my love for her outweighs that.

"Okay," she whispers. She motions toward the blanket. "Is that enough to keep you warm?"

"It's enough. If not, I'll snuggle with Tucker."

She laughs. It's a shy one. "Good night, Adrian."

I can't stop myself from placing another kiss on her forehead. As she leaves the living room, she sways her hips from side to side, as if her goal is to fuck with me.

I give Tucker a pat on the head before spreading the blanket on the couch. I pull my shirt over my head and drag my socks off my feet. I kicked my shoes off earlier before we started the first movie.

Essie left the TV on, which is fine with me since I won't get much sleep anyway. I move a few different angles, attempting to make myself comfortable, and turn on *The People's Court*. It's my go-to show when I can't sleep.

I'm not through even one full episode before I hear footsteps down the hallway. The kitchen light flips on, and I watch Essie fill a glass of water.

She turns to me, resting her back against the counter as she takes a sip. "Are you comfortable?" Another sip.

I make a show of displaying the limited space I have.

"All right," she groans. "Since you insisted the couch was so uncomfortable, I'll share my bed."

You don't have to ask me twice.

I tug the blanket off and stand. "Did you fake come in here for water to ask for a snuggle buddy?"

She covers her mouth with her hand, most likely disguising her smile, and shakes her head. "Absolutely not."

"You want me to come in there and sleep with you, don't you?" I tease.

She shrugs. "Make a big deal about it, and I'm rescinding my offer. So, the couch or my bed?"

40

Essie

My decision-making skills should be heavily evaluated.

I'm inviting Adrian back into my bed.

The man who broke my heart.

This is a *very, very* bad idea.

My excuse? It'd have been rude if I made him sleep on the couch when I had plenty of room in my bed. My mom has always said to treat houseguests well.

Plus, he'd probably snore, keeping Tucker awake, who really needs his rest to heal.

My feet pad against the floor, a rush hitting me as Adrian follows me to my bedroom.

He stands in the doorway, waiting for me to change my mind.

The lamp on my nightstand and the TV—volume turned low—are the only light sources.

I open a drawer, snag a tee, and toss it at him. "Put this on."

He catches the tee, holding it up. "Do you think this'll fit me? I'd be better off grabbing my shirt from the living room."

"No way. Outside clothes are not allowed in the bed. It's an unwritten rule I abide by seriously."

"Do you have anything sexier I can wear then?"

I roll my eyes.

"Blue tie-dye isn't exactly my color."

I roll my eyes again, more dramatically this time.

"Is that what you're wearing?" He motions toward me.

"Uh, yes?" I tug at the bottom of my tank. "What's wrong with this?"

"Babe, not that I'm complaining, but your shorts show half your ass."

"And?" I definitely chose these pajama shorts to mess with him.

Look what you're missing.

Look what you messed up.

"Does that mean I get shorts that show half my ass?"

"You're in your boxers!" I throw out my arms toward him. "I see *more* than half your junk."

He smiles, and as if his cock appreciated my comment, I notice it twitch beneath his briefs.

He whistles. "I think he knows you're talking about him."

"Oh my God. Please never refer to your cock as *he* again."

"Do you have a better nickname?" He leans against the doorframe.

"No!"

"You've seen him before. I think you're qualified to grant him a nickname."

"I swear, I'm losing brain cells having this conversation."

He strolls into my bedroom, drops my shirt on the dresser, and pats the bed. "All right, I'll let you sleep on the nickname thing tonight, and you can tell me tomorrow."

I hold my thumb and pointer finger a few inches apart, and my voice suddenly sounds hoarse. "You're this close to getting kicked out of my bedroom."

He chuckles. "I'll be on my best behavior."

I watch him, wishing I had *some* regret for letting him into my bedroom, but I don't.

He pulls back the blankets that aren't turned down. Making

himself comfortable in the same spot he used to sleep, he waits for me to join him. When I don't, he pats the bed again.

I tiptoe back to the bed and slide underneath the covers. His body heat next to mine instantly relaxes me.

We make ourselves comfortable, and when he wraps me in his arms, I don't stop him.

Instead, I snuggle in closer.

I don't wake up with regret for inviting Adrian into my bed.

I do wake up feeling Adrian's erection pressing against my ass though.

Memories of us in my bed swarm my thoughts.

Us naked, touching, making love.

It all felt so perfect then.

Just like last night, I'm ready to make another bad decision.

I want this man more than I've ever wanted anything.

I try to stupidly convince myself it's just *sex* I want, but that's so wrong.

This morning, though, I'll pretend.

Biting on my lip, I grind my ass against him.

He stirs behind me, not fully waking.

I do it again, harder this time.

Heat travels through my veins when a moan escapes him.

I feel the rumble from his chest vibrate against my back.

Groaning, he tightens his arms around my waist and jerks me closer.

I shudder as he runs his tongue along the lobe.

"Are you sure you want this?" he whispers in my ear.

I'm not exactly sure what *this* he's referring to. But right now, I'll take anything, so long as he's touching me.

"Yes." Moaning, I lick my lips and grind against him again. "But I want us to do it like this."

We need to stay in this position. I'm afraid if I look at him in the face, I'll break down.

He lowers his hand down my stomach, underneath my shorts, and cups my pussy. "So wet," he murmurs. "So wet for me."

His hand doesn't stay inside my panties long.

I frown at the loss, and just as I'm about to complain, he curls my leg around his thigh.

"Much better," he grumbles, his hand immediately returning to my panties.

I throw my head back, resting it against his shoulder while he slowly draws his finger through my wetness.

He does it so teasingly.

Torturously.

This man won't make this easy on me this morning.

"Please," I beg, lowering my hand and gripping his wrist.

He doesn't allow my attempt at controlling his speed.

Instead, like the pain in the ass he is, he moves slower.

"Please what?" he finally asks, sinking a thick finger inside me.

"You know," I mutter. "Please."

"Please *do this*?" Adjusting himself, he thrusts another finger inside me.

I feel so damn full.

The angle is awkward.

I can tell he'd rather us be in a different position, but he's making it work.

He's giving me what I want.

"Yes," I cry out. "*That.*"

He manages to slide another finger inside me. His other hand trails up my stomach to cup my breast, rubbing his palm against my sensitive nipple.

My body shakes as he fingers me.

His pace moves from slow, to fast, to slow.

Gentle yet so damn intense.

I wiggle my ass against him.

His cock grows harder.

Jerking against my ass, as if begging for its own release.

My pussy is so wet that I can hear his every movement.

His thumb massages my clit, and it doesn't take long for euphoria to flow through my body. I feel heavy against the mattress yet light at the same time—as if I weigh nothing.

No. No. Stupid body.

I want this to last longer.

I want this to last forever.

"Let go," Adrian says, nearly panting. "Let it out, baby."

Even though *I* don't want it to end yet, my body listens to him, unable to take it anymore.

I whimper, hardly able to breathe, and he quickens his pace, moving relentlessly.

His hand on my nipple, his thumb on my clit, and his fingers inside me send me into overdrive. There's no fighting it any longer.

I dig my nails into his wrist as pleasure shoots through me.

My body shakes.

He groans, his teeth grazing my ear.

I wish I could see the expression on his face.

Wish I could see how turned on he looks when touching me.

All my nerve endings come alive, and I moan his name as I come undone.

His hand leaves my shirt, and he grabs my tangled hair in his hand, pulling my head back to devour my mouth.

"Let me move us, baby," he says, sucking on my neck. "I promise, in a different position, I'll make you feel even better."

"Yes," I gasp, still coming down from my high but wanting more. "But only if you're inside me in the next three seconds."

"I can do that." He chuckles, rolling us over.

Suddenly having no patience, I push his briefs down in the process.

But then I press a hand to his chest, stopping him.

He raises a brow, his briefs caught at the knees.

"I want to do it this way." I flip onto my stomach.

Adrian, getting the hint, helps pull me to my knees.

We've done it missionary.

In the shower.

But we've never done it like this.

I want all my firsts with him since I'm unsure if we'll have any more seconds or thirds. This might be the last time we touch each other.

"Jesus," he hisses. On his knees behind me, he runs his hand along my spine, tracing it down my back. "God, you're beautiful from every single angle. I wish I could worship your body every second of every day."

I stick my ass up farther in the air. "Then, worship me, Adrian."

He grips my hips, holding me in place with one hand, and holds his cock with the other. I wiggle in anticipation, waiting, and my hands go to the headboard when he thrusts inside me.

My entire body inches up the bed.

I move against him, meeting him thrust for thrust, coming more alive with each one.

He fills me up perfectly.

Fucks me perfectly.

We find our rhythm.

My face hits the pillow and headboard, but I don't give a shit.

He suddenly stops.

I peer back at him over my shoulder.

"Shit," he hisses, slowly pulling out. "I forgot a condom."

I shake my head, hair falling in my face. "We forgot a condom."

"No, it's my dick. My responsibility." His forehead creases in concern. "I should've been more responsible."

"Keep going," I plead. "I'm on the pill. I'm clean."

"So am I." His chest heaves as his breathing grows heavier and heavier.

I push my ass out. "Then, get back inside me."

I don't have to ask him twice.

He pushes my hips up farther, sliding against the sheets closer, and rams his cock inside me.

This time, he's not as gentle as before.

"I love fucking you bare," he says between pants.

"Yes," I say, struggling to balance myself on my elbows.

"I can feel every inch of you, Essie. Can you feel me?"

I tuck my head into the pillow. "Yes, *every single one*. Please keep giving it to me."

"Fuck yeah," he grunts before smacking my ass.

This Adrian is a different Adrian than I'm used to.

He's usually gentle with me during sex.

But I like this.

I like him taking control.

It doesn't take long for pleasure to override me again.

"I'm there," I yell, attempting to look at him, but he's fucking me too hard. "FYI, I'm about to become useless."

"Let yourself go," Adrian says. "I'll do all the work."

Our moans are loud.

Sweat covers my sheets.

The sound of his body smacking against mine nearly sounds like porn.

Each pant of his is raspy and strained.

They get harsher each time, along with his movements.

My knees weaken, and he holds me up as I nearly collapse onto the bed.

I fall apart beneath him, and he keeps fucking me.

And fucking me.

And fucking me.

My head spins until, suddenly, he freezes behind me.

"Where do you want me to come, Essie?"

"Huh?"

"Where do you want me to come? I'll pull out."

"No!" I yell. "Come inside me."

I also want this first to be with him.

"Fill me with your cum, Adrian."

A long groan, along with my name, falls from his lips.

His body shakes behind me, and even though I might be exaggerating, I swear I feel his cum release inside me.

Then, slowly, he pulls us down and helps me to my back.

I attempt to catch my breath, but I am unable to speak.

Resting his arm over my stomach, he runs his thumb over my scars.

Massaging them.

It's relaxing, and my eyes flutter shut. I'm ready for a nap.

"Come on," he finally whispers. "Let's get you cleaned up."

He helps me out of bed, my hair a hot mess, and we walk to the bathroom.

"I'm sorry," I say. "I don't want it to seem like I'm giving you mixed signals. I just got so caught up this morning."

I'm also in love with you, is what I want to say.

That's why I begged you to touch me, to fuck me, to come in me.

I want every part of you.

I'm too scared to tell him that, though.

This will only end one way—heartbreak.

There's this broken part of my heart that can't trust him.

Adrian grasps my waist, pulls me up, and settles me on the bathroom counter. "Baby, you don't have to explain yourself to me or anyone." He smooths his hand over my knotty hair. "It's okay. I won't hold you to thinking this is anything more than you want it to be." He plants a careful kiss on my lips. "I'm playing by your rules here."

I look down at my feet. "I wish you'd played them before you hurt me."

"I didn't mean to," he says, his voice scratchy. "I never wanted to hurt you."

"But you did."

"I'm sorry," he pleads. "Give me another chance."

"I don't know if I can trust you," I whisper.

"Tell me what to do to earn back that trust."

"I honestly don't know that either."

He sighs, resting his forehead against mine. "I'll find it. I'll make it up to you, Essie. Let me prove to you I'm trustworthy enough for your love."

41

Adrian

The Blue Beech Fall Festival is straight out of a movie.

Autumn vomited all over the town.

Everything smells like cinnamon and pumpkin.

There are hayrides and people selling food and crafts, and a live band plays on a makeshift stage. The festival starts downtown but travels down roads that are lined with booths, people, and parked cars.

My abuela put me in charge of her bake sale booth. She's selling her sweet bread and guava pastries. Both are my favorites.

Fellow Blue Beechers stop by her booth, grabbing samples, and almost all compliment her sweets. More than half buy something. When my abuela lived alone, she stayed at home most of the time. I love seeing her make new friends here.

She swats at my arm. "Oh, look who's over there."

I turn to where she's pointing to find Essie standing in front of a cider booth, talking with River and her dad.

"Essie!" she calls out, cupping her hand around her mouth. "Come here and try my pastries!"

Essie turns at the sound of her name, looking toward us. Smiling, she heads in our direction. River and Rex follow her.

"I'd love for you to try this," my abuela says when they reach us. She hands Essie a sample before doing the same with the guys.

River and I offer each other a head nod, and I shake Rex's hand, telling him it's nice seeing him again. River would probably laugh in my face if I attempted the same formalities with him.

Essie bashfully peers over at me like I wasn't naked in bed with her less than twelve hours ago.

I lick my lips, feeling like I can still taste her on them.

"This is amazing," Essie groans after taking her first bite of a guava pastry. "I'll take one, or two, or three. Whatever my options are."

Rex bites into his pastry, nodding in agreement.

River does the same, giving my abuela a thumbs-up.

"As a man married to an incredible baker, I have to say, these are delicious," Rex tells my abuela. "I'd be in the doghouse if I didn't buy some of these for her." He tastes the sweet bread next. "Some of this too."

"Valeria, I'm requesting you bring these to all bake sales and festivals," Essie adds.

My abuela stands up straight, a prideful smile on her face.

I introduce her to River and Rex. Instead of shaking their hands, she skips around her booth to wrap them in hugs.

I can't stop myself from doing the same with Essie. "You look damn adorable," I mutter, smiling at her pink scarf and black beanie with poofs on the top, resembling animal ears.

She returns the smile. "Thank you. This is what they call fall festival chic." Her gaze coasts down my body. "I have to say, it looks like you're falling into the Blue Beech fashion trend."

I glance at my jeans before pulling on my flannel sweatshirt. "I also went for fall festival chic."

These clothes are ten times more comfortable than suits and ties and are slowly becoming my regular attire. I still dress professionally in the office, but unlike the city, I'm not worried about running into clients outside the office while casually dressed.

She smiles before motioning toward the booth. "Please tell me you know how to make those."

"I do." I grin.

"Really?"

"No."

She frowns.

"*But* you can come over to my abuela's, and we can have a bake date together. She'll teach us."

"Is that your way of asking me out on a date?"

"If it works, absolutely. If not, I'd like to give it another shot."

"Let me get back to you on that."

"You have my number."

I wink at her, and she shoves my shoulder.

For a moment, it's like we're the old Essie and Adrian.

The ones who could joke with each other with no expectations or hurt.

"Now, listen," my abuela says to Rex, catching my attention. "How about you show me to your wife's booth so I can taste those chocolate chip cookies you've been raving about?" She looks over at us. "I'm sure these two can watch the booth until I get back."

"Well—" Essie starts.

"Oh, you got this." She flicks her hand through the air. "Be right back."

"Grab some cookies for me," I call to her as she starts walking away. "To pay for my wages here."

My abuela laughs, giving me an *I'm helping you out here* look.

"I must admit, Valeria is quite the trickster," Essie says, joining me behind the booth.

"She only wants what's best for her grandson."

I hold out a piece of sweet bread, offering it to her, and she takes it in her mouth.

"Mmm," she moans, swallowing it. She does a once-over of the booth and snags one of my business cards. "Look at you, adding solicitation with the snacks."

"She put them up there, not me." I smirk. "You can add yours there as well. I don't mind sharing real estate."

"I prefer not to bribe people for business. Though it seems to be your thing."

"Hey now, those sports tickets were *not* a bribe."

"Says every single person accused of bribery."

"I'd purchased them for a game, but my abuela told me I couldn't cancel our dinner plans to go. So, I thought I'd put them to good use."

"Bribery," she sings out. "To get into the partners' good graces."

"Did I think it'd prevent them from firing me at any time?" I shrug. "Yes, but I didn't think it'd score me a promotion. All that was in my head was, if they fire me at any point, that would kill any chance of my making amends with you."

Foster stops at our booth, interrupting us, and smiles smugly. "Is it this common to see two people in competition with each other *this close*?" He grabs a pastry and takes a bite. "I'd be happy to welcome you into our family, Essie. You know what I'd also be happy about?"

Essie stares at him warily.

"Tell Ava to go out on a date with me."

Essie snorts. "Not happening. You just want to do that to mess with River. We know you're not in love with her."

"Oh, come on," he groans. "Of course I'm not *in love* with her, but I do enjoy hanging out with her."

"You know she and River have *something* going on."

"Yes, but she deserves more than a hookup every now and then," Foster argues.

Essie snaps her mouth shut for a moment, as if she can't dispute that.

Foster taps the booth, drags a hundred from his pocket, and

lays it down before taking an assorted bag of pastries. "Tell your grandmother these are delicious." His gaze cuts to Essie. "And tell your brother to stop being an idiot, or I'm asking Ava out."

"Damn," Essie says as Foster walks away. "I had no idea he was so bossy."

"When …" I stop to correct myself, holding up a finger. "*If* my abuela comes back, want to walk around here for a bit … hang out?"

"Yes," she whispers. "But only on one condition."

"Yeah?"

"Let's pretend everything is okay between us. Tomorrow, we'll go back to figuring out real-life problems."

"All right." I slide my hands together. "I can work with that."

We can't pretend forever. Eventually, we will have to revisit the Earl problem.

I cock my waist against the booth, hiding her from the crowd, and then press my lips to hers.

She steps back for a moment, as if in shock, before kissing me back.

"Everything being okay means I get to kiss you," I say, more confident than I should be. I don't know what level of *pretending* we're at.

"Fine," she says, faking annoyance before smacking a quick peck to my lips. "We can consider kissing normal."

"Oh, look at you two," my abuela says.

I swear, she does this shit to mess with me.

She had to choose *this moment* to make her return known.

Terrance is now next to her, smiling as his gaze pings between Essie and me, and they're both holding a bag of cookies. A cup of hot chocolate is in my abuela's free hand.

"Terrance came over to take your job," my abuela explains while Essie stares at her, wide-eyed. "You two go have your fun."

I grab Essie's hand and walk her away from the booth. I swear, I hear a squeal coming from my abuela as she watches us.

Essie laces her fingers through mine. "Have you ever attended a fall festival?"

"I haven't," I say as we pass the hot chocolate stand.

"What do you think about it?"

"It's *something*."

"Is that a good or bad something?"

"It's a something that tells me I'd love to stay here in Blue Beech for as long as I'm welcome."

"What made you ever feel unwelcome?"

I shoot her a *really* look.

She gasps, placing her hand to her chest. "Not me. I've been the captain of the welcome commitee with you."

"In the beginning? Hell no, you weren't."

"Not many people would be jumping for joy if the man who had broken their heart came to their town *and* also stole the business they wanted to buy."

"Hey, I didn't steal anything. I had no idea you wanted Terrance's firm. All I knew was that the firm gave me a chance to come here, where I knew you'd be." I spin us around, moving us in the opposite direction. "But I must admit, the longer I've been here, the more welcoming you've become."

"Well, I'd better be the only one who's *welcoming*."

I whistle. "Is that a little jealousy coming from you?"

"I don't know. Would *you* be jealous if I were *welcoming* someone else?"

"Abso-damn-lutely. Jealousy isn't a common trait for me to have unless it comes to you."

She bows. "Then, I'd like to say I'm honored, counselor."

I grin. "I love it when you speak legal talk to me."

As we move farther into the festival, I start seeing familiar faces.

"Aunt Essie!" a shrieky girl's voice calls out.

We turn to find a little girl running in our direction. Easton follows close behind her. A stuffed cow is in her hand, and her face is painted like a giraffe.

She runs into Essie's legs, and Essie bends down to hug her.

"This is Jasmine," Essie tells me. "Easton's daughter."

When Jasmine pulls away, I notice the resemblance to Easton.

The same dark hair and nose.

I've heard Easton mention his daughter a few times. I think he's the only one with a child in Essie's circle of friends.

Jasmine holds up her stuffed animal. "I won this!"

Easton laughs, coming up behind her.

Jasmine frowns, biting into her lower lip. "Okay, my daddy won it. But I picked the prize!" She waves the cow in the air. "And now, we're about to get a caramel apple!"

Easton hugs Essie and then says hi to me. "They have a caramel apple station over there if you're interested?"

Essie pays me a glance, and I shrug.

"We might stop by on our walk back," she tells him. "I'll burst if I eat another bite." She points toward my abuela's booth. "Make sure you stop by there and try the pastries. They're delicious."

Easton salutes us. "You two have fun."

I've also learned Easton is a man of few words.

He and Jasmine head toward the caramel apple stand, and Essie and I keep walking toward the town circle, which is decorated with scarecrows and pumpkins. We pass a table with a sign that says *Pumpkin Contest.*

It's lined with the best pumpkin art I've ever seen. Growing up, I could barely carve a pumpkin, let alone create one into a teakettle or Frankenstein.

"Did you participate in that?" I ask, jerking my head toward the table.

"I absolutely did not," she says. "I tried one year and pretty much got last place. Even the preschoolers did better than me."

I chuckle.

We say hi and wave to people, and I'm surprised when some know my name. I know I shouldn't be since I'm now a businessperson here, but people remembering me makes me smile.

We're at the town circle when Essie stops at a bench. Something I like about the circle is that there are memorial tokens of people. A statue of a child holding a balloon. A plaque on the ground, celebrating the first town doctor. A dog statue, donated by a local artist for the town K-9 who passed away after serving for twelve years.

We sit, and she taps her foot against a plaque on the ground.

"We raised money to have this bench put up in memory of Ethan after his death," she says.

She knows she doesn't need to explain who Ethan is.

I already know so much about him.

What I don't know is exactly what they were.

"Were you two close friends or ..." I lower my arm along the back of the bench over Essie's shoulders.

"He was failing English and hired me to tutor him. As we spent time together, we became close friends. We were opposites, but he was so fun. We were never anything more, though."

She kicks her feet out and scuffs her boots against the concrete. "His friends spread rumors about us, and because of them, some of the town believes that we were sleeping together. Most of that talk has died down after some years, but it was still hard. They blamed me for him dying in the accident."

She shrugs like she doesn't care, but I see the hurt on her face.

I squeeze her knee. "Essie, nothing with the accident was your fault."

"I know. It's just ..." A shuddering breath leaves her. "Can we not talk about this tonight? We're pretending, remember?"

"We can't pretend forever," I say tenderly. "Sooner or later, we have to talk about this."

She curls her hand around mine on her knee. "Tomorrow night. Can we do it then?"

"Tomorrow night it is."

My stomach curls, tension tightening inside it, the fear of losing her returning.

We sit there for a few minutes, both of us silent.

She sniffles, her eyes watery, and I wipe away her tear with my sleeve. I take her hand back in mine, wanting every second I can have to touch her.

We spend the rest of the night exploring the festival.

I bid in the silent auction. The proceeds are going to a class field trip to Washington, DC, where nearly every business in town donated something.

Essie and River donated an Xbox and custom game remotes.

Callie donated a gift card to her bake shop.

Ava donated a free CPR class.

Jax and Amelia donated a gift card to the brewery.

And Easton's was a basket of gift cards to nearly every business in town. Essie explains that his business, the one he took over from his father, rehabbed heavy machinery equipment, so donating something from there isn't exactly easy.

I love how everyone is so nice here.

How they help others.

I never want to leave this place.

We stop for hot apple ciders and take a break under a large oak tree. The tree has started losing its leaves. Some are on the ground, beneath our feet, while others flutter in the wind. Looking up, I stare at the moon coming through the bare branches and smile at this new life I'm forming.

Like this tree, when spring comes around, I hope my leaves will be different.

That Essie will forgive me, and we'll be together.

That I stay here in Blue Beech for good.

"Next year, you'd better give me a heads-up so I can donate to the auction," I tell her, wanting to feel even more part of the community.

I went from wanting to dominate in corporate law to the desire of a simple life in a small town with the woman I love.

Essie leans against the tree trunk and pauses mid-sip of her cider. "Does that mean you'll be here next year?"

I inch closer to her. "I'll be here for as long as you'll have me."

"Don't you mean for as long as *Blue Beech* will have you?"

"No, *you*, Essie. I can't live here in this town, seeing you and knowing you'd have been mine if I hadn't messed up. If I lose you, this place will only remind me of my biggest mistake. I want to stay in Blue Beech so we can build a home and life together. My dream life is growing old with you and being the happiest couple in this damn town. I want you to be mine *here* forever."

The words feel good as they leave my mouth.

As if the feelings came straight from my chest and bloomed into words I'd wanted to say for so long.

Her eyes lock on mine, but she doesn't say a word while staring at me in pain.

I know that look because I see it in the mirror whenever I think of losing her.

She rests her hand on my chest, and her voice is close to a whimper. "Let's enjoy the night and have all the serious talk tomorrow, okay?"

I nod, attempting to read her emotions, but I can't.

Will she or won't she let me try to heal her heart from the hurt I caused?

But all I can do now is agree and go with her plan.

"Okay," I whisper, taking the chance to run my lips over hers.

Tonight, she's mine.

Tonight, our problems don't exist.

The rest of the night goes smoothly. We see her friends and sample ales at the brewery's tent and sit at a picnic table, eating food and talking. This is slowly growing into a circle of friends I don't want to lose either.

And as the night ends, as bad as I want to ask her to spend the night, I don't. We need to stay at our own places because tomorrow will be rough.

I need to be ready for it.

42

Essie

After having one of the best nights of my life at the fall festival, I tell Adrian good night—okay, *kiss* him good night—and ride home with my parents and River.

We help them unload the car from my mom's booth, where she sold cookies for my grandfather's church. Instead of going to our cottages when we're finished, River and I stay to hang out with my parents.

River and my dad make a drink at the wet bar and talk business.

"I saw you with Adrian tonight," my mom says, handing me a throw blanket as we curl up on the leather couch in the family room, making ourselves comfortable. "River told me what happened."

"River has such a big mouth," I grumble. "So much for twin secrets."

She sits next to me, stealing some of my blanket. "He was worried about you."

I pick at a loose strand in the blanket. "Sometimes, I wish people would worry about me less."

"As your mother, I promise you, that'll never happen. The same with your father."

I fluff a throw pillow and prop it behind my back. "Will you tell me Dad's and your love story again? It's my favorite."

I need something uplifting tonight.

My brain needs a break from its constant anxiety about what'll happen tomorrow.

I feel a knot forming in my belly, just thinking about it.

She laughs, her face brightening, as if she's already reliving the memory. "I swear, your father should've never told you that as a bedtime story."

"Why? It's my favorite fairy tale."

"I hope someday, your favorite fairy tale will be yours when you get your happily ever after."

My shoulders slump. "If that ever happens."

"It will, honey," she says with absolute certainty.

"It seems my Prince Charming preferred to hurt me." I shut my eyes, wishing I believed her words.

"I'm so sorry." Her voice is heartfelt, but there's still a dose of sadness. "It's hard, giving someone your heart and them not cherishing it like they should. But if Ethan's death taught us anything, it's that time shouldn't be taken for granted. We can't take temporary anger as our final decision without giving a chance of forgiveness."

I relax against the couch, lowering my chin so my eyes don't meet hers. "Who said I gave Adrian my heart?"

"Oh, I know my daughter," she says around a laugh.

"Love sucks." I throw my head back.

"Sometimes, yes. But it tends to correct itself."

"Like you and Dad."

"Like me and your dad."

"Now, let me hear my favorite fairy tale."

She gives me what I want and recites their love story. It's been my favorite since I was a kid. Like she said, my dad would use it as his fairy tale at night.

Whenever she tells me, she takes painful pauses, keeping some details from me. Their love story wasn't easy either.

She and my father went to high school together here in Blue Beech and were complete opposites. He was the popular bad boy, and she was the studious daughter of the town's preacher. They became best friends after he attempted to bribe her to write a paper. After that, they were inseparable. They attended the same college, but from the way my mom's voice drops when she talks about it, I know something traumatic happened to her there. She dropped out and moved home, but neither of my parents will ever tell me why.

It took them a while before they got together, but she said once they admitted their feelings to each other, their love took off from there. My dad says my mom saved him, while she says the opposite.

I long for a love like that.

A love that, even with flaws, is beautiful.

It might even be compared with perfection.

I pull myself up to sit on my knees and lean forward to hug her when she's finished.

Using my sleeve, I wipe a tear from her cheek.

She does the same with mine, only with her thumb.

I collapse back onto my butt, and she smiles at me.

River and my dad join us, and we watch a movie.

A movie I can barely concentrate on.

I couldn't even tell you the main characters' names.

Tomorrow will decide how beautiful or ugly my love story with Adrian will be.

The following morning, I'm in my office drinking coffee when Lainey knocks on my door.

"Come in," I call out even though the door is already halfway open.

She steps inside, her hair halfway falling from her clip and her eyes sleepy. I think we all stayed at the festival a little too late last night.

I saw her and her boyfriend snagging many samples from the brewery's tent.

"I have someone here asking about representation. She doesn't have a meeting," she reports. "Do you want to see her, or I can schedule her in for another time?"

As of right now, my client list is currently sitting at zero.

Brielle has been my one and only.

I move a stack of paperwork to the corner of my desk. "Did she give you a name?"

"Jenna Marvin."

I silently blink at her.

"I can tell her you're unavailable," Lainey says, clearly reading the shocked expression on my face.

"No. You can send her in."

She scurries out of my office, and seconds later, she leads Jenna into my office.

No one says a word.

Why is she here?

The only thing I can think of is divorce representation.

Her husband is a straight asshole.

Not as bad as her high school boyfriend, though.

Thankfully, he moved away a long time ago.

Maybe she heard about my success with Brielle and thinks I can help her too.

Lainey, getting the hint again, backs out of my office, not bothering to shut the door.

Jenna scratches the back of her head, searching for words.

"What can I do for you, Jenna?" I ask, helping her out.

She looks relieved at my starting the conversation. "I'd like to hire you for representation."

"For what?"

"I'm, uh ..." She glances back at the door, as if she doesn't want anyone to overhear her words. "I don't exactly know how to *legally* say this, but I need an attorney because I know someone committed a crime, and I never turned them in."

Technically, depending on the crime, it might not even be a serious offense.

I motion for her to sit, and she tiptoes into my office, carefully sitting as if expecting someone to pull it out from beneath her.

"What was the crime?" I ask, grabbing my pen and notebook.

She waits.

"Jenna, we'd have attorney-client privilege. You came to me for help, and you can't be that vague. If I don't know everything, I don't know how to help you."

She folds her hands in her lap and stares at them. "I never told anyone I know who really killed Ethan Leonard." She raises her chin, halfway looking at me. "And it's not the man in prison for it."

43

Adrian

"Hey, man," River says, tossing his bag onto a corner pub table at Down Home Pub. "I hacked into as much shit as I could, studied Earl's bank statements, and even managed to get into his emails sent while he was in prison."

The server comes to our table to take our drink orders.

Both of us opt for a water, wanting a clear mind to discuss every Earl detail. I need to know as much as I can before meeting with Essie tonight.

River waits until she returns with our waters before opening his bag and drawing out a folder. "First off, I want to comment that Earl had a Tumblr account where he reposted puppies, positivity quotes, and meditation tips. He also wrote in it like a diary."

"Any posts made from the night of the accident?"

"Yeah, it was about how he was trying to give up drinking."

"That didn't happen."

"The time stamp was *after* he left the bar, and there were so many grammatical errors in it that there's no way a man typing that badly could drive." Shaking his head, he pulls out a sheet of paper and dramatically slaps it onto the table as if starring in a damn *CSI* episode. "Look at this police report. I found it in an email in the police force's inbox. It was never turned over to prosecutors or his defense attorney."

I pick up the paper and read over the email thread between two officers. They interviewed a man who said they saw Earl's truck at a gas station, but he wasn't the man behind the wheel. He said there were multiple people, but he couldn't make out their faces. Another officer added that they'd messed up by not taking fingerprints from the vehicle, but it was too late now.

"Not one witness who saw him after he left the bar," I comment, reading over them again, wanting every detail to burrow itself in my brain so I don't forget it.

"They only saw *his truck*." He scrubs his palm over his forehead. "The gas station didn't have cameras, and unfortunately, the clerk working that night is no longer alive. But he did tell police Earl never came in to buy gas or anything else. Why would his truck be at the gas station if he wasn't buying anything?"

"Prosecutors could say it was to clean up after the crime."

"The truck didn't have damage on it then."

"He was preparing for the crime, then," I fire back.

"Whose side are you on here? First, you were on Earl's, but now, you're arguing against him."

"I'm an attorney. It's my job to look at *every* side and take in every angle that another attorney could argue."

"If we circle back to the Tumblr posts," River says in annoyance, "a week before the accident, he wrote that Blue Beech no longer felt like home to him. He was considering convincing his grandmother to sell the house and move. People here made him feel like an outsider. He'd started a custodian job at the local movie theater and wrote that people treated him terrible there. One post said that a teenager threw a slushy on him, and the friends took pictures to post on their socials."

"Was the teen Ethan by chance?"

"No idea, but I knew Ethan. He wasn't like that."

"You were friends with him?"

"He wasn't like that," River grits out. "He wasn't even involved in the little prank that got Earl fired. In fact, he was pissed his friends had done it. If Earl killed Ethan, it was because he was collateral damage—because I know for damn sure that Ethan wasn't one of those dickheads who fucked with Earl."

I nod, grabbing a pen and jotting down everything River says.

"Now, onto his prison emails."

"Jesus, man. How do you know how to hack into all this shit?"

"Insomnia," he says, as if it's an obvious answer. "And boredom. I was hacking into classified documents at twelve. My mom is still mad at my dad for teaching me this."

He goes on to say that in every email, Earl maintains his innocence. In his emails to his grandmother, he begs for her to leave Blue Beech, fearing that whoever set him up will hurt her. He also became pen pals with a woman. She was who contacted the PEP.

He goes on with more details—some of them useful, some not.

And, as if saving the best for last, he pulls out a blurry black-and-white photo.

"There was a camera on one of the deserted roads," he says. "The landowners liked to watch for wildlife." He stabs his finger against one photo. "Here, you can see three people getting out of the truck. Just like what the witness from the gas station said. Either two other people were with Earl—and let's be honest; Earl wasn't as skinny as any of these people in the photo—or a group of people stole his truck. None of them match his grandmother either, if people try to argue she was involved." His finger slides across the photo to the date in the corner. "Same night, same time, everything."

I rest my elbow on the table and massage my temple. "If not him, then who the hell are these people?"

They all have different builds.

All three are wearing baseball caps, hiding their faces.

How do you put this together, especially after all these years?

I pause, fishing my phone from my pocket when it vibrates. "It's your sister."

River throws his hand out toward it. "Answer it, dummy."

I flip him off before hitting the Accept button. "Hello?"

"Adrian," Essie says, frantic on the other line, "I need you to come to my office *now*."

44

Essie

Jenna stares at me nervously after I end the call with Adrian. "Am I in trouble? Did you call the police?"

I want to scream at her.

Kick her out of my office.

Tell her to go fuck herself in as many ways as I can come up with.

How could she?

She knew this for years and did nothing.

Let an innocent man go to prison.

Held the truth from a family mourning their son.

From me.

I don't know the entire story yet.

After she told me the wrong man was in prison, I told her to stop talking.

I need an attorney to be here with me.

I need *Adrian*. He knows just as much about this case.

"I called someone to help," I explain, my pulse speeding.

Needing to do something with my hands, I flip my phone over on my desk.

Then do it again.

And again.

Jenna stands.

"Sit down, Jenna," I snap, both of us shocked at my hostility.

She drops back into her chair.

"I didn't call the police. I called another attorney to come help with"—I pause, gesturing toward her and hating that my voice breaks—"this."

Adrian, please get here fast.

I unlock my phone to call him again, but stop.

Taking my call will only delay him further.

Not even a minute later, he rushes into my office.

For some reason, River is with him.

If I wasn't shaking and on the edge of a panic attack, I'd question why.

Lainey comes up behind River, uncertainty on her face of what to do.

I nod a silent *Everything is okay* and gesture for her to leave and shut the door behind her. The less people who hear this conversation, the better.

Which includes River.

Out of all people, why would Jenna come to me?

Adrian wrinkles his nose, coming to my side.

As far as I know, he doesn't know my history with Jenna.

He doesn't even *know* Jenna.

River, on the other hand, knows exactly who she is.

He presses his lips together in a grimace, not taking his eyes off her, and crosses his arms. He looks almost like he's standing guard between her and me.

"Tell them what you told me," I direct Jenna.

She squirms in her chair, warily looking at us. "Why would I say anything in front of them? I came here to talk to *you* about help."

"River, out," I say before mouthing, *Sorry*, to him.

"You can't be serious?" He scoffs. "I don't trust her with you."

I lay my hand over my chest. "I'll be okay. As attorneys, we need to speak with her."

River scowls at Jenna before leaving my office and slamming the door behind him.

"Jenna, this is Adrian," I introduce. "He's also an attorney."

She starts to offer him a friendly wave but drops her hand when Adrian doesn't wave back.

I'm sure he got the hint Jenna is no friend of mine by River's reaction to her.

"Adrian has worked with the Prison Exoneration Program, the organization that picked up Earl's case."

Jenna's shoulders tense.

I peer up at Adrian. "Jenna came here, asking for representation. She claims Earl isn't the one who caused the accident that killed Ethan."

Adrian's eyes slip to Jenna, untrusting, as he steps behind my chair and rests his hands on my shoulders. "Jenna," he says, his voice soft and comforting, "who caused the accident?"

"Isn't this a conflict of interest?" Jenna asks. "You're literally helping the other side."

"No, my *mom* is working on his case. But if you tell us what you know, it'll save all of us a lot of work and give us a chance to help you out. You asked Essie for representation. In order for her to consider, she needs to know what she'd be representing."

Jenna bites into her lower lip.

"If you'd rather speak to my mother, who I can have subpoena you, or the police, we can arrange that," Adrian tells her.

"Do you promise I won't get in trouble?" Jenna runs a hand over her face, smearing her red lipstick.

Mascara remnants are on her cheek. Her clothes are rumpled when she's usually always put together. She looks like she hasn't slept in days.

"We can't promise anything," I tell her. "You told me you *know* who killed Ethan. Not that *you* killed him. If you help us, the police, then whoever your attorney is, will fight for a deal where you won't face any criminal charges."

Tears fall down her cheeks, and she sniffles.

"Who caused the accident?" I say, feeling like I'm moving into interrogation mode more than I should. But I can't help it.

Adrian squeezes my shoulders—a silent agreement that I am.

All I need is for her to tell me.

Tell me that I've been wrong for so many years.

That the monster in my nightmares isn't who it should be.

"It was Greg," Jenna finally says. "Greg and his friends." She covers her mouth with her hand, as if she never thought those words would leave her mouth.

I lose a breath, shocked I'm keeping my cool and not running out of the office to hunt down Greg.

I'm also shocked I'm not screaming at Jenna.

It's probably because Adrian is with me.

Having him here helps keep me calm.

"Was it an accident?" I ask her, feeling like I already know the answer.

"I didn't expect it to go as far as it did." She shakes her head, refusing to meet my eyes.

Greg was Jenna's boyfriend in high school. He played football with Ethan, and they ran in the same circle. But as far as I knew, they weren't super close. Ethan even called Greg a douchebag a few times for the prank that had gotten Earl fired.

After Ethan's death, Greg even made a speech at his funeral, speaking for the football team. He graduated, earned a football scholarship, and moved.

"Why did he do it?" I ask her.

"Because of me," she whispers.

Adrian squeezes my shoulders, walks around my desk, and takes the chair beside Jenna. "Why because of you?"

"I hooked up with Ethan at a party one night. We were both drunk. Greg found out and was pissed. The entire football team gave him hell for it, saying he wasn't man enough to fuck me, and I had to go look for sex elsewhere. He broke up with me, but I begged him to take me back." She blows out a long breath, regret crossing her face. "He claimed Ethan broke *bro code*."

"*That* was his reasoning for killing someone?" I bite out.

"Yes." She lowers her head. "Greg and Jayden were drunk one night and complaining that Ethan was a crap friend and thought he ruled the school. That's when they came up with their plan to cause the accident. I don't think they wanted to kill Ethan, just scare and hurt him. They said if Ethan was hurt, it'd hurt his ego, and he wouldn't be able to play football anymore."

"How'd Earl get brought into it?" Adrian asks.

"Earl was Josh's idea. The guys knew they couldn't hurt Ethan without having someone to blame for it. They obviously didn't want it to be them. Josh was suspended from the football team after Earl told on them for partying on the field. A scout was scheduled to watch him play at one of those games, costing Josh a possible scholarship." She squeezes her eyes shut. "I swear, the plan was for Ethan to maybe break a leg, not *kill* him."

Maybe break a leg?

Jesus.

They killed Ethan for something that petty?

Put me through hell over a high school hookup and missed football game.

"I helped them," she says, her words barely audible.

I lean forward, resting my elbows on my desk. "What do you mean you helped?"

"I snuck into Earl's truck, stole his key, and had it copied for Greg. I also, um … I dropped them off in the woods, so they could walk to Earl's house and steal his truck with the copied key. After they ditched his truck, I'm also the one who picked them up."

Silence takes over the room after her last word.

Adrian focuses on me. His only concern is how I take this.

"Why?" I ask, raising my voice. "Why would you help?"

"I thought it was some stupid prank, I guess. I didn't know

they were going to kill him. I didn't even find out Ethan was dead or you were in the car until everyone in town started talking about it. I just wanted my boyfriend back." She wipes a tear from her face. "I was a stupid girl in love."

And with that, everything I'd thought I knew just went up in flames.

45

Adrian

I've never been so shocked in my life.

Not even when I found the phone in my father's box.

Jenna played a large part in a murder and hurt the woman I love.

Her actions put Essie through grief, hell, and pain.

And also took an innocent man's life too damn soon.

I've never been a violent man, and I don't know who Greg and his friends are, but I want to kill them.

"You lied to me when you came in here," Essie tells Jenna. "You didn't only know who committed the crime. You *helped* them commit the crime. You're an accessory to murder."

Jenna stares at her, speechless.

"Call the cops." Essie's stare cuts to me. "They need to know this."

"Does that mean you'll be my attorney?" Jenna asks, her voice hopeful. Her back straightens in her chair.

Essie shakes her head. "Absolutely not."

Jenna's mouth falls open. "But—"

"There's too much conflict of interest, Jenna. And honestly, there's no way I could work with you or attempt to protect you. You killed someone I cared about and ruined my life. If you tell the police everything, they'll work with you. They'll either find you a public defender or you can ask the officers to give you a list of attorneys."

I leave the room to call the sheriff's department, asking them to come to Essie's office.

"What the hell is going on?" River asks, stopping his conversation with Lainey and walking over to me.

"I'll tell you about it later." I run a hand over my forehead.

This changes everything.

Essie has new demons in her nightmares.

All I want to do is hold her in my arms and make her feel better.

The police don't handcuff Jenna while leading her from Essie's office to the squad car, most likely not wanting to make a scene.

Nosy people are already standing along the sidewalk.

I follow the officer to the station, and River drives Essie home in her car.

Even though I'd prefer not to spend another moment with Jenna, I don't want her to change her story when she speaks to the detective.

On the drive, I call my mother, telling her everything.

She's speechless for a moment, taking every detail in. "She saved us a lot of work. You know, this isn't uncommon for us. Sometimes when news hits that we're reopening a case, the guilty party comes forward. I don't know if it's from guilt or they want to be caught on their own terms."

"What happens with Earl now?" I ask, swerving into a parking spot.

"I'll handle that. How's Essie?"

"I think she's still processing everything."

She sighs. "I'm sorry. I'll send one of my attorneys to the station, and we'll work with Jenna. Go be with Essie."

"I'll leave the station when your attorney gets here." It might seem like I'm doing too much, but I don't want Jenna to lie.

She, along with her piece-of-shit friends, will go down for this.

The police don't question why I'm here, most likely assuming I'm Jenna's attorney. I don't bother correcting them.

Jenna keeps her head down while reciting the same story she told us in Essie's office. When she's finished, the sheriff sends out a warrant for the arrest of her accomplices.

All of them need to face the consequences of their actions.

And I need to be there for Essie every step of the way.

46

Essie

I pace my crowded living room.

Adrian is at the precinct with Jenna and hasn't returned any of my texts.

I want to know what she tells them and their responses. She kept her secret for years. I wouldn't put it past her to try to change her story.

Why she came to me for help will forever confuse me.

I was the other victim in the accident she'd caused.

I don't know if she came to me out of guilt or if she truly believed I'd be out of my mind and represent her. After seeing her face in the restroom, I'd bet it's a guilt thing.

River, Ava, and Amelia are settled on my couch with their attention pinned on either their computer or phone. They're researching everything they can find about Jenna's accomplices. Ava is also texting her dad for information. He and my uncle Kyle—Callie's dad—worked for the police department before starting their own detective agency.

All three guys moved after graduation. Greg scored a football scholarship, then lost it not too long after. Josh joined the military, and no one knows what happened with Jayden. They weren't my friends, so I never kept up with them.

I truly believed Earl was responsible for the accident.

Guilt knots in my stomach.

I regret not doing better research, especially after I learned the PEP took his case. It should've been a sign for me to study it.

"Greg still lives in Iowa," Ava reports. "Divorced, two kids, works construction."

"He's also had multiple DUIs," River adds. "Three aggravated assault and battery charges and a domestic violence felony." He curls his lip. "What a piece of shit."

We all nod in agreement.

"All signs definitely point to him being batshit crazy enough to do what Jenna said," Amelia says.

I stop pacing when my phone beeps with a text.

Adrian: Leaving the station now and headed that way.

As relieved as I am that he's coming here, there's still a sense of nervousness. We planned to talk about the Earl situation tonight, and now, everything's changed.

Yes, he didn't tell me about seeing Earl in prison or his involvement with PEP, but now, it feels like so much stuff has happened that him keeping it from me seems almost small. Also, if he had told me immediately when he saw my name and walked away from the case for me, then maybe we'd never found out Earl was innocent.

"I just found Greg's ex-wife's socials," Ava says. "Let me see if I can DM her and ask if she knows where he's at."

I sit down at the kitchen table and start reading over Earl's case notes. I shut my eyes, and in my head, I try to match up the prosecutor's timeline with what happened that night.

They listened to my 911 call, so most of it lines up with my memories.

But now, I'm questioning everything.

Everyone's attention moves to the front door when Adrian

walks in. He gives the three on the couch a head nod and kisses the top of my head before taking the chair next to mine.

The cottage goes quiet.

My friends know what happened between us. Thankfully, no one has mentioned it tonight or given their input. This is something I need to figure out on my own.

"Want to go to the brewery and stalk the lowlifes there?" Amelia asks the room, but the question isn't directed at me or Adrian. "Drinks are on me."

"You guys go ahead," I answer. "I'd prefer to stay in tonight."

"I'm game," River says. "I'll need something mixed with an energy drink, though. I'm not going to bed until I find Greg."

"Right there with ya," Ava says, shutting her MacBook and securing it under her armpit.

The three hug me and tell Adrian goodbye before leaving.

After they shut the door behind them, my heartbeat quickens.

"How are you feeling?" Adrian asks me.

"Okay," I whisper, shoving my MacBook away and rubbing my eyes. "I mean, given the circumstances. I'm relieved Jenna finally told the truth. I'm also mad at myself for not doing more research when the accident happened. I completely believed everything I was told."

"Essie," Adrian rasps, "you had no idea he wasn't guilty. You were a teenager, for Christ's sake. You never saw the driver. You saw a truck, and that's what you told the police. You didn't pick him out of a lineup. You told them what you saw. They did all the work from there."

My shoulders slump. "I've told myself that in my head all night, but it doesn't change that almost a decade of his life was stolen from him."

"And now, we'll give that back."

"You tried to do that, and I got mad at you for it."

"No, you got mad because I wasn't up-front about it. Don't you dare put that blame on yourself as well. You didn't get mad at me for helping with Earl's case. You got mad that I *kept* it from you, which is understandable." He shakes his head, clasping his hands together and resting them on the table. "Don't let me off the hook for that."

"Adrian," I murmur and go silent.

I don't know what to say.

"I hurt you, Essie," he goes on, his voice choking up. "I begged you to give me a second chance after my first fuckup and then messed up again. Both times, I could've easily protected your heart had I told you. But I wasn't, and that's something I'll always regret."

"Why should I trust you with my heart again then?"

"You shouldn't."

I wince, drawing back in my chair.

"But I'm begging you to. One more chance. I know it's asking a lot. It'd be you trusting your heart with someone who didn't cherish it before."

I sit there, my back straight, and my gaze rests on his.

There's an apology in his eyes.

Remorse.

"Okay," I say. "One more chance."

Some people might say I'm letting him off too easy.

Maybe I am. But at this point, I don't care.

I know what I want.

Cutting Adrian out of my life would be like cutting out a piece of myself. He makes me feel comfortable and secure in my own skin. I've loved him for years, even when we weren't together.

"Keep me accountable," he goes on, his tone stern. "Make me be a better man for you, or drop me. The moment I saw you, I knew you were who I'd been looking for my entire life. I don't want to lose you."

Tears are in my eyes.

Jesus.

Do these things ever turn off?

After all this chaos passes, I swear to God, I'd better not cry for a year.

Unless it's from stubbing my toe or something. But still, I should be stronger than that too.

Adrian presses his hand to his chest. "I'm yours, Essie, until the day I die. I love you." He stands, moving to my chair, and pulls me to my feet.

We face each other, our mouths only inches apart, and I trace my finger along his lips. "And I love you. I'm *yours* until the day I die."

47

Essie

Two Months Later

"Earl McGrey, a man wrongly convicted of a crime nearly a decade ago, will walk free from prison today," the reporter says, standing in front of the courthouse, wearing a bright yellow raincoat with the hood up.

The camera pans to Earl walking down the steps. Paula and a group of attorneys are behind him, holding umbrellas over their heads.

"Earl, how does it feel to be free after all these years?" the reporter asks him.

She reported on his story when he was first sentenced. I remember she was very biased and made sure her viewers knew she believed he was guilty.

Honestly, I hope Earl doesn't even answer her.

I scoot in closer to the TV. They've only shown his mug shot from years ago when the news broke about his innocence. Staring at him through the screen, I see the tenseness in his face.

He looks down at the microphone with sunken eyes. "All I'll say is that I'm happy justice is finally being served, and I wish that my grandmother were here for this moment." He peers up at the sky as if talking to the heavens. "From day one, she fought for my innocence. I hope those responsible will receive the same harsh punishment I was given. Maybe more since they not only committed the crime but also let another man go down for it. They stole a decade of my life and put my grandmother in an early grave." He tips his head down. "That is all."

Poor Earl.

Another reporter asks if he'll return to Blue Beech, but he ignores the question. He ducks his head, and an attorney guides him away from the crowd to a black SUV.

The night Jenna was arrested, River and Ava found Greg. They drove to his beat-up home and sat outside until the police arrived. Greg didn't go easily. He pulled out a gun, fired two shots, and threatened to murder everyone else and himself. They Tased him and dragged him out of the house.

Josh was still serving in the military, and according to Paula, they took him off base, and he's been arrested.

Jayden died in a car accident five years ago after being hit by a drunk driver. The irony.

I refused to help Jenna. So did Adrian.

She was given a public defender, and the prosecution gave her a plea deal to testify against the others. She ended up with immunity, which pissed me off. She was just as involved as them.

Adrian found an apartment closer to town, and Earl moved back into the loft where he was staying. Pete and Agnes had no problem renting the place to him. Turns out, they weren't trying to steal his home. They wanted to help his grandmother. They even told her she could stay there until her death, and they'd just keep their horses there.

I turn off the TV and toss the remote onto the couch when someone knocks on my door.

"Come in," I call out, standing.

Adrian walks in and smiles.

"You know, you don't have to knock."

"This isn't my place, so yes, I do."

I bite my lip, taking him in while he walks in my direction. *God, he's so damn hot.*

He wraps his arms around my waist when he reaches me. "If a certain *someone* would move in with me, we wouldn't have to have this conversation every time I knock."

Now, I think he does it to mess with me.

That's about the 39,439th time I've told him knocking was unnecessary.

I run my fingers along his collarbone. "I'm still considering."

"And I'm still waiting." He grabs my hand on his collarbone and kisses it. "The invite is open indefinitely."

"Glad to hear there's no expiration date."

We rotate between staying at each other's houses. Thankfully, we haven't had a case against the other again. Someone tried, but Adrian turned them down. He hands most cases to me anyway, which some people find odd when they reach out to him for representation.

I tease him that it's because he's afraid of a little competition.

It's really because he's started helping his mother at the PEP part-time.

Chills run up my body, and I stand on my tiptoes to kiss him. "Happy birthday, my love."

"You've said that to me already," he says against my lips. "You said it when I woke up this morning, after morning sex— which was an amazing gift, by the way—after lunch, and after lunch sex."

I wind my arms around his neck. "Are you saying you're tired of hearing it? Should I forget my plan of birthday sex tonight too?"

"Hell no. I love hearing your voice *and* definitely love the sex."

I lower my hand to rub his cock through his jeans and smile as it hardens. "God, I love you."

"I love you more." He presses a kiss to my nose while

thrusting his hips forward. "And I have to say, you look sexy as hell in that dress and even more when you're teasing my cock."

"This is your favorite dress, right?"

"Yes, because it holds a great memory."

"Hmm ..." I move my lips to his neck. "Remind me what that memory is again."

"When you got crazy drunk and rode my dick in nearly every inch of this place." His cock jerks as he slips his hand under my dress. "God, you make me so fucking hard," he groans, this one strangled.

"It sucks we have to leave," I whisper against his skin.

"It's my party. I can be late if I want to."

"It's rude." I gasp when he turns us, pushing me against the wall, and shoves his hand up my dress, into my panties.

"I'd rather be rude than walk in with the biggest hard-on in my life," he grumbles, pushing my panties down my legs and flinging them over his shoulder.

"Fine," I say with a fake moan of annoyance while lowering my hand to unbuckle his pants. "But we need to make it quick."

"I got you," he says, attacking my mouth with his. "I know exactly what you love, where your sensitive G-spot is. I'll get us there in no time."

He nips at my lips, biting at the corner as I shove his pants down. A million sensations flush through my veins. We've had sex so many times, but my body always throbs for him. I'll never get enough of him.

My hand flies to his hair, pulling at it, when he hitches my leg over his, squats, and thrusts inside me.

"Fuuuck," I moan, gripping his shoulder with his first stroke.

He grunts in my ear, pinning me against the wall, and starts fucking me wildly. He tilts his hips up—he wasn't kidding when he said he knew exactly where my G-spot was. The man has mastered every sensitive spot in my body.

"Please," I beg.

"Please what, baby?" he groans in my ear before shoving my hair off my shoulder and sucking on my skin there.

"Fuck me harder," I gasp.

He bites into my skin and pounds into me.

Our bodies hit the wall with so much force that photos shake.

I scrape my nails down his back and then push them into his bare ass. He takes one of my hands, pinning it against the wall, and straightens his back while circling his hips, his cock hitting every angle I want.

"I'm close," I say, peering up at him.

His eyes are closed, and his lips are pinched together.

"Yes, Essie, take my cock," he says, moving faster and grasping a fistful of my hair. "Let me fill your pussy with my cum for my birthday."

I hold his face, digging my nails into his cheeks, and kiss him as my body comes apart. It takes him only a few more thrusts before he releases inside me.

"Hello!" someone calls out, knocking on the door.

"Please tell me you locked the door behind you," I whisper to Adrian, fear in my voice.

"I didn't lock the door behind me," he whispers.

My mom knocks on the door again. "Are you in there? I thought I'd catch a ride with you since your dad and River are meeting us at the party."

"Jesus," Adrian hisses. "And you don't think it's a good idea to move in with me?"

I tap his shoulder. "Oh, please. She'd probably show up there unannounced too."

At least she didn't barge right in.

I'd be mortified if she found us like this.

His face squeezes as he slowly pulls his cock out. I stare down, licking my lips and momentarily forgetting my mom is outside the door. It's already hard again. Adrian never has problems going multiple rounds.

"Just one minute," I yell as Adrian lowers me from the wall. "I, uh ..."

I nearly trip as I start scrambling to find my panties.

Adrian scoops them up, tossing them to me, and shoves his cock inside his pants. I hurriedly pull them on.

"Going to the bathroom really quick," Adrian says, signaling to his pants.

I nod, attempting to fix my hair on the walk to answer the door.

As soon as I come into my mom's view, she looks at me in confusion.

All I can say is, thank God my dad isn't with her.

It's more than obvious I was just fucked.

"You look nice," she says, the words slowly leaving her mouth. "Though, I do have to ask, did you lose your hairbrush?"

I hear Adrian snort and look past my shoulder to find him leaving the bathroom.

"No." I fight with the tangles. "I couldn't find my boot and had to reach underneath the bed for it. My hair got tangled up, and I didn't get a chance to fix it."

Adrian really needs to stop taking his orgasms out on my hair.

I snatch my bag and sweater. "Welp, we'd better go before we're late."

My mom nods, fully knowing the situation. "You take a minute to do that. I need to grab something from the house and will meet you at your car."

"An A for the lie," Adrian says in my ear, coming behind me after my mom leaves. "Good thinking."

"I'm always quick on my toes," I comment. "Just like you're quick in bed."

He swats my ass. "Oh, I'm punishing you for that later."

48

Adrian

"Happy birthday!" everyone shouts when we walk into the brewery.

Essie attempted to keep the party a surprise, and I think some people assume it is, but she's not great at secrets. She kept accidentally blurting things out, like she needed to text Callie about the cake and that River had better make sure he was in town.

All our friends are here.

It's nice to call them that now.

They've all accepted me with open arms.

Sure, the few girls didn't at first, compliments of Essie, but now, we're all close buds.

The parents are here as well.

Carolina didn't mention what she'd nearly walked in on during the car ride, but you could tell she knew something by the expression on her face.

Amelia and Jax closed the brewery tonight to throw my party. He's behind the bar, slinging drinks. A birthday banner hangs above his head. A cake, finger foods, and plates are set out.

Country music bellows from an old-school jukebox, and

most of us are seated on stools at one long table that you'd see in a school cafeteria.

We all bullshit with each other, catching up on our lives.

"The party is here!"

I turn around at the sound of my abuela's voice. I smile, seeing her walk in with Terrance and my mother. Lately, I've seen my mother more than I ever have. She takes every Sunday off to have dinner with us.

My abuela has been on a mission to convince her to move to Blue Beech.

Do I think it'll happen? Probably not.

It's too far from her second home—her office.

My abuela has also tried setting her up on dates with guys here.

She declines them all.

I don't recall my mother ever dating. Even after all these years, she hasn't moved on from my father. They met when she first moved to the States. She was young and only spoke Spanish. He lived across the street, helped her learn English, and she said he pretty much taught my abuela and her everything they needed to know about becoming Americans.

She can't move on from the good memories of my father.

There are more of them than bad.

I don't blame her. I did pine over Essie for almost a decade, but our situation is also different. He's gone forever, and I wish she'd find love again.

Moving on is hard.

Scary.

Trying something new is even harder.

I hope, with time, she'll find happiness.

That she'll stop revolving her entire life around work to forget her loneliness.

"All right, so I have to tell everyone something," Ava announces to our table.

Everyone turns quiet, and Jax moves out from behind the bar. He stands next to Amelia and kisses her cheek.

"I was offered a really good position at a different hospital," she says. "It's a few hours away."

Everyone's attention goes to separate places.

The other parents go to her parents, waiting for their reaction.

Most of ours cut straight to River.

He winces, his face flushing, and I can tell he's replaying Ava's words in his head.

"We're so happy for her," Lauren, Ava's mom, says.

Gage, Lauren's dad, nods in agreement.

Though I can tell he also has mixed feelings about it.

"What?" River asks, setting his beer on the table. "Surely, you're not going to take it?"

Ava looks away, running her finger along the rim of her cup. "It's a huge opportunity. I'll be working under a really great mentor."

"But this is your home," he says, the hurt clear in his voice.

Ava steps closer to him. "I'll still come home on the weekends and stuff." She does a once-over of the brewery. "You all know I'll never fully move away from here."

"Yeah, but ..." River is quiet for a moment, searching for the right words.

He finds them—I can tell.

He just doesn't want to say them in front of other people.

"No." He shakes his head.

"Well, that's a very insightful response," Ava says.

"You know what I mean," River argues. "You can't leave us."

Man, I feel bad for the guy.

"He means you can't leave *him*," Mia points out.

Ava steps closer to him. "You travel for work all the time."

River downs the rest of his beer before answering, "Yes, but I always come home. This is *our home*."

Ava starts walking to him but suddenly halts, as if she just now realizes they have an audience. "Nothing is official yet," she tells the room. "I told them I'd give them an answer when I decide."

River looks like he's been told the worst news of his life.

He needs to get his head out of his ass, stop wasting time, and admit he wants to be more than friends with benefits.

"How about another round?" Jax asks, breaking the tension. "We have a new beer we've been working on. You guys want to be my testers?"

"Hell yeah," Ava says, her excitement somewhat fake.

River rubs the back of his neck.

Just as Jax starts passing out beers, Foster comes up behind me.

"Happy birthday, bro," he says, slapping me on the back.

"Thanks." As I move in my stool, I see a blonde woman standing next to him.

"Oh my God, Sydney!" Callie yells, jumping off her stool and rushing toward us. "I didn't know you were back in town." She hugs Sydney tight and says something about how much she's missed her into her shoulder.

"In case you didn't hear, this is Sydney," Foster says to me, my abuela, and mother. It seems everyone else knows her.

Sydney smiles wide and waves. "Hi." She skips over to my abuela and hugs her from behind the chair. "I've heard so many good stories about you. Foster says you're, like, the funniest person ever."

My abuela grins and mouths, *I like her*, to Foster.

"Everyone loves Sydney," Callie says.

"Does that mean everyone is here now?" Mia asks, glancing at the doorway, as if nervous Trey will walk in and ruin her night.

I've started learning how to read my new friends.

Essie has also filled me in on some of their history.

Though she swears she can't say anything about Trey and Mia.

River takes the chair beside Ava but pretends to focus on his phone. His brows are furrowed, and he looks ready to leave.

"I think that's everyone," Ava says. "*Unless* Easton wants to invite his nanny."

Easton, who's on his phone, but not pretending it, lowers it from his face. "What?"

"You've been texting her all night," Ava says.

"He texts her all the time," River adds, ready to back up Ava even though he's not happy with her.

Easton glares at River and uses his phone to point at him. "He doesn't know what he's talking about. Of course I text my nanny, the person who I trust to watch over my daughter."

"They're not only nanny-related texts," Ava says. "I know this because Jasmine showed me something on his phone, some weird YouTube video where grown-ups fake pretend to play babies—which is kinda weird, BTW—and one of the nanny's texts popped up. It *was* not about Jasmine or a babysitting schedule."

"Oh, you and the nanny," Sydney says, plopping down on a stool, and Foster stands behind her. "Super cute."

"Since when do you have a nanny?" Essie asks.

Everyone's attention is pinned on him, as if he's now our favorite gossip.

"Work has been busy, and now that Uncle Hudson is stepping down"—he shoots Mia a glare, as if it were her fault since it's her dad—"all the work is on me. I need help on the days my mom can't babysit. Plus, the nanny also helps out around the house." He shrugs. "You guys are making a big deal out of nothing."

"Let me just add that the nanny is hot as hell," Ava adds with absolute certainty, a grin spreading across her face. "Like model gorg."

"Can we not talk about my employees like that?" Easton narrows his eyes at her.

"I'm just curious why you didn't invite her to the party," Essie, always my nosy one, says.

"We're in a bar," Easton says, doing a sweeping motion of the brewery. "I can't bring my daughter here. Hence why she needs a nanny in the first place. If she came, what would I do? Hire a nanny's assistant to watch her?"

"Fair point," Foster says.

"You could make her an executive nanny and hire people underneath her. She'd be the boss of them," Callie suggests.

The smiles on their faces tell me they're really going out of their way to give Easton a hard time. I like it since he's usually the one who's the most straitlaced out of the group.

"She's just his nanny," Willow, Easton's mom, says, shooting him a sympathetic look. "I'm actually the one who hired her. He has so much on his plate, and he needed a breather."

"All right, let me see a picture of this nanny," Essie says, wiggling her fingers like she wants someone to hand over the evidence.

Easton shakes his head and sips his beer. "Let's talk about someone else's life, please. I'm over here, just taking care of my daughter."

"Found it!" Ava holds out her phone and shows everyone.

"Okay, she's super hot," Essie says, showing the picture to me, as if asking me to agree.

Hell to the no.

"You're the only woman I think's hot," I tell her.

"Good answer, good answer," Foster says as if we were in a game show, and he slaps my back.

"I'm blocking you all from my business," Easton grumbles, snatching Ava's phone and tossing it back to her.

Ava grabs her phone before it falls to the floor. "Hey, since I'm the part-time babysitter and great-cousin for the Jas-Monster, you can't do that."

My mother leans into me. "Are they always this rowdy?"

"Yes," I say, shaking my head and laughing.

"I love it," my abuela squeals. "You all make me feel young again." She peers at me with affection. "I'm so happy we're here."

"Me too," I murmur to her. "Me too."

This place has changed my life.

I never knew this kind of happiness before I came here.

It's after one in the morning when Essie and I get back to my apartment.

Since Tucker is at my place tonight, we're crashing here. It's half of a duplex and closer to town, only ten minutes from Essie's office.

I've been on Operation Convince Essie to Live with Me. We practically live together anyway.

I sold my condo in the city and became a Blue Beech resident. Even though I loved my condo, I wasn't sad when it sold. It was a relief and a hope for new beginnings. The duplex isn't as lavish as my old condo, but it's actually more comfortable.

I shut the door behind us, and Essie tosses her purse onto the couch. Tucker dashes toward us, jumping at Essie's ankles, and she bends down for him to give her a *welcome home* lick to the cheek.

"I'm sooo full," she says, pressing her hand to her stomach. "I swear, Callie puts crack in her cakes. It keeps you coming back for more slices."

I circle my arm around her waist to drag her toward me. "Thank you for tonight."

Having friends who care this much is new to me.

Sure, I've had friends, but none who've remembered my birthday, bought me gifts, or baked me cakes.

She plants a kiss on my lips. "Oh, this was just your first birthday. I didn't have as much time to prepare. I'm big on birthdays, so expect fun for every single one."

I chuckle. "I can't wait, baby."

"Are you ready for your gift from me?"

She breaks away from my hold to grab her purse and takes out an envelope. All her attention is on me as I open it.

I unfold the paper, and my heartbeat jolts as I read it. "Are you serious?"

"So serious." She struts toward me, pulls me onto the couch, and then straddles me.

The paper is still in my hand as she makes herself comfortable.

I read it again, like I never want to forget everything it says.

"So, what do you think, birthday boy?" she asks, running her hands up my arms.

"You know I've been game for us to merge firms before I even moved here." I hold out the paper and read the business proposal she typed out. "Thank you for making this the best birthday gift ever." I place three small pecks against her lips and drag her body closer.

I groan, throwing my head back, as she grinds against me.

"Which gift made it the best?" she asks, dropping her head to kiss my neck.

"All of them. You giving me a second chance, throwing me a party, this business proposal. All of them make me feel like the luckiest man in the world."

"Well, you make me feel like the luckiest woman in the world, so it seems we make the perfect couple."

God, she's perfect.

And she's giving me the perfect life.

49

Essie

Two Months Later

Earl was released from prison a month ago, but we've yet to see each other.

I'm standing in line at the local pharmacy when I notice a magazine with his face on the cover. The headline has **INNO-CENT** written in bold writing.

The woman in front of me is rummaging through her purse for a lost coupon. I look over my shoulder when someone steps behind me.

My body freezes when my eyes land on Earl.

It's not that I've been avoiding him. Luck has just been on my side.

Sometimes I've considered visiting him, but I was too nervous about how he'd react.

Does he hate me?

Does he blame me?

Plenty of people in his situation would.

I don't want to be a reminder of his past and the trauma he went through at the hands of my classmates.

He's wearing a baggy sweatshirt with a Carhartt logo and

ripped jeans. His attention is on his phone. He doesn't even notice me.

That changes when the woman in front of me starts cursing because she still can't find her coupon. She drops her bag onto the counter and starts removing its contents.

He looks at her, then at me, and his eyes widen.

There's no turning around and pretending I didn't see him without making it obvious that's what I'm doing. It's either I ignore him, talk, or run out of the pharmacy.

"Hello, Essie," he says, luckily making the first move for me. His voice is kind. There's no animosity.

"Hi," I squeak out, playing with my purse strap and tapping my foot.

He slips his phone into his pocket and leans into his cart. "How are you?"

"I'm okay." I grip the box—my only item—in my hand. "How are you after, uh"—I bite my lip, hating that I sound as nervous as I am—"everything?"

"I'm happy to be home."

"That's good. Blue Beech is happy to have you back." I hope my words don't sound ungenuine.

Earl was welcomed back to town with open arms. Though it kind of pissed me off with some people. He was treated like shit for so long. A lot of people here owe him a huge apology.

Including me.

"I'm sorry, Earl—" I start to say, but he interrupts me.

"I don't blame you," he says, blunt and straightforward. "You and I were nothing but collateral damage in their plan. Both of us victims." He scoots his cart closer. "Please don't have any guilt for what happened to me. Paula told me what you did when Jenna came to you." He bows his head. "Thank you for that."

I gulp. "I appreciate that, and welcome home."

He tips his hat toward me. "Glad to be here. I thought I'd never miss it, but it's good to be home."

"Next!" the cashier yells as Coupon Woman finally pays and storms away with her cart.

Even though I stopped paying close attention, I'm pretty sure she didn't find her coupon.

The cashier gives me a scrutinizing stare as her gaze slides from the box I'm purchasing to my ringless finger.

Okay, rude.

She grumbles out my total, and after paying, I wave to Earl before rushing out of the pharmacy. My UGG boots crunch against the snow on my walk to my car.

I toss the bag into the passenger seat, and just as I buckle my seat belt, my phone rings.

"Hello?" I answer with a slight shiver.

I forgot to heat my car, and it's starting to get cold AF here.

"Hi. May I please speak with Essie Lane?" the woman on the other end asks in a friendly tone.

"This is she."

"It's Mary from Dr. Hedges's office. You're on the waitlist to meet with him about scar reconstruction surgery. Dr. Hedges has some cancellations, if you'd like to schedule a consultation with him."

I stare down at my stomach, then at the package in the seat, and then back to my stomach. "Thank you for following up, Mary. But I think I'm okay."

"All right," she chirps. "Have a great day and let us know if you change your mind." She ends the call.

I lift my shirt and coat to peer at my stomach again, no longer hating the sight of my scars.

I've grown into accepting them as part of me.

I'm beginning to love the skin that I'm in.

If I had surgery, it'd be like all the work I'd done, loving myself, would've been for nothing.

I smile when I approach our law firm, Castillo and Lane at Law.

Adrian and I went back and forth on whose office to stay in. While I loved mine, Adrian's—Terrance's before—had history. I'd worked there in high school. It brought Adrian to Blue Beech, and people in town are familiar with it.

It has two offices compared to my one.

I also like that we'll be keeping Terrance's work alive.

"Hi, pretty," Ralph greets me when I walk in, swatting snowflakes from my hair.

"Hey now," Lainey says, shooting him a frown. "I'm *her* secretary, which means I'm the one who's supposed to greet her like that."

I grin. "How about *both* of you can call me pretty?"

"I'll take it, *pretty*," Ralph says.

"Although I don't really need my ego stroked and think we should keep things more professional," I add, and they crack up laughing, as if that's realistic.

While Ralph and Lainey are professional with clients, they have no problem butting into our business or arguing with each other. They even have lunch cook-offs here, and we always have birthday dinners.

I never want my workplace to be like Adaway and Williams.

I'll never be a boss like them.

I head across the lobby straight to Adrian's office.

The door is open. He's on the phone, and he waves me inside when he notices me. While we have separate offices, he has an L-shaped desk in his with a computer on each side. I work on the other computer since I'm in his office more than my own. I'm normally only in mine if we're meeting with a client.

"I'll call you back," he tells the person on the other line as I shut the door behind me.

He rises from his leather chair, sets down his phone, and kisses me. "Hello. I have to say, you're late to the office today." He swats my ass. "We can't have that, Ms. Lane."

I pat his cheek, and he frowns at my cold hand. "I've been brainstorming, babe."

"Uh-oh." He grabs my arm, leading me to the desk and situating me between his legs after sitting on the edge. "Brainstorming about what?"

"About us moving in together."

He cocks his head to the side, waiting for me to go on.

"What if I said yes?"

"That'd make me a very happy man."

I hold up a finger. "We just have one problem."

He raises a brow.

"Both of our places are only one bedroom."

"Do you want an office there?"

"No." I shrug, grabbing his hands and pulling back some. "Just another bedroom."

"Are we having guests?"

I grin. "I wouldn't say *a guest*. Something more permanent, actually."

"River?" I lose one of his hands when he scrubs it across his face. "Oh God, is this some twin thing where you come as a package?"

"No." I laugh, knowing he wouldn't believe me even if I said yes to that. "We need a room for a nursery."

He blinks, as if not getting it.

"A nursery," I repeat, drawing out the word.

He goes completely still. "Wait ... are you ...?"

I nod, losing his hold when I walk backward to grab the plastic bag from my purse.

His gaze is pinned on me when I hand it to him.

A pregnancy test is inside.

"Hell yes," he yells before sweeping me in his arms.

He kisses me.

Again.

And again.

And again.

So many kisses that I lose my breath.

I've never seen a grin so big on his face when he inches back.

The pregnancy wasn't planned, but we haven't been careful.

Condoms have pretty much been nonexistent.

It wasn't the smartest decision, but I like feeling him without a barrier.

We tried the pull-out method, but both of us forget half the time, too caught up with each other.

"We're having a baby," he says against my lips.

"We're having a baby," I whisper.

My body has gone through so much.

I've loved it, hated it, and loved it.

And soon, it'll give us a child too.

50

Adrian

Four Months Later

I'm going to be a dad.

Essie and I are going to be parents.

Holy shit. I still get excited each time I think about it.

My dream life keeps coming true.

Essie and I are together.

We share a firm.

We're in a town we love.

"All right, just in case some of you don't know, pink means they're having a girl, and blue means a boy," Ava explains as Callie carries out a cake.

One side of the cake has blue frosting with a blue bootie drawn in icing.

The other side is the same, only pink.

River relaxes in his chair and grins. "Thanks, Doc. We really needed those medical terms."

He shares the same excitement for Essie's pregnancy as we have. He keeps saying he can't wait to be the best uncle ever and introduce the kiddo to video games.

Ava stares at him in annoyance. "I still don't miss you, FYI."

Today is our gender reveal party, and we're having it at
Callie's Bake Shop. Callie closed the shop down. While she
didn't have to add anything pink to the interior, she did hang
some blue banners and streamers from the ceiling.

It honestly doesn't matter to me whether we have a girl or
a boy.

All I want is a healthy baby.

Yes, some people might say that is cliché, but I don't care.

Essie is next to me, absolutely glowing. I can hardly tell you
who's at our party because I've barely kept my eyes off her. While
she doesn't look like she's grown much in her dress, I see it when
the dress is off.

When we're lying on our bed, her in only panties and a bra,
and we talk to our baby. I know Essie's body so well that I see
where it's growing.

She throws her head back, laughing at something Callie said.

I grin. She takes my breath from my lungs every time I look
at her.

Sometimes, I have to pinch myself—a reality check that this
is real and I'm not dreaming.

"I can't wait to have someone to play with," Jasmine says,
jumping up and down with a cupcake in her hand.

"The baby might be a little too small for you to play with for
a while," Easton comments, grabbing a napkin to wipe the
frosting from her cheek.

"Why?" Jasmine frowns. "I play with baby dolls all the
time."

"She does," Ava confirms, a smile cracking her lips. "I saw
her hanging one upside down from the couch the other day. As
your aunt, that's a big no-no, babes."

"Hannah will help me with her," Jasmine says with certainty,
smiling over at her nanny.

Hannah stares at Jasmine with affection.

"Ahh, that's the nanny," I hear my abuela say to my mother.

I'm pretty sure it was meant to be said much quieter, but my abuela, apparently, isn't capable of *quiet* voices.

"She's also his employee," my mom comments.

Her tone is lower, but from the way Hannah's eyes widen, I'm sure she heard her.

"That's just asking for a lawsuit," my mother adds.

We're still working on warming her up.

It's getting there—slowly but surely.

I dip my head toward my mother. "This isn't a company. I don't think we need to worry about HR."

She holds up her hands. "Don't blame me for always considering liability."

"You wouldn't be you if you didn't," I murmur.

She shrugs, shooting me an *exactly* expression.

Callie holds out cake cutters to Essie and me. "Are you ready?"

We take them, but Essie grabs my cutter before I can make another move.

She sets both on the table and captures my hand in hers. "Can we have a minute in private?"

All eyes are on us.

Callie tries to pretend she doesn't think what Essie did was awkward but is doing a bad job at it.

Carolina and Rex scoot in closer in their chairs, as if they know something is wrong.

"Yeah," I say, pinching the bridge of my nose in nervousness. "Of course."

For some reason, some weird dread flows through me.

This feels almost like a bride walking down the aisle and then telling the groom they need to talk. I actually attended a wedding where that happened once.

Essie's hand is clammy, and her boots click against the floor. My steps are slow, my body tense, as she guides me out of the room. She walks us into the employee room and shuts the door.

Her back rests against the door, as if she doesn't want to risk anyone else coming in.

"Essie," I say, taking a startled step toward her, "what's going on?"

"I don't want us to find out with everyone else."

I squint, unsure what she means. "What?"

She sticks her hand inside her bra and whips out a small envelope. It looks the same as the one we gave to Callie—the only person, other than the doctor, who knows our baby's sex.

"I want us to do this privately," she says with full certainty. "Just me and you. I know it was important for our families to plan this, and I didn't want to break their hearts." She inches closer, putting the envelope in both our hands. "This should be intimate. Let's do it right here, right now, and then we'll go back out there and pretend we didn't know."

A smirk stretches across my face. "Sounds good to me, babe."

I'm cool with whatever she wants.

She slowly exhales a breath. "All right, on the count of three."

We count together, "One, two, three."

The noise of the envelope ripping open sounds like my future is bursting through it. We hold the paper in our hands, neither of us looking before the other.

I run my thumb along her hand, our gazes locking, and she nods.

Her hands tremble, and mine shake as we open the paper and read it.

"A girl," she whispers.

I'm glad she wanted us to experience this moment in private.

Because, damn, do emotions take over me.

We're having a baby girl.

A baby girl.

My face softens as happiness washes through me, and I swipe at my nose to hide how I'm getting choked up.

She climbs on her toes for a kiss. "We're having a baby girl."

I kiss her back. "I can't wait to meet our little angel."

She shoves her face against my chest. "Now, we need to go back out there before we worry everyone."

As she pulls away from me, I keep her at arm's length. "Wait, how is my surprised face?"

I pinch my face together, then open my mouth, then clasp my hands over my cheeks—very *Home Alone*–style.

"It's terrible." She laughs. "But it'll have to do."

The first room we paint in our new home is the nursery.

We decided on yellow, like sunshine.

We've yet to select a name.

We're waiting to meet our little girl before choosing one.

We haven't fully moved in yet. The real estate market is limited in Blue Beech. Only four houses were available, and all of them needed rehabbed. Fixing the place up has been my job for the past few months, along with our family's help.

I not only gained friends in Blue Beech.

My family also grew.

Rex and Carolina have been nothing but supportive of us.

I've even started to look up to Rex like a father. I go on trips with him and River, and we try to watch games together when we have the extra time. They've even introduced me to video games, though since I prefer hanging out with Essie to gaming, they always whoop my ass when we play.

Essie's face radiates as she admires the nursery.

She stands in front of the window, sunlight shooting through the blinds, and I lean back on my heels.

Fuck, she radiates beauty in every single way.

This weekend, River and Easton helped me put the nursery furniture together. We also managed to move some of our bedroom furniture. If we want, we can start sleeping in our new home.

She runs her hand along the crib. "I can't believe you guys got all this done in only a few days."

While we worked here, I arranged a spa weekend for Essie and her friends.

Essie is strong as hell, but pregnancy is fucking hard. I've always known it was a lot, but after reading the books, I admire her so damn much.

She's doing most of the work—the *hardest* job—carrying our baby. The least I can do is spoil and pamper her as much as I can.

She steps toward me, straight into my arms, where I always want her.

"This might be the biggest test we've prepared for," she says, turning to rest her back against my body.

I snuggle her in my arms and kiss the top of her head. "I think we might ace this one."

"If we struggle, we have each other to lean on for support." She clasps her hand over my wrist and gently sways us from side to side.

"I love you, Essie."

I lower our hands to her belly. My palm is large over hers, and we both laugh as the baby kicks.

"I can't believe that just happened," she says, tilting her head back to stare up at me. "I think she approves of her nursery."

Here we are, forming our own little family in Blue Beech.

Essie and I have gone through so many ups and downs.

Our journey together made me become a better man for her.

It made me open my eyes and learn from my mistakes.

It helped me find a love that I'll cherish forever.

Fate brought us back together.

It gave us our happily ever after.

ALSO BY CHARITY FERRELL

Blue Beech Series

(each book can be read as a standalone)

Just A Fling

Just One Night

Just Exes

Just Neighbors

Just Roommates

Just Friends

Only You Series: A Blue Beech Second Generation

(each book can be read as a standalone)

Only Rivals

Twisted Fox Series

(each book can be read as a standalone)

Stirred

Shaken

Straight Up

Chaser

Last Round

Marchetti Mafia Series

(each book can be read as a standalone)

Gorgeous Monster

Gorgeous Prince

Gorgeous Villain

Lucky Kings Series

Sinful Sacrifice

Sinful Ruin

Standalones

Bad For You

Beneath Our Faults

Beneath Our Loss

Pretty and Reckless

Second Chance Sweetheart

Thorns and Roses

Wild Thoughts

Risky Duet

Risky

Worth The Risk

ABOUT THE AUTHOR

Charity Ferrell is a USA Today, Wall street Journal, #1 Amazon, and #1 Apple bestselling author. She resides in Indianapolis, Indiana. When she's not writing, she's on a coffee run, online shopping, or spending with her family and fur baby.

Website: www.charityferrell.com

Made in the USA
Columbia, SC
20 February 2025